WILL SURVIVE

THE DEVIL'S OUTLAWS
BOOK 2

BETHANY DAWN

To anyone who ever thought they weren't good enough.

You are.

TRIGGER WARNINGS

This is a series about a 1%er motorcycle club, please expect them to act accordingly. Will Survive is meant to bring awareness to the mental struggles and mental healing after being abused. Triggers include: Mental health struggles, verbal abuse, mentions of gang rape and date-rape drugging on main female character (no on page assault, only past mentions), mentions of forced abortion of unmentioned character, murders made to look like accidents/ODs, mentions of past thoughts of suicide, gore, explicit torture, extreme acts of violence, explicit sex scenes, and recreational drug use.

Will Survive is closely connected to Only The Strong, so some triggers from OTS are included here as well, which are stalking and kidnapping. Chapters 31 & 32 if you'd like to skip those.

If you or someone you know is struggling, please know that help is always available. *I* am always available. Please reach out to health care professionals for appropriate coping mechanisms. What you are about to read is definitely not that.

As always, your mental health matters, take care of it.

PLAYLIST

P.G.N.L - Conor Maynard
ANGELS & DEMONS - jxdn
Dark Matter - Rivals
Paralyzed - Sueco
If I Were A Cowboy - Miranda Lambert
after dark x sweater weather - daddy's girl, creamy, 11:11 music
group
Juke Box - Round2Crew
OHMAMI - Chase Atlantic
UH OH - Tate McRae
Control - Zoe Wees
The Walls - Chase Atlantic
E-Girls Are Ruining My Life! - Bryce Savage
OUT THE ROOF - Chase Atlantic
Wicked Games - The Weeknd
Life's A Mess - Juice WRLD

Playlist available on Spotify @bethanydawnn17

INTRODUCTION

The first chapter of Will Survive takes place one month before the first chapter of Only The Strong. The cliffhanger from Only The Strong will be resolved in Will Survive, just not at the beginning. You need to know Finn and Huntley's story first.

1

———

HUNTLEY

I SLIDE DOWN THE DARK PURPLE WALL, RAISING MY WATER BOTTLE to my lips and taking a long drink. The fans blow the hair that has fallen out of my bun around my sweaty face, and I lean my head against the wall to catch my breath. I watch the other girls spin around the poles and work on different tricks and poses. Our instructor walks around and helps or corrects girls that need it. I see my friend struggle on the other side of the room, near the wall of floor-to-ceiling windows. They're one way, with a design on the outside that blocks the view inside, but inside you can see out clearly. I set my water bottle down and run over to help Farryn. She's stuck in a Jade Split, stalled in her rotation, so I put both hands under her shoulder blades and support her weight, allowing her to drop her leg. I guide her to the floor and she turns around with a smile. "P.G.N.L." by Conor Maynard starts playing through the speakers in the ceiling.

"Thanks," she says, walking to the windows where her water bottle is.

I shrug, putting my hands behind my back and pulling my little black spandex down to cover my small butt cheeks.

"So." She takes a drink of her water. "Some of us from class are going to Second Circle for their amateur night, wanna come?" She raises her eyebrows.

I cross my arms under my black sports bra. "You mean you haven't had enough pole already?" I cock my head, smiling.

Farryn grabs my arms and pulls me forward slightly, bringing me down closer to her height. Her tan hands are such a contrast to my pale arms. "Some of the girls wanted to enter and show their routines to an audience." I stare into her dark brown eyes, biting the inside of my lip. "Come on, Huntley. It'll be fun."

I roll my eyes, sighing. "Fine. What time?"

Farryn beams, her white smile bright. "Ten."

Resigned, I followed her to the locker room. We dress in our street clothes and grab our bags. We walk through the studio together and outside to our cars. I pull the hood up on my cropped black hoodie to cover my white blonde hair, still in its sweaty messy bun on top of my head. It's gray and freezing out. The rain let up today, but the cloudy February sky makes seeing Mt. Rainier impossible. The only view now is the massive trees that tower over every building in town. I get into my Camaro and crank the heat, waving to Farryn as she starts her car and speeds out of the lot.

2

———

HUNTLEY

The steam of my shower hugs my body as I step out and wrap myself in my fluffy bathrobe. I put on body oil and lotion, dry my hair, and do my makeup. All I had to do was dry my pin-straight hair, and add some oil and it was good to go—falling down my back like a waterfall, ending at my tailbone. I did my usual thick winged liner and cat eye false lashes, but added a bright red matte liquid lip. Heading into my closet, I pull on a pair of light-washed, high-waisted boyfriend jeans with big holes in the knees. I roll them at the ankles so they're more of a 7/8th length, add a white crop top, and top it off with a black leather jacket. It cinches at the waist, which helps not drown my thin frame. I step into a pair of red heels—the same color as my lips—and look into the mirror. My eyes are seductive and my sharp jaw moves as I purse my lips. The crop top and jeans show a small sliver of my toned stomach, and the heels put my 5'8" height closer to the height of the average man. Outside of my closet, my heels click on the concrete floors of my small indus-trial apartment. I grab my small black bag from the table beside the door. Taking a deep breath, I disable the alarm and unlock the three locks, and slowly walk through the hallway to the

6

elevator. The last thing I want to do is go to a strip club on the outskirts of town this late at night, or any time for that matter.

Pulling my phone out of my back pocket, I unlock it and click on the Safe Walk app. I walk through the brightly lit parking lot, sliding into my car and locking the doors. Quickly starting my car, I drive to the gate and wait for it to open before driving through town to Second Circle.

Pulling into the gravel parking lot of the club, I park under a streetlight and pull up my app again. I look around the lot before getting out, and almost run to the door. Inside, the club is dark and loud. I pay my admission at the front entrance desk and exchange some money for ones. The velvet curtains part as I step through them and into the main room of the club. It's huge, with three main poles and a large bar along the right wall. I see my girls sitting around one pole close to the bar and I make a beeline for them. My heels click on the tile, and the millions of perfumes mixing together assault my nose.

When Farryn sees me, she rises and gives me a quick hug before we sit down in the tall backed velvet chairs. The walls are dark, with blue and purple neon lights lining the stages and ceiling, flashing around the club. The floor is comprised of dark tile, and is surprisingly not sticky. A cocktail waitress in a maroon corset and boyshorts comes over and takes my order. I place my order and turn towards the pole, watching the beautiful brunette twirl around and then bend backward, slowing the spin. She's good. The waitress brings my drink and I tip her generously.

"Hey Huntley, I didn't know you were coming," Rachel yells, leaning over Farryn.

"Well, I figured since I wasn't working tonight." I shrug.

Farryn moves Rachel out of her face and I stifle a laugh. "Are you going to enter?"

I scrunch my nose at her question. "Hell no."

She rolls her eyes, placing her hand on my chair and leaning into me. "You're the best in class." She's able to talk at a normal level instead of yelling now.

I cock my head and look at her out of the corner of my eye. "I don't want everyone to watch me."

"What's the difference between you up on that pole in spandex and you at Mickey's in short shorts and a push-up bra?" She counters.

"At Mickey's, I'm *behind* the bar and I'm wearing a shirt over my push-up bra," I say, turning to face her now. "I just don't want all of these guys watching me, okay?" I soften my voice.

She nods, finally relenting. We watch a few more sets, all of us tossing out several dollars to each girl before the announcer comes over the loudspeakers. "Alright, alright, you fucking degenerates, are you ready for some new blood?" He rumbles through the microphone. We applaud loudly, as does the rest of the club, along with whooping and hollering from a large group of super intoxicated men from in front of one of the other stages. "That's what we like to hear down in the Second Circle of Hell!" He yells again. "So if you dare, make your way to the dressing room in the back of the club to get signed up and changed." He stops talking and turns the music back up.

A few of the girls from our group get up and leave for the back of the club. "You're not entering?" I ask Farryn when I notice she's not following the other girls.

She shakes her head. "No. I think I pulled something in my Jade Split in class. My thigh is fucking killing me." We both laugh at her. She's always pushing herself harder than she probably should, but she's not used to having to work too hard for things, so when she does she just fights harder.

There's a loud commotion at the front doors, and everyone in the club turns to watch the group of men enter through the velvet curtains. Their bodies take up the entire entrance, the light from the hallway not even shining through the curtains as they spread apart for the men to walk through.

The Devil's Outlaws.

They're laughing loudly as they walk confidently into the room. Everyone stops; all talking ceases, and we all just watch them. They walk through the club, heading right towards us to the seats across the stage from us. They give one look to the guys already sitting there, who quickly grab their drinks and scurry away, making way for the seven men in leather cuts to sit down.

Rachel saunters onto the stage in front of us in a white bra top that wraps around her stomach, and shimmery pink boy shorts, and she seems to break everyone's trance with the Outlaws. "ANGELS & DEMONS" by jxdn reverberates around the club, and Rachel starts to climb the pole expertly, twisting her body around it. Our group claps loudly and throws money onto the stage. But then I feel it—the prickle of someone watching me.

My eyes scan the club. Everyone is watching Rachel and the other girls on the other two stages. Then, my eyes land on him. The biggest of the Outlaws is sitting directly across from me on the other side of the stage, and he's staring right back at me. When I lock eyes with him, he doesn't look away; he doesn't smile; he just stares. We're locked in this stare-off and I blink my eyes slowly. My breathing picks up, making my chest rise and fall faster and faster. This man is beautiful. He has slicked back black hair and a clean-shaven face. The twirling neon lights catch on two nose piercings and tattoos on the side of his head. He brings his hand up to wipe the corners of his mouth slowly, pulling his bottom lip with it, and I notice that tattoos extend down his hand onto his fingers. When his hand lands back in his lap, I see that two thin chains and tattoos cover his neck too. The contrast of dark tattoos and the clean, tan skin of his face make his jaw look impossibly sharp.

Oh my God. Who the fuck looks like that?

Rachel straddling his lap breaks my trance, and I blink rapidly to regain my wits. She lays her hands on his shoulders and grinds on his lap, but he doesn't take his eyes off me. His giant hands land on her hips, and he lifts Rachel off of him—fully off of the ground—and sets her in the man's lap next to him. He takes a drink of his amber liquid and continues to watch me.

I'm so overwhelmed, I stand and quickly walk to the bathroom. I squint my eyes against the harsh light of the bathroom —it's such a dramatic change from the dark lights of the club. I walk to the sink and tear off my leather jacket, laying it on the counter and turning on the cold water. Placing a damp, cold hand on my forehead to cool myself down, I lean against the counter with the other.

Holy shit.

I don't know why I couldn't look away from him. His eyes were so intense and I felt pulled toward him. I couldn't stop it.

I pull my jacket back on and walk out of the door, back into the club, and immediately crash into a hard chest. Before I can apologize or look at who I just walked into, I'm being pushed back into the wall in the narrow hallway. All of the muscles in my body lock and my blood turns cold.

Fear.

I'm well acquainted with that feeling. I ball my fists, but before I raise my hand, I look into the eyes of the man in front of me. It's him. I drop my hand, falling into his spell again. He's still a good five inches taller than me, but with his hands on either side of my head, caging me in, and him leaning into me, I can see his dark blue eyes.

As blue as the ocean and just as deep. I could get lost in them.

"Were you going to hit me, Angel?" He asks, his cologne and minty breath wafting over me. *Fuck he smells good.*

I clear my throat, steeling myself. "Do you just go around touching women without their permission?" I snap.

His tongue slowly traces his bottom lip. My eyes leave his deep blues to watch his mouth, and his plump lips slowly slide into a smirk. "You ran into me. I'm touching the wall." I run my eyes down his body. He's wearing a black long-sleeve shirt under his Devil's Outlaws cut, dark jeans, and dark boots. He leans down next to my ear, his voice dropping to a husky whisper. "Do you want me to touch you?"

"No!" I snap, placing my hands on his hard chest, shoving him away from me.

He stumbles backward a step, and I squeeze through the small gap between us, leaving the hallway.

"What's your name?" He yells out to me over the music.

I don't turn around to answer; I just raise my middle finger in the air and keep walking. I pass by my chair, tapping Farryn on the shoulder and motioning toward the door. She pouts, but I don't care. I'm leaving. He'll come back soon to join his friends, and I don't want to be here when he does.

3

FINN

I RUB MY INDEX FINGER ACROSS MY LOWER LIP AND WATCH THE blonde woman walk through the club and out of the door. Fuck, she looks like an angel with white blonde hair, sharp features, and those fucking intoxicating eyes.

I don't chase women. I don't need to. But I'm about to chase this girl to the ends of the earth.

I noticed her for her beauty, but her eyes are what held me. When you've seen what I've seen, *done what I've done,* you start to recognize when someone isn't all there—when parts of them are dead. I've never seen such emotionless eyes from anyone before. They matched my own.

I pull Mason out of his chair by the back of his cut and direct him to the office in the back with my hand on his shoulder. When we're inside, I push him into the chair in front of the computer.

"If you want my vote at your patch in, I need you to do something for me." I lean over the desk, my hands gripping the edge. He nods quickly, his tongue darting out to wet his lips. Poor Prospects, they're still a little new and scared. "Find that blonde that was sitting across from us. I want her name, where she works, who her friends are, who she's fucking, and anything else you can get me." I take a seat in the chair opposite him, letting him know this is happening right the fuck now. "Let's see if you earned your degree, Prospect."

Mason clears his throat. "Yeah, okay. I just need to go get my laptop out of my pickup. I'm pretty sure this thing still has Paint installed on it." He hooks his thumb to the ancient monitor sitting on the desk. Probably an accurate assessment.

"You have three minutes," I say, watching him. I slide down into the chair, spreading my legs wide, and think about the beautiful siren that just threw my world into a fucking tornado.

Mason hurries back into the room and sits down behind the desk again, laying his laptop down gently and opening it. I stand and walk to the back of the room, next to the desk, where a small shelf has a few bottles of alcohol. I grab the scotch by the neck. Who the hell was in here drinking scotch? Ronan's old ass. When I don't see any glasses around, I return to my seat and raise the bottle to my lips, taking a drink and closing one eye at the burn it leaves in my throat. The only noise in the room is Mason's fingers tapping his keyboard at lightning fucking speed, and the distant sound of the music from the club. The office is pretty well insulated, so you can still hear loud shit, just in case something popped off in here, but it's definitely muffled.

"Huntley Novikoff. Works at Mickey's, lives in the Ridgeview Apartments, apartment 3C, and attends Ridge State as an Accounting major. She's twenty-three and in her senior year, and she has a black Camaro registered to her. Raised by a single dad, mother split after birth. Her socials are locked down and I can't find any relationships, friends mostly include the girls she was here with tonight." Mason rattles it all off like he's reading the weather. Casual as fuck. He'll fit in fine.

I nod my head slowly, reciting all of the information to memory. "I'm impressed. Don't fuck up and you got my vote." I rise from my chair and leave the office, taking the nearby backdoor out of the club. I don't want my brothers to question where I'm going.

Stepping outside into the dark night, the cold takes my breath away. My boots crunch over the loose gravel as I slide into my Hellcat and drive to the heart of town. Ridgeview Apartments are nice, with a gated parking lot and security cameras all over the place. I scan the third floor, not knowing exactly which one is 3C. A few windows are illuminated by lights; some normal lights, others are neon lights, and the rest are completely dark. I can't see if her car is in the lot from across the street.

A matte black Audi R8 with bronze wheels slows next to me and stops. Rolling my eyes, I roll my window down, leaning my head against my headrest and slightly turning my head towards my annoying brother.

"So now you have to resort to stalking girls to get some pussy? Yikes." Saint's irritating fucking voice yells from the driver's seat on the further side of the car. Callum sits in the passenger seat, trying to contain his laughter behind a smile, but fucking failing as his shoulders shake.

"Fuck off, Saint." I try to subtly glance at the third floor again, but the sound of a car door opening pulls my attention back to my brothers, who are just sitting in the middle of the road next to me.

Cale walks around my car and opens the passenger door, sliding in next to me as Saint slams the gas in his Audi and speeds away.

"I don't know what the fuck I'm doing, Cale," I say with a sigh.

He chuckles. "Being a creeper."

I turn my head toward him, the streetlight shining off one

side of his face. "I am being a creeper, aren't I?" We both laugh at my expense.

"Major fucking creep. Now come on, let's go see what we can get into before I'm forced to make a citizen's arrest on your creeper ass." He raises a flask to his lips while I shift into drive and slam the gas pedal, leaving the white haired-angel behind.

4

———

HUNTLEY

I thank him and grab my large coffee, shoving a few bills into his tip jar. I hold my hot coffee in my cold hands as I take the stairs up three flights to get to the second floor from the basement, the sweet smell of baked goods following me the whole way. The library is quiet, but packed. The hushed whispers and tapping on the computers are soothing to me, which is why I like to study here sometimes, just to get a change of pace from my apartment. The tall ceiling—twenty feet tall at least—with pale yellow wallpaper and deep red trimmings compliment the red marble hallways, which lead to a wide open area filled with heavy wooden tables and chairs, rows of computers, and of course, rows upon rows of books. And this is just the second floor. Floors three and four and filled with even more stacks.

I work for a few hours, getting the majority of my assignments done for this week. Packing up my laptop and books, I start for the back entrance of the building, closest to the parking lot. I cross through the stacks when I abruptly stop, as all of my breath is yanked out of my lungs.

No matter how long it's been, he's instilled this feeling into me for the rest of my life.

Fear.

And this one is bone deep.

I turn around to run the other way when I ram into a hard chest. I slam my hand over my mouth to muffle my scream. Big hands grip my upper arms, keeping me from falling backward toward the ground. My panic dies out at the sight of the eyes I meet when I look up.

It's him. The man from the strip club. The Outlaw. His thick, clean, dark brows pull together, and his lips flatten. I slow my breathing and shove his hands off of my arms, taking a small step back, but I only end up pushed against the stack, looking up at him.

"Did I scare you?" he asks quietly.

"No," I answer honestly. He doesn't scare me. There are only three people who scare me, and he isn't one of them.

He smiles, and it's nice. "Good. I don't want to scare you."

"Are you a student?" I ask, looking over my shoulder to see where *he* is.

I look back in time to see the Outlaw following my line of vision. "Are you hiding from someone?" He looks back at me and cocks his head to the side.

I raise my chin. "No." I lie, but then I hear my tormentor's voice and footsteps getting closer. I hear him laugh, and my stomach rolls at the sound. I grab the man in front of me by his leather cut and turn us so he's standing between me and the end of the aisle. I pull him down closer to my face. "Don't kiss me," I whisper.

He puts one hand on the bookshelf above his head—the top shelf—and the other on my hip. "Why not?" he whispers, inches from my lips. His hand burns through my jeans and makes my skin tingle.

"Because I would hate to be banned from the library for kicking your ass." I glare up at him.

He laughs, his chest shaking with his deep rumble. "You could at least ask my name before manhandling me, Angel." The footsteps fade away and I let go of the man's cut, my hands shaking. "Who are you afraid of?" His eyes harden, the playful look gone.

"No one. Didn't we have this discussion a few days ago about touching women without their consent?" I swat his burning hand off of my hip.

Not even realizing it had fallen until now, I swipe my bag up off of the floor and step around him to leave the aisle. I finally take in a deep breath when I'm away from him and can breathe in something other than his heady cologne.

———

"DARK MATTER" by Rivals pumps through the speakers in the ceiling. I throw myself around the pole when the beat drops, with my back against it. I spread my legs into a straddle before tucking and grabbing the pole and inverting, straddling again. I right myself and climb to the top of the pole, spinning slowly the whole time, before inverting again and pressing my foot to the pole in a Russian split. I tuck into the pole again and slide down, stopping myself only a foot from the ground. I place my hands on the ground, leaving my thighs clenching the pole. Slowly pushing against the pole with my outer thigh, I shift my body into a handstand straddle, and then place my feet down one at a time next to me. Swinging my body upright, I catch Farryn watching me from her pole next to mine.

"That's my bitch!" She claps her hands slowly, grinning from ear to ear.

I roll my eyes. "Yeah, yeah, shut up." She follows me to the window to grab our water bottles.

"The Devil's Outlaws were sitting across from us at the strip club last Thursday," she says over her bottle.

I swallow greedily. "I know. I ran into one of them when I left the bathroom, and then again yesterday in the library."

"Really?" She flashes her eyebrows, biting the side of her lip. "Is he hot?"

I shake my head and sigh. "I mean yeah, but it's kind of weird that he keeps showing up."

"Well, technically, it would be normal for him to be at the club, they do own it. But you are right on the library thing. Maybe he's taking some classes?" She guesses, following me back to our poles.

At the end of class, we walk out together like always. I shove my hands into the pocket of my big hoodie, waiting for Farryn to fish her car keys out of her gym bag. "Oh, that's a nice car," she says. Her eyes follow a gunmetal gray Hellcat that's riding down the street.

"Yeah, it is," I answer absently, walking to my driver's side door.

She leans her back against her door, crossing her arms. "What are you doing this weekend?"

"Working." I lean my arms against the roof of my car.

"Shoulda known." She rolls her eyes, smiling.

I open my door, tired of standing in the cold. "I have next Friday off."

Farryn grins. "Good. Keep it open for me!" she yells as she gets into her car. I follow her, starting my own car and turning the heat all the way up.

5

———

HUNTLEY

"Good morning, ladies." I swing my gaze across the people spread out on the thin mats. "And gentlemen," I amend. "I'm so glad to see all of you here on this early Saturday morning." I smile at the two guys standing at the back of the group. "My name is Huntley, and this is my second semester teaching this self-defense course." I smile. The group is bigger this semester. I schedule the class at the beginning of the semester so that I can hopefully get new students in here before they start going out or walking around a dark campus by themselves.

I want to supply them with helpful knowledge before they can become a victim. I've brought up offering the class a second time each semester and adding one or two classes during the summer, and the woman who schedules my classes said she would pass it up to the University President.

We run through several defenses; how to get out of holds and how to defend themselves properly. It's something everyone should know. This world is a scary place, and no matter how safe you think you are, you could always be in danger.

"Okay, I'd like everyone to take a seat, drink some water and relax." My assistant, Brad, the poor guy I always rope in to

20

helping me demonstrate this class, brings two chairs over for us both to sit in. I take a seat next to him and start talking to the group. "We need to talk about other safety tips. These are things I'd suggest you start doing in your everyday lives to help protect you that much more." I sigh, and look around at my students today. They're so young. Most of them are freshmen, but some are returners. We shouldn't have to live like this, constantly in fear. They don't deserve this. "I'll go over the basics first. Never go to a party or bar alone, and never leave without your friends or let your friends leave with someone they don't know. Do not accept open drinks from anyone, but really don't accept *any* drinks from anyone. Always watch the bartender make your drinks yourself. Never ever leave your drink unattended. Don't even trust your friends to watch it; they might take their eyes off of it and not realize it. If you leave a drink, throw it away and get a new one. If you're going out to meet someone you've never met, tell at least one, preferably two people where you're going, who you are going with, and what you're wearing. Send them the person's phone number, address if you have it, and some of their social media profiles. Please don't wander around alone, especially at night, too often. Always lock your doors, and don't sit in your car and wait around after getting inside." I pull my phone out of my bag that my helper brought over for me. "There's this great app that I use when I'm walking alone." Swiping the screen unlocked, I click on the app and talk them through it. "You set a simple pin when you download it, and when you start walking, riding in a vehicle with someone you don't know, or just feel unsafe, you hold down this button with your thumb until you get to a safe location. Then you take your thumb off." I pull my thumb away from the screen. "And you have fifteen seconds to enter your pin." I let the time count down until almost zero and enter my pin. "If you don't enter your pin in the allotted time, the app will send your last current or last pinged location to the police." My phone vibrates in my hands. "When you type in your code, you'll get a text saying the app team is glad you made it to your destination safely." I smile politely at everyone staring up at me. "Please, if you're uncomfortable carrying a small weapon of some sort, like a taser, pepper spray, or a self-defense keychain, always take your keys with you. They can fit between your knuckles and act as a great weapon." I set my phone on the floor next to my bag. "Any questions before we dismiss?"

A blonde with a short bob to my left raises her hand. I point to her. "I thought RSU was one of the safest campuses in the state?"

My ponytail swishes across my back as I turn my head to think of a proper response. "Places aren't dangerous, it's people that make them dangerous. You could be in the safest place." I make quotation marks with my hands in the air. "But if someone is there who wants to harm you, they're going to."

I dismiss the class and pack up my things into my gym bag. Waving to Brad and pulling the hood up on my cropped hoodie, I push through the heavy glass doors of the University gym and walk to my car. The air smells sharply clean, and it burns my nose with its chill when I inhale.

WARMTH WRAPS me into a snug blanket when I step into my dad's house. The spicy smell of chili fills my nostrils from the front door, and I know by the clangs of cooking utensils against my dad's large stock pot that he's in the kitchen. I kick off my Converse by the front door and walk into the kitchen to the left, finding my dad exactly where I thought I would: standing over the pot on the stove, stirring the food.

"Hey, daddy." I take a seat at the kitchen peninsula and watch him work.

He turns and sets the spoon on the holder. "Hi, Princess." He walks to me and gives me a long hug, the embrace settling all of my nerves and causing my body to relax into his strong hold. "How are you doing?" His deep voice rumbles as he leans against the kitchen counter and watches me.

Smiling, I answer him. "I'm going good, daddy. Is dinner almost ready?" I ask, eyeing the large pot.

He chuckles, turning and walking back to the stove. His navy tee shirt and jeans fit him perfectly. I don't know why my dad never remarried after my mom left us; it's not like he's ugly as far as dads go. "Yeah, get the bowls and let's eat."

Sliding off of the padded stool, I step around the peninsula and grab two bowls out of the overhead cabinet. Handing one to my dad, he scoops the chili into the bowl and then hands it back to me, kissing me on the temple as I take it from him.

He joins me at the small, round kitchen table and we eat in peace. I catch him up on my classes and work, and the self-defense class I taught today.

After dinner, we make our way into the living room to watch a movie together, eating popcorn and lounging; me on the large couch and my dad in his recliner, as usual. While I'm slipping on my shoes to go back home, he slips a folded-up bill into my hoodie pocket.

Taking it out of my pocket, I unfold it and stare at the hundred-dollar bill. "I don't need this, dad." I extend my hand with the bill so he'll take it back. "I'm doing fine."

He keeps his hands at his side. "I know you're doing fine taking care of yourself, but you're my baby girl and I want to help you sometimes." He continues to refuse to take the money back. "Buy yourself some extra groceries, some new clothes, oh, or some new boxing equipment. Just treat yourself, Huntley."

Knowing I won't win this fight, I slide the bill into the pocket of my black joggers. "Okay. Thank you, daddy."

He pulls me into a tight hug and kisses the top of my head. "I love you, Princess. Be safe, text me when you get home."

I reluctantly pull away. I love my dad and I hate leaving him. Even though we live in the same town and I see him almost every week, it still sucks. "I will. I love you too." I twist the door handle and step onto the front porch. My dad steps out behind me and watches me get into my car and back out of the driveway, not going back inside until I've driven away.

6

———

FINN

The low din of conversations and a random song play through the digital jukebox when I step into Big Dawgs. I turn to the left and see my dad hunched over the grill in the back with the new cook, flipping a burger and talking to the kid with a big smile on his face. I walk behind the bar and pull open a door on the fridge, grabbing a beer. I pull my phone out of my back pocket and check my notifications. I ignore the texts from the cut sluts and scroll to the one from Cale, letting him know I'm at the bar. An older couple walking to the register pulls my attention away and I slide my phone back into my pocket and place my bottle next to the register.

"How was everything tonight?" I ask, taking the receipt from the man's hand. I type in their order number onto the screen and pull up their tab.

"Finn, is that you?" The elderly lady asks.

I look up from the receipt, into her sweet, hazel eyes, recognizing my childhood babysitter immediately. "Yes. Hi, Mrs. Long." I smile, stabbing the receipt onto the holder. I switch my gaze to the man next to her. "Mr. Long." I dip my head in respect.

"Oh, Finn!" Her face scrunches into a big smile. "Come give me a hug, big man!"

I laugh deeply. "Yes, ma'am." I walk around the long bar and wrap her in a gentle hug. I tower over her, which is how I got my nickname from her. I was always large for my age. She hangs on for a while, whispering how much she's missed watching me and how much she misses my mom. My throat starts closing and I have to cough to open it. No one's talked about my mom in a long time. She finally lets go of me and I turn to shake her husband's hand.

"The Outlaws?" He asks, pointing to my cut with his head.

"Yes, sir." I stand tall, not at all ashamed of my club or my brothers.

He pauses, slowly nodding his head. "As long as you stay safe." He smiles a small smile.

"I always do, Mr. Long." I look down into his eyes.

"Is that my deviant son?" My dad yells, walking out of the kitchen and drying his hand on a paper towel.

He wraps his arms around me and claps my back hard. The old man still has to show that old age hasn't softened him. My dad's only a few inches shorter than me, with blonde hair and ice-blue eyes. Honestly, he looks more like Cale or Saint than like me, the exception of our build. I got my looks from my mom: dark hair, dark blue eyes, thin nose.

We pull apart, but he holds his hands on my shoulders, looking into my eyes like he does every time he sees me. Like he's making sure I'm still here. Losing my mom almost killed him. If he lost me too, I don't think he'd survive it. "Hi, dad." I smile.

"Hi, buddy. I missed you." He grins and slaps my arm once more before letting go and walking behind the bar to the register. He regards the Longs and slides my beer to me when I take a seat at the bar a few seats away from the register.

I love my dad. He's always been one of my best friends. He took me to get my first tattoo at sixteen, even though my mom about killed him when we got home that night. It was my parents' wedding date on my ribs. Still got it, and I won't ever cover it. He's always supported whatever I wanted to do, even if he didn't agree with it. He let me make my own mistakes, but was there to support me through putting the pieces back together. My parents have always been involved in my life; attending all of my plays in elementary school, wrestling matches, or football games in middle and high school. Now my dad caters club events or hosts them here at Big Dawgs. He treats everyone who comes into this bar like they've been life-long friends. He's the best kind of man there is; the kind of man I wish I was.

"Are you married yet?" Mrs. Long asks, standing next to me at the bar.

My dad snorts, tapping at the screen of the register. "Not for a lack of trying. I don't know how many girls I've tried to set him up with in hopes that he would settle down." I take a long drink of my beer. Here we go.

Mrs. Long smiles. "Oh, I don't think Finn needs any help meeting ladies."

"I'm working on it, dad." I sigh and take a drink.

My dad's head snaps to mine, his eyes wide. "You're dating someone?"

I smirk and take another drink, making him wait for an answer. Serves him right. "I'm working on it."

"Are the guys coming?" My dad asks, leaning his thick arms against the bar in front of me after the Longs have left. My dad likes tattoos, but he's clean compared to me. He just has one sleeve.

I swallow the pull I just took. "Yeah. Cale, Saint, and Ro."

He nods and turns around to pull bottles of beer from the

fridge, a short tumbler, and Saint's favorite Vodka down from the shelf. He sets all of our preferred drinks out and the guys make their way in, one by one, in the next few minutes.

We find a table and order, smacking small talk while we wait for our food. "We're hosting the O'Connell family on Friday," Ronan says, biting into his burger.

Callum takes a pull from his beer. "Your Irish cousin?"

Ro nods, chewing. "Distant, but yeah," he says after swallowing.

"Ronan finally decided to let family into our ammo biz." Saint pops a small breaded shrimp into his mouth.

Ro's mouth curves into a grin, while he looks at Saint from the corner of his eyes. "Killian just inherited the family from his father and is moving operations to the States." He looks around at all of us. "I know you've all met a few times before, but I want to show him and his guys a good time. Make them feel welcome here."

"Come on, Ro. When aren't we a good time?" I smirk above the lip of my bottle.

Ronan ignores me; he's used to us by now. "The four of us will take Killian and his cousin, Conor, to the warehouse to show them the operations. I want the Prospects to plan the party and put it on while we're out. We'll meet them back at the club-house when we're done." Saint pulls his phone out of his back pocket, probably to summon the little fuckers right now. "This party is important."

"So their top rocker is contingent on their ability to throw a rager?" Saint smirks. His smirk is fucking evil; it never turns into anything good.

Ronan turns his head to stare at Saint, deadpan. "Would we want anyone in the club if they couldn't?"

"Fuck no!" Callum and I yell at the same time.

Ronan's deep laugh reverberates out of his chest. "Good. Now let's go play some pool. You two blonde fucks versus us." He motions between him and me.

7

HUNTLEY

THE KNOCK AT MY FRONT DOOR BREAKS MY THOUGHTS, AND I TURN away from the large mirror in my closet. Checking the peephole, I turn the locks and open the door to a smiling Farryn. But her smile slowly drops as soon as the door fully opens and she looks me up and down.

"Oh no. This won't work." She runs her finger down my body.

"What do you mean?" I look down at the soft, oversized white sweater and tight black jeans—really tight black jeans.

She pushes through my door, walking straight to my bedroom. "You gotta show some skin for an Outlaw party!" She yells over her shoulder as she walks.

What? No. No, I'm not going. "First of all, I am showing some skin, and second, why are we going there?"

"That small triangle of stomach where you tied the sweater doesn't count. And because I've always wanted to party with the Outlaws, and I guess Rachel hooked up with one of the Prospects after the amateur night, and he invited her and whoever she wanted." I find her in my closet flicking through my clothes. "The whole class is going."

I calm down a little. A group of girls that I know are better odds. Farryn hands me a new outfit. "But I like what I'm wearing. You know I don't like to stand out."

She crosses her arms and purses her lips. "You're going to stick out more wearing what you're wearing now." I scan Farryn's outfit, a black, mesh, long-sleeved top with a maroon bra under it, skin-tight black leather mini skirt, and maroon Doc Martens.

Sighing, I grab the clothes from her and walk into my bathroom to change. I pull on the lace black bodysuit—the sides and back have no lining so you can see through the lace—and the distressed black jean shorts.

Farryn is sitting on my bed when I walk back through the door. "Much better." She nods her head, smiling.

"I'm going to freeze," I state, walking into my closet and grabbing an acid-washed denim jacket and my white converse. I already had on my usual thick winged liner and lashes, but I add a deep maroon lip.

She eyes the final outfit when I step out of my closet, her hands leaning back against my bed, holding her up. "That'll do." She smirks.

"Gee, thanks." I roll my eyes, leaving my room with her trailing behind me, cackling.

Farryn waits while I lock my door and we walk to the elevator together. "Thanks for driving tonight," she says as she leans against my arm in the elevator.

I loop my arm around her. "Anything for your alcoholic ass." I kiss the top of her head, and we laugh together. Farryn and I snark at each other all the time, but she's the closest thing I have to a best friend, and we've grown close in the last six months since I started going to the pole studio.

I pull up to the giant gates of the Devil's Outlaws' clubhouse. A tall man with floppy brown hair walks toward my car and I roll my window down.

He leans his arms against the window and his spicy cologne hits the back of my throat. His brown eyes sparkle, and he slowly runs his tongue across his top lip while he looks over Farryn and me. "Are you ladies lost?" The words roll off of his tongue.

Farryn leans over me, smiling up at the man. "Rachel invited us."

He nods, smiling, but his eyes quickly dart behind Farryn. I turn my head to see what he's looking at and see another man walking around my car, carrying a long stick. "Open your trunk, please." He smiles at me.

"What are you searching my vehicle for?" I narrow my eyes.

He pauses, looking between my eyes. "Weapons."

My mouth opens slightly. Where the fuck did Farryn bring us? "Why would someone bring weapons to a party?" My brows knit together.

He stands straight, shrugging one shoulder. "You can never be too careful with outsiders."

I look at Farryn and she's biting the side of her lip. She shrugs. I let out a breath. "Okay," I say as I click the button to open my trunk. It's empty, except for a roadside emergency kit, blanket, and a change of clothes. The blonde guy closes it again soon after.

"I'll see you ladies inside." The brunette motions for an older man and a guy with a hood over his head to slide the gates open.

We drive through slowly and immediately see the sea of bikes and cars. After finding somewhere to park, Farryn and I walk hand and hand through the parking lot toward the club-house. There are outdoor heaters and fire pits set up around outside, and people are standing around drinking or sitting around the fires, talking and playing card games. Several kegs and coolers are stashed around the lot. We find a cooler with some unopened beers and grab a can each. Farryn pulls me toward the large, square building where music and screams and laughter pour out from. "Paralyzed" by Sueco plays while we walk through the giant room. Farryn was right, I would have looked like a nun in my sweater and jeans compared to the rest of the girls in here. They're all wearing little shorts or skirts, with bras or bikini tops, and some are only wearing pasties. Farryn spots our group of girls from class and drags me over to them, lounging on a big couch at the back of the room. I perch on the arm of the couch, my arm resting behind Farryn. My eyes scan the room. There are several round tables with chairs around them, a long bar, and a pool table. I'm people watching, ignoring the conversation between my classmates, when my eyes fall on him. I didn't realize I was looking for him until I found him, and my eyes stopped searching. He's walking down a set of stairs to my left. His eyes scan the room, much like mine were before, and he looks bored. Emotionless. Until his eyes land on mine. He stops midstep, his head falling to the side and he leans his shoulder against the doorframe, crossing his arms, watching me. His eyes fall down my body slowly, and it scares me.

It scares me because he doesn't actually scare me at all.

His touch doesn't repulse me; his scent doesn't make me panic. The noise and the people fade away, just like they did at the strip club. We just watch each other. Finally, he breaks eye contact, motioning to the bar with his head and then he turns to walk toward it, without checking to see if I follow him. Should I? I raise my beer to my lips—It's empty. Well...

"I'm going to the bar to get another beer. Want anything?" I ask into Farryn's ear. She nods and holds up her can. I grab her empty can and dump them both into a large trash can on my way to the bar.

It's not hard to figure out which one he is. He's bent over, his arms resting on the bar, but he's bigger than anyone else here. The Devil's skull with snakes coming out of it every which way proudly displayed on his back. I walk to stand beside him; waiting for him.

He looks at me over his shoulder. "You stalking me?" He asks, a small smile in his voice.

I scoff. "Don't you wish?" I raise my hand to get the bartender's attention.

A pretty girl with pink hair hurries over and I give her my order. "I wouldn't mind it." He shrugs as the bartender comes back with mine and Farryn's beers and quickly pours another round in the man's glass without him saying anything.

I laugh softly, shaking my head. This guy has an answer for everything. "Why were you at the library last week? Are you enrolled?"

He takes a drink, and turns on his arm to face me, still leaning against the bar on his forearm. "No. I own a body shop and I was dropping off a customer's car to them on campus. I had heard there was a room in the library that looked like the Great Hall in Harry Potter, and I wanted to see it." Makes sense. That's every Freshmen's first stop when they set foot on campus for the first time.

I turn to face him at the same time that a shorter man, about my height, shoulders past me, knocking me into the bar. It didn't hurt, but I glared at him anyway.

"Sorry." The shorter man smirks, running his eyes slowly down my body as he passes. His gaze feels like slimy fingers sliding their way across my skin. Chills run down my body and I feel my stomach knot with nausea.

I grab ahold of his arm, intending to get him to turn around before knocking the smug look off of his face, but as my arm makes contact, the massive man is yanking the shorter one back by the back of his neck, slamming his head into the bar between us. I meet his eyes, and they're wild. His big chest rises and falls quickly and his thin nose flares, but still, he doesn't scare me. We're locked in each other's gaze once again, like a trance.

"Finn, what the fuck?" The man against the bar tries to yell.

Finn, I suppose, applies more pressure to the back of the man's neck, causing a choking sound to leave him. I watch him squirm against the wooden bartop, his eyes starting to widen with the realization of what he's done.

"You don't touch what belongs to me," Finn growls next to the man's ear. *Hang on, what?* "Apologize to her." He bites out, yanking the man up by his neck again and directing him to stand in front of me.

"I-I'm sorry," he stutters. His eyes are saucers, and his eyebrows are practically in his hairline.

"You're sorry for making her uncomfortable." Finn squeezes harder and the man yelps.

"I'm s-sorry for m-making you uncomfortable." The man squeaks.

Finn shoves him away from us so hard that the man lands on his hands and knees in the giant berth that the rest of the party-goers have created around us. "And you're fucking fired."

The man stands with his jaw dropped. "But you're not my boss." He accuses.

"You think Saint will allow a perv to work in his fucking tattoo shop?" Finn steps into the man's space, and the man has to drop his head back to look up at the giant. "I don't think so." Finn pulls him in even closer by the collar of his shirt. "Get the fuck out of my clubhouse while you can still walk." Finn releases him and he runs out of the building, people parting for him. Finn turns around and I open my mouth to ask him what the fuck that "belongs to me" shit was about, but I stop when I see him climb onto the bar and whistle loudly. "Listen the fuck up!" he bellows through the room, and I swear the walls shake. The music cuts out and everyone falls silent, their attention solely on the man standing on the bar. "If anyone so much as looks at my Old Lady, you will answer to me. If I find out anyone has made her uncomfortable, it will be the last thing you ever do." I look at my friends at the back of the room, they're all staring at me with mixed expressions, confusion being the majority. When I meet Farryn's eyes, I shake my head, because I don't know what the fuck is going on either. "Pass that around, because that's the only fucking warning I'll give." He jumps off of the bar with a loud thud, the barstools next to him shaking with the impact. Finn looks down at me from over his shoulder and walks away without a word.

I follow him through the crowd. He can't just make some declaration like that and then walk away. When we come to a wide hallway, I grab the back of his cut and slam him into the double door. Well, it would be a slam for a normal sized person, but for him, it was more of a suggestive redirect. "What the fuck was that?" I hiss, fisting his tee shirt in my hand.

He smirks and runs his tongue across his plump bottom lip. My eyes briefly trace the motion before I remember that I'm upset, and I snap my eyes back to his. "He made you uncomfortable, so I made sure no one else would again."

"I don't need you to save me." My voice turns to ice. I don't need *anybody* to save me anymore.

He shakes his head. "No, you don't, but you deserve someone who will." He places his hand under my chin and strokes my jaw with his thumb. "You are beautiful, and you deserve to feel that way without trying to cover up." With his other hand, he removes my hand that's clutching my jean jacket closed. I didn't even realize I was attempting to cover myself with the hand that wasn't holding a death grip on Finn's shirt. I release both fabrics like they're burning me, and cross my arms under my chest. "Don't close yourself off to me." His thumb rubs my jaw again and I smack it away.

"Did you claim me back there?" I glare into his ocean-blue eyes.

He rubs the back of his neck, his eyes moving to the ceiling. "Uh... No—"

"What? Do you think I'm going to fall to my knees for you just like that? Like all of the other girls around here because you showed me some attention?" I hate him. A typical man, thinking that because he did someone a favor, he's owed something. I don't owe anyone anything, and this man can fuck right off if he thinks I'm going to bend over and take him because he threatened everyone. Even though that's something I've always yearned for; someone to stand up for me even though I'm perfectly capable of standing up for myself.

Finn chuckles and I almost hit him in his perfect fucking face. "You've already proved that you don't do anything *just like that*." He leans down and gently kisses my cheek, and the scent of his cologne catches in my throat, making my breath stop. He moves to my ear. "But when you do fall to your knees for me, Angel, I hope it's with every ounce of attitude and fire that you have in you right now," he whispers.

Then he steps around me and goes back up the stairs that he came down minutes ago. I stand there, speechless, just staring at the double doors in front of me.

8

———

FINN

THIS GIRL. THIS FUCKING GIRL IS GOING TO BE THE DEATH OF ME. The way her long legs move across the room, her tight, thin body, waist-length hair—fuck, she's a goddamn dream. And her attitude; she's not intimidated by me, or charmed, for that matter. She drives me fucking crazy, in all the best ways. I had to step away from her, or I was going to throw her over my shoulder and lock us in my room, not letting her leave until she shelved that attitude and was on her knees in front of me like a good girl. Well, that's not completely true. I never want her to lose her fire, especially when she's in my bed. I stomp up the stairs and slam into my old bedroom, right across the hall from Cale's old room. I land on the bed on my back, staring up at the ceiling. I pull my lighter out of my pocket and spin it between my fingers. The bass from the music bleeds upstairs, through the door to the hallway I left open. I light my joint and take a few tokes, listening to the moans from Leo's room. Between the blonde downstairs and the sex surrounding me up here, my balls are hurting, so I decide to head back downstairs and get another drink. I step into the hall and pull my door shut, locking it. Taking another drag, I turn and spot the object of my obses-

38

sion at the end of the hall, her back turned to me, her long, straight hair swishing as she walks. *Please tell me she was not up here looking for an open room and an open brother.* "Can I help you find something, Angel?" I yell down the hallway at her. She quickly spins around, her eyes wide, like she was caught. *Goddamn it.*

Her hair flares out around her. "No, I was actually looking for you." She crosses her arms over her chest.

The moans start in Leo's room again, and my anger subsides. He was still occupied with whoever wasn't the girl in front of me. I knew that was illogical—it couldn't have been her, the moans started shortly after I came upstairs—but it still didn't stop me from worrying. "Me?" I ask, taking another toke. "Why?" I breathe the smoke out through my nose.

"I'm not sure yet." She takes a step toward me.

I nod and turn to unlock my door that I just locked. I push it open and walk back inside, leaving the door open for her to decide if she follows me. The light on the bedside table casts a dim glow around the room, and I sit at the head of the king bed, my back against the wall. Just when I'm about to give up hope that she's coming, she slowly walks through the door. She looks around, taking in the room, finally landing on me on the bed. Her body tenses and she crosses her arms. "Do I make you uncomfortable?" I ask on an exhale of sweet smoke.

"A little," she whispers. Her blue eyes boring into mine.

I lean over to the nightstand and pull open the drawer, taking out the Glock I leave here. I click out the magazine, making sure it's full, and slam it back in. Making sure the safety is on, I toss it to the end of the bed. "The safety is on, but you can turn it off. You can also leave the door open, and take a seat in the desk chair." I lean back against the headboard again, watching her. Hoping she stays.

Huntley looks around the room one more time before slowly

walking—no, gliding, like the fucking angel she is—to the bed. She picks up the gun in her delicate hand, turning it side to side, and I think my dick almost rips through my jeans at the sight of her handling it. She finally sets it on the bed and perches next to it.

"Why do we keep running into each other?" Her head cocks, eyeing me.

"Fate." *Slight stalking.* Kind of, the library really was a coincidence. I was lost in the library looking for that damn fucking room when I saw her in between the stacks, and I couldn't stop my feet from moving towards her. She pulls me in like a fucking magnet, and I'm powerless to resist. I don't know what the fuck is going on with me. I think it's just the allure of the chase since I've never had to do it.

She cocks her head, and her long hair brushes against the bed, the white blonde stark against the black comforter. "I don't believe in fate." I watch her dark lips while she talks, loving their movement.

"Why not?" I ask, leaning forward to offer her the joint.

She eyes the joint for a long time, finally leaning forward to take it from my outstretched hand. Our fingers brush for that brief second, our eyes locked on each other, and something passes between us. I'm not sure what, but I've never felt anything like it in my life. She places the joint between her pouty lips and inhales. "Because I refuse to believe something is cruel enough to send you the best thing in your life, and the worst. People just suck. Don't mitigate their actions by giving them something else to place the blame on."

"All people are terrible?" I take the joint back from her.

She looks away from me, focusing on the open door to the hallway. "Most are."

Leaning my head against the wall behind me. "What about me?" I ask.

Huntley turns her head to look at me again. She's on the edge of the bed, her arms behind her, holding her up. She slowly runs her eyes down my body and back to my eyes. "Depends on how tonight ends."

"Why are you in my clubhouse tonight?" I bend one leg and rest my elbow on it.

Huntley turns her torso toward me, still using one hand beside her to hold herself up. "Partying like everyone else."

"You didn't look like you were enjoying it much," I say, offering her the joint again.

She takes it. "You're the one hiding upstairs." God, her voice is so fucking smooth, like silk spilling from her lips. "Besides, I work in the night life industry, I stopped partying for myself a long time ago."

"Where do you work?" I try to sound like I'm making small talk, even though I already know exactly where she works, and how long she's worked there. I drew the line at getting her schedule, though. That felt too stalkery.

She takes the joint from me again. I might light another one just to have an excuse to keep touching her. "Mickey's." She answers after a beat.

"Can I come see you there sometime?" Since when do I ask permission to do anything?

She raises her brows, her lips sliding into a smug grin that makes me want to wrap my hand around her thin throat and kiss it right off of her face. "If you tip well."

A laugh tumbles out of me. I shouldn't have expected anything less from her. "I tip real well, Angel."

Knocking at the door draws our attention away from each other. It's Cale, leaning against the frame. "Finn, Church is starting." He inclines his head towards the stairs at the opposite end of the hallway.

I nod silently, and he turns to leave. Huntley hands me the

roach and I take one last hit, stubbing it out in the ashtray on the nightstand next to the bed. I turn back to see Huntley extending her hand toward me again. "I'm Huntley," she says.

I shake her hand. "I'm Finn." Fuck, I love touching her.

She chuckles. "Yeah, I got that when you were shoving that man's face into the bar."

I growl low in my throat, remembering that fucking idiot. "The little fuck deserved it." Standing from the bed, I offer her my hand. She stares at it for a minute, biting the inside of her lip, before she finally places her delicate hand in my callused one. I guide her to stand, but I don't step back. Our chests press together and I bend down to whisper in her ear. "I'll see you around."

I feel something cold press into my abs. The barrel of my fucking gun. I take a curious look down at my gun held in her hand, and she pushes me back with it, making room between us. "See you later, Pretty Boy." She cocks her arched brow and smirks. Placing the gun in my hand, she walks past me and out of the door. *Holy fuck.*

9

FINN

THE MUSIC THUMPS LOUDER WITH EVERY STEP I TAKE DOWN THE stairs, but my mind is still in my room with Huntley, my Angel. Pushing open the double doors to The Chapel, everyone falls silent and all eyes fall on me. Great, I'm the last to arrive. Saint starts a slow clap, and every eye slides to him and slowly back to me, confused as fuck, and I mean, me fucking too. This is a little extreme for being a few minutes late. Fuck, maybe I was saving a life or something, being a fucking stand-up citizen.

"How's the Devil's Outlaws Washington Chapter's first Old Lady?" *Shit, I kind of forgot about that.* Not completely though, she is mine.

Rubbing my hand over the back of my neck while every one of my brothers laughs at me, I walk to my seat and sit down. Cale leans over the armrest of his leather chair, and I hold my hand up to silence him. "Shut the fuck up." He snickers as he pulls away. Fucking shithead. I gesture to Tobi at the end of the table.

Saint shakes his head, his lips pursed. "Tobi is like ninety, he's not in our generation."

"Hey, jackass!" Tobi scolds, interrupting Saint.

"Besides," Saint continues. "They barely talk, so she doesn't count."

"Congratulations," Ronan rumbles, a small smile tugging at his lips. "When you're ready to make it official, let us know." I nod my head, my fingers fishing for the lighter in my pocket. I don't like being the center of attention, especially when there's more than just my brothers in this room right now.

Killian and Conor O'Connell sit opposite Cale and me. They are watching the room with their piercing gazes; Killian's eyes a deep green, and Conor's such a pale blue, they almost look like ice.

"So what did you think of the warehouse?" Ronan starts.

Killian turns to Ronan. "Very impressive, but you already knew we would go with you. Family stays with family."

"When will the rest of the family be on U.S. soil?" Saint asks from beside Killian.

Conor steps in. Dude looks like a fucking teenager, but he's only a few years younger than us—no more than twenty-one. Killian is my age, twenty-five, and he inherited the family business earlier than most. His dad wanted to expand operations to the U.S., and believed Killian was ready. Killian chose his younger cousin as his second. "The last of 'em should be here by the end of next week."

"And what type of arrangement were you thinking?" Saint continues, Ronan seeming happy to let Saint lead this. He leans back in his chair at the head of the table, keeping an eye on the two Irish cousins standing behind Saint, Killian, and Conor— and not for Killian and Conor's sakes.

Killian turns his body to face Saint. I would too—all that head turning shit would put a crick in my damn neck. "A big shipment at first, and then as needed. We haven't got much pushback to expanding and don't anticipate many enemies."

Saint looks to Ronan—we all do, he's our President. "Okay,"

Ronan finally says. "Leave us to vote on it and I'll give you our final decision when we've made it." Killian, Conor, and their goon cousins leave the room, leaving just my brothers and me. "All in favor of taking on the O'Connells, raise your hands." One by one, we all raise our hands. There aren't any negatives to taking them on. They're less likely to turn on us, being a distant relative to Ronan. They're young kids who aren't set in their dumbass ways, and are more willing to work with others. Plus, they're not total psychos who will go around just popping people with our bullets. "All in favor. We move forward with the O'Connells." Ronan slams the wooden gavel onto the wooden table with the devil skull with snakes engraved into the middle. We all rise from our seats, except for Ronan and Saint, and slowly make our way out of The Chapel.

My eyes scan over the bodies standing and moving around the clubhouse. I don't see her long, white blonde hair anywhere, so I walk into Purgatory. The red lights dance around the black room, illuminating the women moving on the stage and dancing on the men sitting in the chairs surrounding it. I quietly leave; nothing in here catching my attention anymore, and make my way upstairs back to my room. Maybe she waited for me there. The hallway is empty. Not shocking, only brothers are allowed up here—and of course, whoever they bring with them. I step into my room, the door already open, and find it empty. She left. I turn around, walk down the stairs, and back through the clubhouse to the parking lot. There isn't any reason I want to be here anymore.

I pull down my long driveway, driving into my home shop, and turn off my Hellcat. I walk across the even pavement and onto my wooden porch, unlocking the back door. The interior of my house is bathed in darkness, and that's not just the lack of light—everything is black; the black marble kitchen counters, the black subway tile backsplash, the couch, the coffee table, the walls in the open plan living room. I drop my keys into the organized drawer holding the keys to all of my vehicles and make my way through to the master bedroom on the other side of the house. The long hallway is dark with dark walls, and the double black doors with silver hardware open into my large owner's suite, where a giant low bed with LEDs lights the bottom and the perimeter of the ceiling; blue tonight. I strip, leaving my clothes on the floor—other than my cut, which I laid over the black velvet footrest at the end of the bed. I step into my bathroom; black herringbone flooring, with a large, black, tile steam shower. I brush my teeth at the counter and then shuffle back into the bedroom. I fall into bed and fall asleep immediately, remembering the feel of my Angel's fingers against mine, and the cold press of my gun when she held it against my stomach. *Goddamn, she's better than any dream my subconscious could create tonight.*

10

HUNTLEY

THE SOUND OF GLOVES SMACKING BAGS FILLS THE AIR OF THE LONG, rectangular boxing gym as I pummel the heavy bag, over and over. I punch with my right hand twice, switch to my left, deliver a quick kick with my left shin, then a final blow high on the bag with my right leg.

"That's it, Lee!" My old instructor cheers as he claps me on my very sore shoulder. They burn with the hits and kicks I've been exerting over the past hour.

"Thanks, Tyler," I say, unstrapping my gloves and pulling them off.

He stands beside my bag, his bulky arms crossed and his stance spread wide. "We haven't seen you here in a while."

Bending down to drop my gloves in my bag and pull out my water bottle, I take a drink, still squatting next to my duffle bag. "Yeah, I know. I had some energy to burn this morning." I use a towel to wipe the sweat from my chest and the back of my neck.

"Yeah, I could see the crease between your brows from across the gym." His mouth forms a wide smile, his perfect white teeth popping against his tanned skin. His deep laugh tumbles out of him when I throw my sweaty towel at his head. He catches it of course. Douche. Tyler tosses the towel back to me. "You wanna help me demo some combinations for the class? He gestures behind him to the group haphazardly throwing punches at the bags at the end of the long gym.

"I can't, I'm sorry. I have to go home and shower and nap before work tonight." I give him a half smile. I trained with Tyler at his gym three days a week for almost a year, before I dropped to start taking pole instead. I still come in when I'm in a mood or stressed or need to burn some energy.

Last night with Finn was... nice. Which scares me. I don't have *nice* interactions with people. Really the only person I've let in in a long time was Farryn.

I sling my bag over my shoulder, accepting Tyler's offered hand. "No problem, Lee. Be safe tonight!" He pulls me to stand.

"Always." I smirk before he turns around and walks over to his gathered students.

———

FLOPPING onto my bed in just my white fluffy towel, I grab my phone and open Instagram. I post the video Farryn recorded last week in class and then start scrolling through my feed. As if without thought, my fingers move to the search bar, but once my thumbs are hovering over the keyboard, I realize I only know Finn's first name. How could I find him? Wait, he mentioned something about a body shop, right? I swipe out of the app and click on Safari instead. I google body shops in Merrill Hill. I clicked through a few before opening Evans Body Shop's website. A few photos are posted on the website, and I immediately recognize the thick muscular arms in one photo. I pick him out instantly, despite his head being hidden behind the open hood of the car he's leaning into. Okay, Finn Evans. I take my findings back to Instagram and search for him by name. He pops up and I click on his profile. Thousands of followers, and only following club brothers and car profiles.

His profile is filled with lots of aesthetically pleasing pictures of cars; pictures of him with a man who looks a little like him; but mostly pictures of him with that guy that interrupted us and others wearing The Outlaw cuts. I scroll back to the top and hit the follow button before I can think about it anymore.

The room is dark, the only light coming from the small white lamp on my bedside table. The black-out curtains keep all sunlight out of my room and coat it in complete darkness. My feet sink into the white shag rug as I step across it to my closet to slip on some soft shorts and an oversized tee shirt. I pull back the black comforter and toss the white fluffy pillows to the floor so I can crawl into bed for a nap before work tonight. Blowing out the cinnamon apple candle on my nightstand—I don't care if it's March, fall scents are always in season—I sink into my mattress and close my eyes, thinking of that big, tattooed biker that keeps finding me wherever I go.

11

HUNTLEY

"YOU WANT ME DOING SHOTS TONIGHT? BUT I'M SUPPOSED TO BE behind the bar." I yell to my manager, trying to be heard over the pulsing bass reverberating around Mickey's.

"I know, but two shot girls called out and you'd make better tips on the floor anyways!" She smiles, like that alone will convince me.

I sigh and nod my agreement. The shot girls always do make more tips, and I haven't had any of them complain about handsy customers in a while. Why the hell not? I push past people and head to the main bar downstairs, walking behind to grab a tray and place several shots on it.

When my tray is full, I balance it on my hand and leave the safety of the back of the bar, stepping into the fray of bodies. Eyes follow me and people stop me to buy shots. When my tray is empty, I walk back to the bar and refill it, repeating this several times. About an hour in, I'm starting to realize that the higher tips aren't worth the monotony of serving shots. Behind the bar I got to talk to the other bartenders and customers. I was making different drinks, and experimenting with new ones. Out here, I'm just trying not to be shoved over and spill my shots all over myself. I make rounds around the downstairs area, the patio, and the rooftop. The cool air hits me when I take the last step onto the rooftop for the millionth time tonight. The black, mesh crop top and black, high-waisted distressed shorts doing shit all but make me freeze every time I come up here.

Shuffling from foot to foot, I wait for the bartender to place all of the tiny plastic shot glasses on my tray. Big, warm hands grasp my waist and I feel a warm breath ghost over my neck. I spin around, my hair fanning out around me as I go, and pull my fist back in a punch. I swing at whoever thinks they can touch me, but Finn catches my fist in his large hands inches from his nose.

"I'm starting to think this is how you say hello." He smiles, still holding my fist.

I yank it away, glaring at him. "How many times do we need to have the conversation of consent and boundaries?" I hiss.

Finn smirks. "I was about to say hello, but you resorted to violence before I could." I roll my eyes, turning my back on him to grab my tray. "If I buy all of those, would you be able to take a break and sit with me?"

"I suppose." I sigh, it's been hours and I wouldn't mind a break. "Twelve dollars," I say, holding out my hand.

"Keep the change." He places a fifty-dollar bill in my hand, and I hand him the tray after placing the bill in my black waist bag.

Finn sets the tray back down on the bar, motioning over the bartender. "Free shots for whoever wants them. Huntley's taking a break."

"Sure thing." The bartender says, taking the tray back to where he was working.

I follow Finn to his table, where there are only two chairs and one is already occupied by that blonde guy who interrupted us last night. Finn falls into the other chair, staring up at me with a smile.

"You two look pretty cozy, you gonna give your chair up for me?" I cross my arms and stare at Finn.

A devilish smirk slides onto Finn's face and I just know he's gonna come back with something annoying. "Baby, I am your chair." *Knew it.*

"Do these lines really work for you?" Jesus, why does anyone fall for this shit?

His tongue moves along his bottom lip, accentuating his smirk. "Usually I don't have to say anything, my body is typically doing the talking."

"I'd thought it'd be your pretty face that girls usually fell for first." I sneer. Why is this conversation making me jealous? I don't even know this guy.

He grabs my hands gently, holding them in his. "No one's ever made it that far, that's why you're perfect for me." He stares up at me, his deep blue ocean eyes watching me carefully.

"If I sit, you have to massage my shoulders." I can't believe I'm giving in to this, but I can't help it.

"Angel, if you're in my lap I'd do whatever you want me to." He gently pulls me forward, and I obediently sit in his lap, sideways so I can see both him and his friend.

I watch as they talk. Finn's thumb gently rubs back and forth over the exposed skin of my outer thigh, leaving a burning trail along the way.

I feel Finn shift underneath me. He leans forward, holding me still as he whispers into my ear. "I like talking to you, I want to keep seeing you."

I turn to look at him, his blue eyes capturing me for a moment before I remember what he had said. "You act like this is a date."

"Then let me take you on one." He counters quickly.

I laugh softly, the thought of him showing up with a bouquet of flowers and in a suit flashing through my mind. "Have you ever even been on a date?"

"No." He shakes his head. "But I want to go on one with you." I stare into his eyes, trying to find some sliver of a lie; any red flag to make myself run away from him, but I can't.

Finn's eyes quickly divert behind me and I turn to follow his line of vision. "Cale, where the fuck are you going?" he yells, as Cale quickly stomps towards a short redhead and some guy towering over her, grabbing her arm. She's beautiful, with her long, soft waves flowing down her back. I stand to intervene as well, but Finn places a hand on my shoulder to stop me as he passes me by, following after his friend.

That kind of pisses me off—I don't need anybody to protect me. I turn on my heels and walk back to the bar; my break is over. I figure the little redhead is safe with the two scary bikers, insert eye roll, and that she doesn't need my help as well. I lean my elbows against the bartop, waiting for the bartender to finish with a customer.

"Let's go on our date now," Finn says as he suddenly leans against the bar next to me.

I look around the rooftop. "Can't you see I'm working?" I snap at him.

"You can go." The bartender steps over to us at that time. "Marisa finally showed up for her shift."

"I can bartend then," I say, taking the red flannel from around my waist and sliding my arms through it.

He bites his lip. "We're too full tonight, just take off with your boyfriend."

I sigh. I had already made more in tips than what I normally would, so I could leave early and still make rent this month. "He's not—"

"Let's go, Angel." Finn takes my hand.

I yank it back. "Where are we going?"

He smiles and steps closer, his hands landing on my hips, but I don't have the normal urge to brush him off. I like the feeling of his warm skin against mine. "Where do you want to go?"

I think it over. What are we going to do? Go to the movies? Go back to his clubhouse? No, that's not me. "Show me something that means something to you. Don't take me to wash your Harley or get a tattoo. Show me something real." I raise an eyebrow, challenging him.

Finn looks to the sky and bites his lip. After a moment he finally looks back at me. "Okay, I got it. Let's go." He grabs my hand and pulls me down the stairs and through the bar.

We walk along the wide, bright sidewalk of The District, passing bar after bar, pushing through the crowd who are switching bars, or just getting into The District, probably after partying at a house party after the game today. Just as we're about to pass The Sticks, Finn pulls me inside.

The sunken dance floor is busy with bodies moving together and the porch around it has people standing around watching or sitting at the high-top tables.

"I never took you for a country fan," I say, walking beside him to the bar.

He orders us two beers and then turns to watch me. "I'm not really, but it was the only place I could think of in The District."

"So why here then?" I look around the bar. People are laughing and joking, dancing together, and there's even a mechanical bull in the far corner where people are standing around yelling and cheering as a young guy holds on for his life.

The bartender leaves our drinks on the counter and Finn pulls out a bill to way overpay him. He takes a long drink, and I don't think he's going to answer me. "My mom was from Texas and she loved to dance." His eyes drift to the dance floor beside us. "She taught me, and at every wedding we went to in Texas, she made my dad and me two-step with her. My dad hated it, but he loved her, and the way she would light up on the dance floor made it worth it." His mom and I have something in common. I love to dance too, ballet when I was little, and now pole. He takes another drink. "I haven't danced since she died, but I want to, with you." My heart melts out of my body. I didn't even think I was capable of feeling anything like this again. I don't know what to say. What do you say to someone who just bared that much of his soul to you? His mom sounds like she was the light of his and his father's lives, and he wants to share this with me. I thought he would take me to his favorite bar, or up to Look Out Ridge and tell me he lost his virginity there. This is so much better. I nod my head and let him lead me to the side of the dance floor. "Have you ever two-stepped before?" He asks.

I shake my head. "No, but I'm a dancer so I can pick it up quickly."

His lips slide into his cocky smirk. "Is that why you were at The Second Circle? Scoping out our talent?"

Finn takes my hands and places one on his shoulder and holds the other in his tattooed hand. "No. I meant I danced when I was younger, but I take a pole class now for fun. My friends wanted to do amateur night."

"If I Was A Cowboy" by Miranda Lambert switches on next and Finn leans into me. "You'll take two quick steps forward, and one back, then repeat. It helps to keep your steps short and I'll lead the pace." I nod and we start to move slowly to the music, and I watch our feet while I get used to the motion of the dance. He moves so surely like he's been doing this all of his life, and I guess he kind of had. When I finally raise my eyes, confident in my steps, I connect with Finn's eyes, which are already watching me. "Wanna pick up the pace?" He asks, smiling. I nod mutely, and when the chorus hits again, he almost doubles our speed. Leading us in a circle around the dance floor with the other couples, the room moves around us, the air blowing us by as we dance together. His chest pressed to mine and his eyes watching me. I love this. I giggle—actually giggle—because I'm having more fun than I have in a long time. Finn's loud laughter matches mine, his face lighting up more than I've seen yet.

The song ends and I frown looking around. "Can we do another song?" I ask, not wanting to leave the dance floor.

"Of course, Angel." Finn pulls my body into his and leads me into another rhythm to match the next song.

We dance like that, pressed to each other, my eyes roaming from Finn's to the couples moving around us, until the DJ calls for last call. I snap my head up to look at Finn. We've been dancing for two hours and I didn't even realize. It only felt like a few songs. "I didn't realize we'd been here that long," I say, pulling my head back so I can see into his eyes better.

"Me either." He chuckles. "Wanna go grab some food?"

"Food too?" I laugh.

He shrugs one shoulder, already leading me off of the dance floor. "Aren't you supposed to get food on dates?"

We walk through the doors and the cold hits instantly, the wind chilling me. "I suppose." I wrap my arms around myself.

Finn notices and slides out of his cut, handing it to me. I take it and look at it in confusion. What did he want me to do with this? It doesn't have any sleeves. I look back at him to ask why the fuck he gave me this, when I see his black hoodie sliding over his face, the hoodie pulling his tee shirt with it and showing off a chiseled tattooed stomach. He's completely covered in tattoos, from mid-stomach down to the waistband of his jeans. I blink a few times to get my brain to start working again. *Holy fuck, that's hot.* He hands me the discarded hoodie and holds out his hand for his cut. We exchange them and I pull his hoodie over my head. It's huge, and hangs to mid-thigh, but it smells so strongly of his spicy cologne. The same one that was wrapping me in a blanket while we were dancing.

"So Chinese or Mexican?" He points in the direction of each restaurant as he says the names.

Nothing is better than late-night tacos... or Lo Mein. "I can't decide, you choose."

"Both then." He smiles and pulls me down the street to Hunams first.

Finn leads me down the sidewalk, carrying two big bags of food, and still holding my hand. We make it to the parking lot and he leads me to a beautiful, gunmetal gray Hellcat. I stare at it as he sets the food on the hood, walks to the driver's side and gets in, starting it. I listen to the loud rumble as he gets out and walks around to the trunk, popping it open and disappearing behind it. The rumble does something to me; my stomach filling with heat as I listen to the menacing sound. This is the same car that Farryn was admiring after pole class a few weeks ago—he really is everywhere. Finn comes back carrying two blankets. He lays one blanket over the hood and sits down, looking up at me from under his long, dark lashes. I take a seat next to him and he lays the other blanket over my bare legs.

"after dark x sweater weather" by daddy's girl, creamy, and 11:11 music group plays from the speakers in Finn's car while we pull food out of the bags and start eating.

"I had a lot of fun tonight," I say between bites.

Finn finishes his burrito in three bites. "I did too." He unwraps another one. "So tonight was a good first date?"

Twirling my noodles around my fork, I nod. "Yeah."

"So you'll let me take you out again?" He demolishes another burrito and reaches for his Lo Mein.

I swallow the bite I took, bringing my legs onto the hood and crossing them. "Yeah, you can message me on Instagram. I followed you today."

Finn slurps his noodles. "I saw that. You're really good on the pole." My mouth drops. "Not sexually!" He hurries to cover. "None of the girls at Second can do some of the stuff you were doing in your videos."

I close my mouth. He's not wrong. The girls at his club seemed to prefer floor work and lap dances over pole tricks. Maybe they made more money that way, I don't know.

"Thank you," I say with a small smile.

We finish our meals—very large and oddly combined meals —but exactly what I wanted nonetheless, and talk more. Him telling me about his club brothers and his shop, and me sharing what I'm going to school for and a little about my dad.

We step into the small employee parking lot behind Mickey's and I lead Finn to my car. I click the unlock button on my fob as we walk up to the side of my car and he pulls the door open for me. I smile in thanks and slip past him. "Goodnight, Finn," I say, his tattooed hand resting on my door.

He rests his other hand on my hip, holding me still; not with force, but of my own volition. He leans down, placing a gentle kiss on top of my head. "Goodnight, Angel. Message me when you get home."

I nod in agreement, and before I can think of it anymore, I lean up and quickly kiss his cheek, pulling away as fast as I went in, and step into my car. Finn shuts the door and steps back, crossing his arms. I start my car and slowly pull away, watching him still standing in the same spot as I drive away. What even was tonight and who is that man? He's nothing like what he looks like. He's gentle and funny. He's fun, and I really enjoyed tonight.

12

FINN

THE TINKLING OF CASINGS AND THE RELOADING MACHINES SOFTLY clinks around the small concrete basement of Cale's warehouse. I'm standing down here with Saint and Ronan while they talk to the manager. They're trying to figure out how quickly we can get something going for the O'Connells, and it looks like we're going to have to hire a few more employees to make up for the extra load. No problems there; money speaks in this town, as does our reputation. Our employees are either too scared or too in love with the money to ever rat on us. Not that it would do them a whole lot of good in this town; they'd have to take this crime way above Merrill Hill PD. I was really only down here to make sure there weren't any issues with the machines, and since there isn't, I ascend the concrete staircase and enter Cale's office through the old red Coke machine.

Cale is sitting at his desk, looking over a few blueprints when I walk through, and I drop into the chair opposite his big desk, extending my legs in front of me. We are sitting in comfortable silence. That's what I love about my brothers, we don't have to fill every silence with something pointless. We just exist with each other, sometimes for each other. I love my dad, and I loved my mom, but it's a different kind of love when you *choose* to love each other. Cale's phone starts vibrating wildly on the desk beside his hand, and his head snaps up from the printed blueprints in front of him to the desktop computer. His eyebrows pull together and his eyes narrow, searching the screen and clicking around with his mouse.

"What the fuck?" he mutters, grabbing his phone and the handgun off of the desk. I follow Cale as he storms out of the office, tapping at his phone furiously. "Leo, Jack!" he yells the Prospect's names and they turn around sharply as we storm to them where they're standing at the huge sliding door of the warehouse. "There's movement on the West side of the shop in the forest. Go!" Cale orders.

Leo and Jack share a look before Leo sprints to the back of the warehouse and quietly leaves through the back door, while Jack sneaks through the open sliding door at the front, both with guns pulled. The breeze blows into the warehouse while Cale watches the security cameras on his phone and I stand over his shoulder and watch it too. Every few breaths, you can barely see the top of someone's head peek around the trunk of a giant tree. My blood rises; someone is watching us. Sneaking around on our fucking property. I clench my fists at my side, watching the screen of Cale's phone. Through the camera, we watch Leo fly through the air and tackle the man to the ground, like a wolf going after its prey. He pummels into him with a brutality I'd never seen in the kid, and I have to admit, I'm impressed. The man tries to fight back, but Leo's blows are so vicious that he eventually tries to just shield his head, not that it does much good. I let out a dark chuckle, watching Leo beat the man unconscious while Jack finally meets them and stands over them with his gun hanging loosely at his side.

Leo and Jack drag the man back, dropping him in the dirt in front of us. Leo huffs heavily, his knuckles dripping blood, and

Jack has a feral look in his eyes that I recognize all too well. I think we just found these boys' roles in the club.

"Put him in the van." I nod toward the black club van. "Take him to the cabin and wait for me." Jack and Leo drag the unconscious man around the side of the warehouse, and I hear the thump of his body landing on the metal back of the van when Ro and Saint walk out of Cale's office. Cale continues to look through camera feeds, probably trying to see if there are any other threats, and I watch the trees surrounding us, listening. I'm a hunter. I watch people and my surroundings. I pay attention to the things that most people ignore. The sounds that carry on the breeze, the bed of leaves that are slightly messed up from faint footprints. The way someone looks away when they lie, or gives too many details to try to convince you; when the small vein in someone's neck pulses harder when their heart rate spikes, and so much more. It's all a part of doing what I do, and I do it well.

"We found someone watching the clubhouse," Cale says when Ro and Saint are close enough. "Leo and Jack have him waiting in the van."

Both of their brows raise, they're shocked, and with good reason. We rule this part of Washington, and it didn't come easy. None of us set this club up, that was before our time. But we inherited it, and we made sure to keep our reputation dirty. It's been quiet for the last three years, the only time things popped off is when I've taken on jobs to gain favors from influential people who need someone gone. It's been quiet since our peace pact with The Kings of Mayhem, the only other club in Washington, but before that... We went at each other hard, and I did a lot of things that I'm not proud of. It's how we lost the majority of our club about three years ago. We killed... *I* killed the Kings Prez, and when the new one moved up, he and Ronan settled on a peace pact.

"You taking him to the cabin?" Ronan, the first to recover, asks me.

I nod, pulling the joint from behind my ear and placing it between my lips, but before I take my lighter out to spark up, I put it back. I'll be leaving soon, no sense in wasting it.

"Let's go take a look then." Ro stalks to the door and we all follow. Saint is keeping quiet, but I know he's plotting; he's always fucking plotting. That's just how his brain works, always putting things in mental boxes and figuring shit out. I've never seen this man make a decision out of emotion, it's always calm and calculated. What's best for the club or our brothers is always what makes his decision.

We meet Jack and Leo at the van. The night is quiet, and the stars and the overhead light in the back of the van are the only lights out here. The tall trees surround us, the only break is for the dirt road that leads out of here and a small trail at the back of the property.

Jack hops into the van and heaves the unconscious man up, tilting his face into Leo's phone's flashlight so we can get a look at his face. We all stay silent, none of us recognizing him, even through the blood and swelling that's already starting to set in.

I turn around without a word and stalk to my bike. The loud rumble calms me. It always has, ever since I heard the first army of bikes roll into my dad's restaurant when I was five. It was that day that I knew I wanted to join the club. They were like the cowboys that my dad watched in his Westerns, but so much more badass. Right before I lift the bike to kick up the kickstand, my mind drifts to Huntley, and how much I know she would enjoy being on the back of my bike.

Leo and Jack follow me through the winding back roads to the cabin. The wind rushes past my face, the trees turning into a blur beside me as I speed toward the club's remote cabin. When I get to the dirt road leading to the small wooden house,

I slow way down. My headlight illuminates the long dark road ahead of us. Around a bend, the trees break and the cabin comes into view. I pull behind the house while the guys pull into the small attached garage to take the man down the hidden stairs into the basement. When I switch my bike off and the sound cuts, the complete silence of wilderness envelopes me. Tilting my head back, I watch the moon through a gap in the trees. I take a few breaths, readying myself for what I'm about to do. You have to lose all humanity to torture someone, and I can turn mine off like a fucking light switch. It's why I'm so good at this; it's why I was chosen to do this job for the club. When the anchor that keeps you chained to the earth is ripped from you, you stop caring about humanity. My mom dying left a hole inside of me that I was never able to fill. I was angry, so angry that my mom was ripped away from us. We needed her. She was good, kind, a loving mother and wife, who baked pies for our neighbors for holidays and volunteered at the homeless shelter often. She bought gifts for the children who didn't have homes on Christmas and was always bringing people in to eat at Big Dawgs, just because they couldn't afford a meal anywhere else. I needed a place to put my anger, and I found it in being the Enforcer for the Outlaws. I know normal people don't get off on watching people bleed out. When someone wrongs them, their first instinct isn't to hunt them down and make a thousand cuts into their chest. I'm not a normal person. I'm fierce, and ruthless, and I won't stop until my family is safe. But there are moments where my old self peeks through, my joking and light self. It's only ever with my brothers and my dad, though. Slowly I swing my leg over and walk to the small garage, taking the steps down into the concrete basement.

Stepping off of the last stair I step into my element, every emotion from my body gone; all but anger. Leo and Jack chained our little plaything to the chair and they lean against the counter on the side of the room next to the sink.

My table is all set out for me, the Prospects having already gotten my tools ready. I reach for the smelling salts and turn back to look at my new proteges. "You can leave, or you can stay and let me teach you exactly what it takes to be an Outlaw." I watch them slowly, moving my eyes from one to the other. Jack and Leo look at each other, a silent agreement seeming to pass between them.

"We're all in, boss," Jack says, pushing off of the counter.

Nodding my head, I step toward the man chained to the metal chair. "That's what I thought. Now let's see who this rat is."

After a few passes of the salts under the unconscious man's nose, he jerks awake. His eyes fly open to land on me, leaning in front of him with my head cocked and an evil smile on my face.

———

THE COOL BREEZE feels like sandpaper against my already irritated and tired eyes. It's been well over thirty-six hours since I've slept, but I had to come here. I was slipping into the abyss. The emotionless black hole that sometimes sucks me in when I kill. I normally pull myself out with a handle of something and a long ass nap, or a woman in my bed, but none of that appealed to me this time. The only thing I could see in my mind was her.

I check my phone for the time, then look around. Waiting for her. I parked my bike in a nearby parking lot and then found this bench to wait on. It's across the street from her apartment building so I can see when she gets home from her last class of the day. I had to come here. I had to see her. After everything that happened in the cabin with the spy, and then the emergency club meeting where Cale found out that his new plaything has a stalker.

The shit we're in just keeps getting deeper. First, a spy that wouldn't crack from a black market agency. No idea who sent them or why someone would be watching us, and now, we're taking on a fucking stalker case too. Cale's about to get into some shit that I'm afraid might hurt him, but he can't see anything but the little redhead he saved at the bar, his hero complex coming out. Flicking my lighter between my two fingers, I wait.

But I guess I'm not all that different, right? I'm hiding on a bench with a hoodie covering my body and face, waiting to watch Huntley walk home. I just need some sleep... and to see Huntley. I won't be able to sleep and kick this funk until I've seen her.

I check my phone again, and when I look up, there she is. Walking through the giant gate that leads to campus, she walks quickly, her phone in hand but her head up, watching her surroundings. Her black backpack, gray joggers, and black tee shirt don't show any signs of the banging body she was showing off at the clubhouse or during our date. She waits with a group of people at the stoplight, and then they all cross the street and she heads into her apartment building, never looking my way. I sit here for a while longer before I finally stand up and walk to my bike. Starting it up, I look at the third floor of the Ridgeview Apartments, and then I drive home. My heart beats normally again and my brain clears from the fog that was surrounding it.

13

HUNTLEY

THE SMELL OF BAKED GOODS AND COFFEE WAFTS AROUND ME AS I walk into the main floor of the University library. I love it here. I take the steps to the second floor, the dessert and coffee smell meeting the smell of books, and I hold in a groan at how amazing the smell is. My table at the back by the giant circular corner of the building is empty, so I lay my bag on the wooden chair next to me and grab out my laptop and books to start working.

After a few worksheets, and getting caught up for my classes this week, I start to reload my things into my bag. But then I remember something Finn had said to me, that he was trying to find the Great Hall when he was here. Pulling my phone from my bag, I click on Instagram and pull up his profile. I click on my inbox and my fingers hover over the keyboard. What should I say? I figure something simple.

HUNTLEY

Did you ever find the Great Hall in the library?

Swiping out of the app quickly, I lock my phone and place it face up on the table, and I wait. I wait for what feels like forever, but really it was only a few minutes. I can't believe I'm practically simping for this man. I don't do this. I haven't been interested in anyone, but he's different. He's stunningly beautiful, yes, but it's more than that. He knows exactly how far to push me to step beyond my boundaries, but not too far that I'm uncomfortable and shut down.

When my phone vibrates and I open my phone so fast, it's embarrassing.

FINN

No, I was distracted by something far more beautiful in between the stacks.

Warmth pools in my stomach and rises to my heart, squeezing it tightly.

HUNTLEY

I'm here now if you want a tour.

He immediately messages me back, like he didn't even close out of the message thread.

FINN

I'm on my way.

I get an idea, a way to keep myself in check, because there is no way I am going to fawn over this man, especially not after only a month of knowing him.

HUNTLEY

Meet me on the third floor in the stacks.

Grabbing my bag and slinging it over my shoulder, I slide my phone into the back pocket of my jean shorts and take the stairs up one flight to the third floor. The entire floor is empty, as it usually is up here. The third floor is full of rows of folklore books and at the back is the giant room that everyone says resembles the Great Hall. It has a towering pointed ceiling with wooden beams running the length of the room, with deep mahogany herringbone flooring. Large wooden tables with wooden chairs around them are arranged down the room, and it has giant mosaic windows spanning from floor to ceiling. Beautiful murals of wooded areas with animals painted opposite the windows so the sun shining through the colorful panes paints the colors even more vibrant. The Great Hall is a complete silence workroom. Most people opt to work on the second floor or in the coffee shop downstairs because they can listen to music or talk to their friends or class partners. This room is completely silent, so the rest of the floor is too.

I place my bag by the entrance to the Great Hall, and then find a stack in the back row in the middle of the room with a good view of the entrance. Sitting on the floor, I cross my legs and lean against the books, waiting for Finn.

About twenty minutes later, I hear heavy footsteps ascend the steps. I climb onto my hands and knees and look over the gap in the books, and there he is. He stands at the entrance of the floor, a black tee shirt, dark wash jeans, black biker boots, a backwards hat, and his cut. He scans the room quietly, a white paper bag in his hands. He starts to move through the stacks, and I quietly rise to my feet and move a few stacks in the opposite direction. He's in the first row of stacks, whereas I'm in the third, and I plan to follow slowly behind him. Halfway through the first row, he steps between the first two rows and continues down. This worked better for me because I have a much better view now. He moves slowly, his steps turn deathly quiet, and now the only thing I can hear is my faint breathing, but I keep watching him, moving away slowly and pausing when he weaves between stacks. The only thing that makes it possible to hide on this floor is the offset arrangement of the stacks. The first and third-row line up while the second is in between, meaning you can't see completely through the floor. I'm watching Finn over the books on the shelves when I see him snap around, and I swear he looks right at me.

"I can smell you, Angel." He calls through the silence of the library. The jolt of his voice and thinking he saw me courses through me, and I take too big of a step back and run into the stack behind me, causing a small sound. He sets into motion at that, his strides increasing, making his way right to me. I turn and run and I don't look back. I get to the end of the room and round all three rows, making my way to the first row and slowing to make my way about halfway through the room. When I finally think I might be safe, I slide into a row and look around the corner in the direction I was originally hiding, listening to any sign of Finn. I lost sight of him in my attempt to make it away from him, and now I can't find him. "You smell so good," Finn whispers in my ear from behind me and I suck in a breath, my eyes going wide.

I feel his warm chest and stomach press into my back and he places a big tattooed hand on my waist, turning me around and pushing me back into the stack. My eyes slowly travel up his body and to his perfect face. The tattoos creep out of the neckline of his shirt and onto his neck, all the way to his jawline. His deep blue eyes penetrate mine and without thought, I rise on my tiptoes and gently place a kiss on his plump lips. He stiffens, and I suck in another breath, quickly pulling away.

I can't believe I just did that. Why did I just do that?

I was so excited about the hiding and the thrill of being caught by him, the kiss just felt natural after the adrenaline. I hear the paper bag land on the floor a second before Finn lifts my chin with tattooed fingers and presses into me. His lips land on mine in a much more brutal kiss. He sweeps his tongue across my lips, encouraging me to open them, and I do. In this moment, I'd do anything for him. Our tongues tangle for dominance, neither of us wanting to let the other have the upper hand. His hand slides from my chin to the side of my neck, and it immediately snaps me out of this moment with Finn and back to that moment in the bedroom of the K Gam frat house. I break the kiss and turn my face away from Finn. I don't want him to see the hot tears that well in my eyes.

It's not his fault. He doesn't know, and I don't want him to know.

I'm not going to let him see me like this; weak, broken, scared. I place my hands on his chest and push him a step back, stepping over the white paper bag on the floor and towards the Great Hall.

"I'll let you shut me out this time, Angel, but don't get used to it," Finn says from behind me, but I ignore him, choosing to walk away instead.

"The Great Hall is this way," I say, not letting myself look back. I take several deep breaths to try to calm my nerves and rein in my tears. I know he's following me; I heard the crinkle of the bag when he picked it up and I can hear his footsteps on the floor behind me. We breach the entrance to the hall and I finally turn to look at him. He's looking around the room, nodding his head. "What do you think?" I ask. "Is it everything you dreamed of?" I raise my eyebrows sarcastically.

"You are," he says, running his eyes down my body and back to my eyes, but it's not in a leering way. It makes me feel powerful, instead of gross. Powerful enough to have captured this man's interest and have held it for so long.

Rolling my eyes, I walk to the wall where I placed my bag and bend to pick it up. When I turn around, Finn is laying out napkins on a table and placing donuts on them. He sits on one side of the table in front of the towering stack of donuts I'm assuming are for him. He looks at me and motions for the chair opposite him. I release a breath and sit down across from him. A glazed donut, a purple sprinkle donut, and a cinnamon sugar muffin sitting on the napkin. "I didn't know what you liked, so there's more in the bag." He takes a giant bite out of the already large donut, eating half in that one bite.

"Is there such a thing as a bad donut?" I ask, biting into the glazed donut. I smile around the bite, I love glazed donuts.

"Creme filled," Finn says around another bite.

I nod my head while I chew. "True."

"Only one thing needs to be creme filled, and it ain't food." Finn smirks and I choke on my bite. Finn barks a loud laugh. We're definitely not abiding by the quiet rule for this room, but no one's up here, so whatever. "I'm just kidding, Angel, don't die on me now."

"If I go by way of donut, I don't think I can complain." I'm able to say after finally forcing my bite down my throat.

Finn shrugs one shoulder while nodding. "There are worse ways." He finishes off what must be his fourth or fifth donut before wiping the edges of his mouth with a napkin. "Anyways, thanks for showing me this." He gestures towards the ceiling and around the room. "I went to a tech school for bodywork and mechanics. We didn't have libraries and shit like this."

I peer into his eyes. He seems genuinely thankful and happy to be here. I'm not used to someone being so kind and interested in me. I shake my head. "It wasn't a big deal, I'm here all of the time."

"Is it hard to study while having to work every weekend?" Finn slouches into his chair, resting his thick, tattooed arms on the table. His hands are clasped together; tattoos cover the backs of his hands, but the fingers are free. A cross with wings on the sides, surrounded by clouds, is on his right hand.

I look away from his hand and back to his face, where a small smile ghosts his lips. "It's not that bad. I try to get all of my schoolwork done during the week so on the weekends I can just work and sleep. I'm very sleep-deprived, but what college senior isn't?"

Finn bites the inside of his lip and slowly nods his head, but when he opens his mouth to say something, he cuts off and pulls his phone out of his jeans pocket, lifting it to his ear. "What's up, Ro?" He talks into the phone, his eyes staying on mine, watching like we so often do. Eye contact seems to be our thing, we can say more with it. No words to get in the way, just pure emotion. "Yeah, no problem. I'll head out soon." He takes the phone from his ear and slides it back into his pocket. "I gotta go to Seattle, Angel, but what are you doing this weekend?"

I start to reach for my bag, sensing this little date, or whatever it was, is ending. "Working," I sing sarcastically. Didn't we already discuss this?

"Right." Finn nods, pushing his chair back to stand. "Well come find me when your schedule clears." He stands and takes a step so he's standing next to the table, towering above me. I lean my head all the way back, watching him. "I'll be waiting for you."

A LIGHT BREEZE blows the hair away from my face when I step out of the English building. The notification for an incoming email appears at the top of my screen while I'm checking my Social Psychology test score. I guess I was able to retain some information from my study session in the library two days ago. Turning it over and narrowing my eyes to try to see through the bright sunlight reflecting off of my screen, an email from my advisor pops up. Sliding the email, it opens so I can read it. She says she has news about a scholarship for me and wants to meet. Since I'm done with classes for the day, I head across campus to the business building. The limestone buildings stand out against the dark green trees and grass. The warm breeze blows my hair off of my shoulders. I check in with the office assistant and not long after, I'm back in her office, sitting in front of her.

"An anonymous donor went through the students in your major and graduating class, and chose you to be their first recipient." She beams from behind her desk. Her round glasses and short blonde hair always perfectly in place. She's been my guide for the last four years; always helping me choose my classes and teachers. She's the one who even convinced me to take on a Psychology minor.

"That's great. What's the amount?" I ask, not sure why I'm receiving a scholarship in my last semester, but who would turn down free money?

She crosses her arms on the desk and leans over them. "Well since it's your final semester and you've already paid your tuition with loans and scholarships, they've offered to pay your rent for the rest of your lease and deposit the remainder into your personal account."

That sounds like a fucking dream! "What are the stipulations?" I ask, wearily.

"Just to keep your same standing in your graduating class, or better." Her smile is so wide that I think it might split her face in half.

"And this is legit?" I continue, still not convinced this is real and happening to me.

Blinking, she gives me a deadpanned look. "Yes, it's legit." She shakes her head. "We've confirmed their income and your rent has already been paid for the remainder of your lease, as well as the monthly deposits already set up for auto-pay." Now I shake my head, because what the actual fuck? "Go ahead, Huntley, call your property manager and your bank."

That's exactly what I do once I step outside of the building, walking down the sidewalk toward my apartment building. She was right. My rent has been paid until July when my lease ends, and the bank confirmed a monthly deposit of eight thousand dollars has been set up by some company that I don't recognize. Holy shit, eight thousand dollars a month? Who the hell is bankrolling me? That's four times my rent, and they're taking care of that too. I tried to ask the bank who the donor is, but they said they wanted to remain anonymous and when I tried to look them up on the internet, I couldn't find any information about them. It's like it doesn't exist. I also call my manager at Mickey's and tell them I'm quitting until the semester is over. I should probably keep my job, but I don't really have a reason to. Not with this new scholarship covering my bills.

14

HUNTLEY

I'T'S BEEN THREE DAYS AND I HAVEN'T BEEN ABLE TO STOP THINKING about that kiss with Finn in the library. I've done everything to try to forget; I've gone to pole, classes, and even the boxing gym. I've completely avoided the library, which is probably why I find myself pulling into the large parking lot of Evans Body Shop. I can't resist him, and if I'm being honest with myself, I shouldn't have to build a wall against someone I like because of what happened to me. Fuck them, I'm not going to give them the satisfaction of controlling my life after that night. If someone interests me, I'm going for it. And Finn interests me a lot. That's a lot of bravado for someone who is shaking because she's so nervous, but I'm pushing myself off of the deep end.

Stepping out of my Camaro, the light posts illuminate the parking lot, and I pull my black high-waisted shorts down and adjust my black cropped tee. I really hope he's here. It's way past normal closing time, and I didn't message him on Instagram again. I just came straight here because I thought if I talked to him then I would talk myself out of coming tonight. "Juke Box" by Round2Crew carries through one of the three large garage doors. The left one is open while the other two are closed, and a car sits in the open bay, the hood open at the front. So that's where I go, the light spilling out from the garage. Stepping inside, I look around, and find the brunette guy from the club party, the one who stopped Farryn and me at the gate. He's watching me, wiping his hands on a red shop rag.

"I recognize you. You looking for Finn?" He asks, a slow smile creeping onto his boyish face.

I cough to clear my throat. "Yeah." He points to the front of the car, and my eyes follow. I can't see anything from the back, the hood obscures the view, but I walk towards it anyway.

"You got a visitor, boss! See you on Monday!" he yells, leaving through the garage door.

When I turn back around from watching the kid leave, I come face to face with Finn. He's walking around the front of the car, some tool in hand, and his eyes narrowed, but once we make eye contact they widen and a smile pulls his lips upward. My eyes drop from his face and I find him shirtless. The tattoos covering his arms and neck span every inch of his chest and stomach and dip down into the jeans hugging his waist, his CK boxers hovering above the band. The word "Outlaw" is written between his hip bones. His chest is wide and hard, and I just stare. Finn is massive; tall with bulking muscles, and a perfect fucking face. I bet he has a tiny dick. There's no way he can be this perfect.

"You're drooling, Angel." He snaps me out of my daze that his body put me in and I feel my stomach tighten with desire, something I haven't felt in a long time.

"I'm leaving." I turn on my heel, but before I can take a step, Finn is there. He gently grabs my upper arm and turns me around.

"Nope, I'm not letting you leave now, I just got you to come to me." He moves his hand to my waist, and I can feel a fire light where his hand lays. He rests his other hand behind my head, his fingers plunging into my hair and massaging my scalp, and his thumb reaching forward to tilt my head back. "Take a ride with me," he whispers, only a breath from my lips.

"To where?" I ask, my teeth biting the edge of my bottom lip. Finn watches the motion and a small groan leaves his throat.

Finn smirks, his eyes sliding down my body and then back to my face. "You'll see." He releases me, but grabs my hand and leads me to the passenger door of the car, which I'm now realizing is his gray Hellcat.

He opens the door and I slide in, the interior smelling like leather and a hint of Finn's cologne. He drops the hood and turns around to pull a black tee shirt from a stool and over his, surprise, completely tatted back, followed by his Outlaw cut. He grabs a heavy set of keys from the table and then opens the door to slide in. The car dips with his weight, and I watch him out of the corner of my eye. The car turns over and the engine rumbles, vibrating the seat beneath me. Finn rests a deft hand on the back of my seat and turns his body to back out of the garage, and when we're out, he exits the vehicle to turn off the light in the shop and press a button to close the large garage door.

He leads us out of town, and we both stay silent. He watches the road, occasionally looking over at me, and I watch him and the trees pass us by. I catch a sign for Seattle, and I figure that's where we're going.

An hour later, we pull into a large parking lot. Cars are parked everywhere, with people sitting on the hoods while others are huddled underneath them, and girls walk by in small outfits. Finn backs into a spot, his body turned to look and his tattooed hand working the steering wheel. It's hot as fuck.

Getting out of the car, we meet in front of the hood, Finn leaning against it and me standing in front of him.

"Did you bring me to the filming of the next *Fast and Furious*?" I cross my arms across my stomach.

Finn chuckles and reaches forward to splay his fingers around the backs of my thighs and pull me to stand between his legs. He opens his mouth to speak, but closes it when something behind me catches his attention. I turn my head and watch a man walk up to us.

"You want in, Outlaw?" he asks, crossing his arms over his chest and standing with a wide stance. I look back at Finn, noticing him already looking at me. He studies my face, running his eyes across every feature.

"Yeah," he finally answers. Pulling out a wad of bills—a very thick wad—he passes it to the man and he walks away, counting the bills as he leaves.

"What did you—" I start to say, but stop when Finn stands. His height towering over me in my white converse.

"You wanna go for that ride, Angel?" Finn's hands slide from the sides of my thighs, where they moved when he stood up, to my waist. The warm breeze ghosts under my crop top and I nod. Not able to think about anything other than the hot trail that his hands have left on my body. I'm starting to love when he touches me. I love that he can never seem to stop touching me, or looking at me. He makes me feel like I'm the only person around when he looks at me.

Finn walks me to the passenger side door again and I slide in, watching him walk around the front and get in behind the wheel. The engine rumbles around us and we slowly drive through the packed parking lot onto the street and into a lineup. There are four cars around us, and the man who took Finn's money is standing in front. The cars in the lineup rev their engines, and the people from the lot line the sidewalk to cheer and yell. Finn messes with the radio, putting on a song, but I don't pay it any attention. I'm too caught up in everything else. The man in front holds up one hand, sticking one finger up, then another, then he flashes a bright spotlight and I'm thrown into the back of my seat as Finn shifts and slams onto the gas pedal. "OHMAMI" by Chase Atlantic penetrates my mind, Finn's song choice finally coming through. High-rise buildings and small manicured trees pass by my window in a blur. We're racing in the middle of the fucking city, and no one is around but us, the five racers. Two cars are ahead of us, and I watch everything; the blurring lights beside us, the cars in front and behind us, and Finn next to me with both hands on the wheel and a completely relaxed demeanor. We overtake the second car on a long curve that causes me to grab the handle on the roof and pushes me into the door. A small smile pulls at the corner of Finn's lips as he rights the wheel and we race toward the one car ahead of us. We take a sharp turn and leave the city, the road turning to a narrow curvy road with tall, thick Evergreens lining the road. The engines roar, but the sound is lost to the expanse of forest surrounding us. We're approaching the back of the car in front of us quickly, and Finn swerves into the oncoming lane as we start to pass him. His car downshifts, gaining speed, and Finn does the same, stepping into the gas as the RPMs raise on his screen in front of him. We stay in this lane—the wrong lane for us—as we make progress on the other car and he pulls forward a little more.

"Finn," I warn when it's becoming clear he's staying in this lane.

"Relax, Angel," he says, a smile on his face but his focus is on the car next to us.

We take another sharp turn and headlights shine ahead of us. "Finn!" I scream.

"Fuck," he hisses, flipping a switch under his ignition and dropping down onto the dirt shoulder.

The Hellcat slams forward, the speedometer quickly rising, as we bounce along on the dirt. Our bodies jostle with the impact of the hits, and the car that was coming our way goes past my window, their horn blaring at the racers. When we pass them, Finn swerves into the correct lane in front of the last racer we had to pass to be in front. My heart pounds in my chest. The near crash, the speed—it's intoxicating. I feel like I'm high. The car behind us must have something similar to what Finn turned on because he catches up behind us, but he's not fast enough. Fifty feet ahead of us, I see headlights lining the road. Another 50 after that, and Finn slows as we pass a pair of flashing lights on either side of us, the car behind us coming in right after us. Finn slows and pulls up next to the man who took his money earlier.

He rolls down his window and pulls a gun from his door compartment, holding it to the man. "The roads are supposed to be blocked. If you ever put mine or my girl's life in danger again, either me or the Outlaws are coming after you." He cocks the gun, returning it to aim at the man whose face has paled and whose eyes are about three times the size. "You fucking got that?"

"Y-yes, sir," he stutters. "H-here's your winnings, Finn." The man hands Finn five thick rolled-up wads of cash.

Finn snatches them from him and opens the middle console, tossing them in and slamming it closed. He rolls up his window and slams on the gas, speeding away from the gathering crowd of racers and spectators. "UH OH" by Tate McRae starts playing through the car speakers.

"I'm so sorry, Huntley. The roads are supposed to be blocked off. I would never have put you in that situation had I known." Finn's voice is rough with anger, his hands clenching the steering wheel tightly, and both eyes narrowed on the road, his beautiful face twisted in a scowl.

I don't know what's wrong with me. The adrenaline, the race, Finn pulling a gun on that guy—all of it turned me the hell on. What can I say, I like Finn's danger. I run my hand over the side of his face, smoothing out his features. He catches my hand and pulls it to his lips, kissing my knuckles. "Pull over," I say.

"What?" Finn turns to look at me, his eyebrows pull together.

I unbuckle my seatbelt and lean over the center console, running my hand slowly down his chest and over his lap, squeezing him through his jeans. Leaning into his ear, I hear his sharp intake of breath at my touch. "Pull. Over," I whisper into his ear.

Finn slams on the brake, his arm wrapping around me to hold me in place like a seat belt, and he pulls off onto the shoulder of the road. Killing the headlights, he pulls me into his lap and I brace myself on his shoulders. We stare into each other's eyes for a moment, the only light coming from the car's entertainment center. Finn looks villainous with the low lighting making his features even sharper than they already are.

Finn grasps the back of my neck and pulls my lips to his. All restraint from either of us is let loose. He bites my lips and sucks on my tongue after pushing his way into my mouth. His hands slide up the bottom of my shorts and he greedily squeezes my ass, moving my hips over his rising erection. I rest my elbows on his shoulders and snake my hands up through his hair. His aggression eggs me on, causing me to grip his hair in my hands and angle his head perfectly for me to try to dominate his mouth. *I love this.*

His hands leave my ass and one slips under my shirt and into my bra. Finn's thumb circles my nipple and his other hand grabs my throat as his mouth moves to my ear and he bites down on my lobe. I freeze, my entire body goes rigid and I want to cry—not in fear, but frustration with myself. It's been months, and I want this so badly. I don't want to be reminded of them, I want to be here with Finn. My body likes what he's doing, it's just my brain that's ruining this for us.

Finn pulls away from my ear and uses his hand around my neck to pull me away from him and he looks into my eyes. I can feel tears start to form, so I grab his wrist and pull it away from me, placing my hands in the passenger seat so I can climb back over into it. Finn stops me, placing his big tattooed hands on my thighs and holding me in place.

"No. You're not running away from me. What the fuck just happened?" Finn rests his head on the headrest and looks up at me.

"I want to go home." I try to blink away the tears, but one falls and I quickly swipe at it.

Finn watches the tear, glaring at it. "I'll take you home, but you have to tell me what just happened."

I try to pry my fingers under his palms, but it doesn't work. "I don't have to do a goddamn thing. Let me go," I hiss.

He removes his hands, holding them up next to his head in surrender, and I climb off of him and into the passenger seat. The absence of his heat underneath me makes me want to cry more and I stare out of the car window, waiting for him to drive me back to his shop and we will never see each other again. Who can come back from this? He's not going to want some fucking tease who cries midmakeout. When the car doesn't move, I look at him. He's turned towards me, leaning his back against his door with his arms crossed.

"I'm waiting, Huntley. Why do you always freeze when my hand is around your neck? What happened to you?"

I shake my head, looking down at my hands and subconsciously pulling the bottom of my shirt lower. Men who look like

Finn don't want someone who is broken. They don't want complicated, and I'm a fucking headcase. "Nothing, Finn."

"I just want to help you, Huntley. Please let me in." His voice is a plea and I can't hold the tears back anymore. They fall down my cheeks and onto my neck. If I come clean he'll pity me, but he'll distance himself.

"I was drugged and raped by my ex-boyfriend and his two friends at a frat party almost a year ago." The air seems to leave the car at my confession. I don't want to look at Finn. I don't want to see the pity on his face—or worse, the disgust.

Finn places his hand gently on my shoulder. It's a whisper of a touch, the lightest he's ever had with me. I look out of the bottom of my vision as he slides it up under my chin and moves my face to look at him. He's leaning over the center console so he's only inches from me. "I'm so sorry that happened to you, Angel." His thumb rubs along my jaw. "You won't ever experience anything like that ever again, beautiful. I won't allow it." I search his eyes. There isn't any pity or disgust, only a fire burning deep within and sincerity. "What can I do for you right now to prove that?" He asks.

"Fuck me," I breathe, blinking the last of the tears away.

Finn lets out a small chuckle before his face returns to the serious expression of before. "Is it your first time?" I turn my face away, ashamed again, but Finn forces it back somewhat gently. "Is it your first time since it happened, Huntley?" He asks again, more sternly this time.

"Yes," I whisper, avoiding his eyes.

Finn lets go and I know he's done with me. "Okay." The car starts to pull away from the shoulder and onto the road again. Fresh tears well up in my eyes, and I look out of my window. "But I'm going to fuck you how you need, not how you want. At least this time."

"What?" I snap my head around to look at him. He's staring ahead at the road, accelerating around the curves of the road.

"We're going to my house. I know you'd be more comfortable at your place, but I have things at mine that I need." He quickly looks at me and then back at the road.

"Okay." I agree, confused and nervous about what I'm getting myself into. I want it though, I'm sure of that.

15

HUNTLEY

WE PULL INTO A WIDE STONE CIRCLE DRIVE THAT LEADS TO A large, gray brick house with a three-car garage and a large shop off to the side. Finn stops the car in front of the low, wide, white porch and double glass doors. Trees surround the property, and deep green, perfectly manicured grass covers the ground everywhere there isn't stone. We're in one of the wealthiest parts of Merrill Hill, in a community right outside of town. Finn opens my door and I step out, following behind him to the front doors. Inside the house is dark, and I can't see anything. I feel Finn's warm hand wrap around mine and lead me through the house, wood flooring beneath our shoes. Finn's phone illuminates his face as he messes with it, leading me down a hallway. Based on the small light from the phone, I think the walls are painted black. Finn stops and drops my hand, opening a door in front of him and stepping through. I follow him in. It's a large bedroom, bigger than my entire apartment. A giant, black bed sits low to the ground in front of me, light blue LEDs run around the bottom of the bed, making it look like it's floating. The same colored LEDs are lined around the ceiling of the room. There's a bay window to my right with two plush armchairs. On my left is a set of double doors to what looks like a large bathroom, LEDs shining in there as well.

Finn sits at the foot of the bed on a black velvet ottoman and takes his cut off. He folds it and lays it next to him. "Your move, Angel." His rough voice rakes over my skin, causing goosebumps to rise over my arms and legs. He looks fucking magical sitting there in the low light.

I let out a shuddering breath. "I don't..." I trail off, shaking my head. I don't know how to do this anymore.

Finn moves forward and rests his elbows on his knees, his eyes holding mine. "You don't want to or you don't know how?" he asks.

"I don't know how," I answer quietly.

He nods, standing and moving to the side of the bed, pulling his shirt off as he goes. "Take off your clothes," he says, his back to me. He pulls his belt from his jeans and they fall to the floor.

He gets rid of the rest of his clothes and reaches into his bedside drawer. I lift my foot and untie my converse, stepping out of them and my socks, and then ditching my shirt, shorts, and underwear. I place my arm across my chest. Even with his back turned towards me, I'm so self-conscious. Other than the doctors on the night it happened, I'm the only one who has seen me naked since then. Finn tosses something onto the table and deftly lands on the bed naked, a small bottle landing next to him as he strokes himself, a condom already encasing his dick. His long legs extend in front of him. His legs are completely covered in tattoos as well, all the way down to his feet. His eyes run over me hungrily, pausing on the arm draped over my breasts. He bends down, his stomach muscles flexing, and comes back up with his black tee shirt in his hand. He extends it to me—no judgment in his eyes, just lust.

I pull the large, soft shirt over my head and "Control" by Zoe

Wees softly plays from speakers in the ceiling. I watch Finn place his phone on the bedside table.

"Please don't make this some sappy thing," I groan, my arm falling to my side.

Finn shakes his head. "I'm not, just trying to give you something else to focus on." His movement stills on his cock. "Come here, baby." His voice, his command, and his body all make a wave of lust rush through me.

I want him so bad, but I'm scared. What if this makes it worse? What if I mess something up? I walk to his side and his hand encloses mine. My knees hit the soft bed as he guides me on top of him. My mouth finds his as he kisses me softly, licking and nibbling on my lips until I open them for him. With one hand cupping the back of my neck, he caresses my tongue with his, claiming me unlike he has before—unlike anyone has before. "Can I touch you?" he asks, pulling away from my mouth, and I nod a second before his mouth is back on mine. He raises my hips gently and starts circling a finger over my clit. Dropping my head back, I moan, my chest starting to rise quickly with my breathing picking up. I start to grind over his erection when I feel something off on the bottom of his shaft. I drop one hand from his broad shoulders and grip his slick condom-wrapped cock, running my thumb along the bottom. My fingers can't even close around his fat cock; he's bigger than my wrist. Finn and I both suck in a harsh breath when I feel eight bars with small balls on the ends running up the long length of his cock. Piercings. His fucking dick is pierced. *Holy fucking shit.* Finn grabs my hand off of his dick and kisses the back of it, placing it back on his shoulder and using his hand to move my hips over him again. I ride him like that, his pierced cock slipping through my pussy lips and his finger slowly rubbing my clit, before I lean forward and rub my clit against his piercings. "Oh, God!" I yell. My pace picks up, an orgasm building in me that I haven't felt in so long.

"No, baby, there ain't no room for him here." Finn's chest rises and falls quickly, his eyes focused on where my pussy is rubbing over his dick. I cum. I cum so fucking hard that my body locks up and I squeeze Finn's shoulders and sit still on top of him. When my breathing calms down he says, "I'm gonna give you some lube, okay?"

I nod, breathless, and he picks up the little bottle next to him and squirts the clear liquid into his hand. Stroking his dick again, he stares at me and then gently rubs the same hand over my pussy, sticking one finger inside of me. I moan as his finger works the lube into me, but he removes it and moves his hands to my waist, lifting me and positioning me over his cock. Fisting his dick under me, I line it up to my entrance and slowly, because he's huge, lower myself onto him, but even with the lube, he's not fitting.

"All of it, Angel," he rasps with his eyes half closed.

"I don't think it's gonna fit," I say in a moan, his dick already stretching me painfully.

"I'll make it fit," he groans as I sink lower, the lube helping to push him inside.

I pause a few times to let myself adjust, but eventually, with both of us breathing heavily, I make it down to the bottom. "Fuck. You're so fucking tight, beautiful," Finn moans.

I rock over him slowly, loving the way he fills me. This is the best feeling in the entire world. I can't imagine how it could get better. The piercings add a very new sensation, and I love grinding my walls against them. Moaning loudly, I lose myself in my pleasure and my body moves faster, back and forth. I cum again, completely without warning. My pussy spasms around Finn's cock and he hisses, his shirt I'm wearing bunched up in his fist as he rides out my orgasm with me.

"Can I fuck you now?" he asks as he places soft kisses up my neck.

"Mmhmm." I nod. My lids falling closed.

Finn wraps his thick arms around my back and moves forward until I'm on my back with him hovering above me. His thick cock never leaves my body. The bed dips as he rests his forearms on either side of my head, his hips moving slowly.

"I've never done this before." His brows pull together and he watches my face.

My eyebrow raises. "Are you a virgin, Pretty Boy?" My voice is deep and full of lust.

His beautiful blue eyes narrow. "Does this feel like I'm a virgin?" He pulls almost all the way out and puts a wave into the motion so he thrusts up as well as in, the head of his cock rubbing against my g spot.

"Ahhhh." My head tips back, my throat exposed to him.

"That's what I thought, Angel, don't doubt me." His voice sounds smug, and he should. That felt fucking amazing. One of his hands grips my chin and pulls my face back to look at him. "I've never fucked slowly." His thumb caresses my cheek. "Not a day in my fucking life."

"Can't you feel it though?" I ask around another moan, his hips doing that roll thing again.

My pussy flutters around him again and his eyes glass over. "I feel everything with you, baby." Then he pushes into me, so deep that I swear I feel him in my cervix and he stills. We never look away from one another. Blue on blue eyes; different shades, different people, but the same fucked up soul. He changed something in me tonight. He gave me a part of my life back—a part of my soul that died the night I wish I had instead.

16

HUNTLEY

Soft footsteps pad across the carpeted floor of Finn's bedroom and the bed dips beside my hip as he kneels on the floor. He rests his elbows on the bed next to me with a warm washcloth. With my head on the black satin pillow, I watch as he gently wipes away the lube from between my thighs and my pussy before placing a gentle kiss on my hip bone.

"I love your ink, baby, so strong and sexy." He's referring to the Medusa tattoo that sits low between my hip bones and up to below my belly button. "Did you get it because—" He trails off, but I know what he's referring to.

I nod my head, watching him out of the bottom of my vision. "Yeah," I croak, my voice hoarse from the amount of screaming I did tonight wrapped around Finn's cock.

The washcloth hits the bedside table and Finn's large body slides up next to mine. "Will you tell me what happened?" he whispers.

I stare up at the ceiling, watching the blades on the fan spin. "Ryan and I met at a house party. He was relentless in his pursuit of me and he seemed like a nice guy. Polished and connected. His dad is a judge. I went to his fraternity parties a lot, sometimes I'd hang out in his room upstairs and watch movies or work on homework, other times I'd join the party. I just wanted to hang out with him and he had to be present at the parties. One night though, I don't know." I let out a deep breath and close my eyes, the night flashing behind my lids and making me squeeze them tighter. "We had been dating for about six months. I never expected it from them, they never gave off any signs." I shake my head, tears pooling in the bottom of my eyes.

"I'm going to kill them," he says, his bent arm supporting his head and he looks down at me.

"I wish." I roll my eyes and stare at the tray ceiling. And I do wish they were dead, I so fucking do. I wish the world would be rid of their vile faces and no one would ever have to endure what I did. Fuck them.

Finn grabs my chin and pulls my attention to him. "Are you afraid of them?" His expression is hard, the same stare I saw in the strip club on the first night I ever laid eyes on him. These are his calculating eyes.

"Every day," I admit, though I really don't want to. I hate having weaknesses. They made me hate having any weakness because they saw one small one and took advantage of it.

His thumb caresses my cheek and I lean into his touch, then his rough hand moves up the side of my face and into my hair, where he buries his hand. "Then I'm killing them. I won't let you live in fear, and I can't live knowing that those rapists are breathing the same air as you." I roll my eyes again, pulling my face away from him. I don't see the point in having a pointless conversation with pointless threats. I don't need that anymore. My head is jerked back towards Finn and he leans in closer, his head cocked to the side. "You don't know what I do for the Outlaws, do you, Angel?"

I remember what his patch said. I saw it the first night when

I ran into him. "You're the Enforcer." My voice is dead, dull with a lack of emotion. I don't want to talk about this anymore.

"What do you think that means, babe?" he continues, not letting this fucking thing die.

Narrowing my eyes at him, I answer. "That you enforce the rules of the club."

Finn slowly shakes his head, a cold expression crossing over his beautiful features, one that slightly scares me. "No. It means I make sure people don't cross the club. I kill people for the Outlaws, have since I was eighteen."

What? "You're not funny." My eyes slightly widen. He can't be serious, those rumors about the club can't be true.

"Do you want me to prove it to you?" His hand leaves my head and he sits up.

Bravado fills me and I rise to my ass as well, still in just his tee shirt and keeping eye contact the entire time. "Yeah." I cross my arms under my chest.

Nodding, he turns and gets out of bed, picking up his jeans he turns to me. "Alright, Angel, get dressed. We're going for a ride."

I climb out of the bed and find my shorts, keeping his shirt. He can't be serious.

Finn turns towards me, shirtless and buckling the belt on his jeans, and staring at me. I want to drool or drag him back into bed to fuck me again. Blinking several times, I just watch him slowly run his eyes up my body from the Converse I just put on, up my bare legs, and finally landing and staying on his shirt that I have no intention of taking off, maybe ever. He smirks before turning away and stepping into the bathroom. I take that opportunity to look around. Walking through the double doors that we entered the bedroom through, I step into the hallway and fumble around for a light switch. When I flip it, a long black hallway extends in front of me. My shoes thump quietly on the gray wooden floorboards that extend through the entire down-stairs of the house. At the end of the hallway is a giant open space living area, a large black sectional that sits close to the floor with a matte black stone coffee table in front of a very large mounted tv. The kitchen on my right, opposite the living room, has a long, black, marble waterfall island with black marble countertops and black cabinets behind it, and all black appli-ances—even the hardware. There's not a speck of color in this damn house. No art on the walls. Just a large wall of floor-to-ceiling windows at the front of the house and another large window at the back by the back door, overlooking a large wooden deck.

"What do you think?" Finn asks, stepping into the living area. The sound of his voice jolts me from my personal tour.

I take another look around the vast room, the vaulted ceil-ings making it feel even larger than it already is. "It's very black." I laugh.

He stands next to me and grabs my hand, and my eyes shift up to his. Tonight was more than just sex, and I think he felt it too. "I don't like a lot of color." He tugs my hand and leads me to the front doors. "Come on, I got something to prove to you."

———

WE PULL onto a dirt driveway and drive for what feels like miles, the only light coming from the headlights of Finn's Hellcat. He said he was going to prove that he's killed people. Is he taking me to his victims' graves? What the fuck am I even talking about? What the fuck am I doing here? Who listens to someone say that they're a murderer and is like "Yeah, take me to your victims' graves?" Oh I know, their next victim. Huntley, you're such a fucking idiot sometimes. When I'm about to throw off my seatbelt and launch myself from the moving vehicle, Finn turns and a small wooden cabin is lit up by the headlights.

The car stops in front, the headlights shining at the front door and Finn gets out, leaving the car running. I'm thinking about sliding over and stealing the damn thing to make my escape when Finn opens my door and offers me a hand. Fuck, I guess I'm going inside to be murdered like the stupid girl that always dies first in horror movies. I can defend myself, there's no doubt about that, but with a guy the size of Finn? Not fucking likely.

When I don't accept his offered hand, Finn rests his elbow on the roof of the car and the other on the open door and leans down to look at me. "Where's your gun?" I ask, crossing my arms, letting him know I'm not going anywhere.

Finn stares at me, turns his head for a second, and then comes back to me. "You think I brought you here to kill you?" I just stare at him, keeping the same position as before. "Jesus fucking Christ," he mutters as he stands up and pulls a gun from the inside of his cut.

He holds onto the barrel and offers me the handle of the gun, and when I accept it he offers me his hand again. This time I accept, letting him pull me out of the car. The grass is short and there are twigs and pinecones littering the ground. The breeze is slightly chilly and goosebumps rise on my bare legs. Holding Finn's hand with one hand and his gun with the other, we take the three steps onto the wooden porch and Finn pulls a set of keys from his pocket and unlocks the little wooden door. He flips the lights on as he walks in and turns to enter a code into a security monitor by the door. I step in after him and look around. It's mostly empty. There's a worn, two-seat, brown leather couch with a small wooden coffee table and an old worn chair with tears in it. A hallway leads off on the left, and at the back of the room I can see a glimpse into the kitchen. It's small and looks dated, the back of a chair peeks around the corner. Finn walks to the back wall of the living room and pulls at a coat hanger mounted to the wall. The fucking wall opens like a goddamn door. The wooden planks make the seam blend in perfectly and it's completely unnoticeable. He flicks another switch and a light turns on in the stairwell. Turning back to me, still standing by the front door, he inclines his head towards the stairs and takes the first step down. Do I follow him? Do I run? What the fuck is this murder cabin? My heart beats out of my chest, but I don't know if it's at the thought of following a potential murderer down into his evil lair, or at the thought of leaving Finn. I follow him because he hasn't given me any reason to fear him. I've looked evil in the eye, watched as they ripped my soul from my body, and laughed about it. Finn doesn't have evil eyes. His eyes are devoted and tortured, loved and full of want. So I follow him.

We walk down a narrow set of cement stairs, the walls and the ceiling are all concrete as well. It's like a concrete box down here. At the bottom is a square concrete room, void of anything but a metal chair in the middle of the room over a drain, a metal cart with nothing on it, and a sink with a few cabinets on the side along the wall. Finn leans against the wall and gestures for me to look around. Tentatively I walk towards the chair. The cement floor under the chair is stained a deep reddish brown.

Blood.

And the drain next to the chair looks like it has rust all along it.

Blood. Oh my God.

I turn and walk toward the large cabinets next to the sink. Opening it, I find a multitude of things; sharp knives in every length and width, scalpels, big water buckets, stained wash clothes, rusty pliers and hammers, a sledgehammer, a blowtorch, and so many other things that I have no idea what they are. This isn't a murder cabin, this is a torture room, and the man I just slept with is the one who tortures people.

I should be scared. I should be turning around and blowing a hole into his knee or chest and making a run for it, but I just stand there and stare into the cabinet of horrors.

"Would you really kill them?" It leaves my mouth without me even meaning it to. My anger at my rapists taking over.

Finn's breath ghosts over my neck, a trail of goosebumps rising in his wake. He moved so silently. But I'm not scared. "There's no 'would' about it. I am, and I'll find out their names whether you want me to or not. No one is allowed to hurt my girl and live." My stomach somersaults. The rage that has lived within me finding a place to live within Finn, and my heart finding the protector that it has longed for.

"I want to do it." I voice my most private thought, throwing it out there where I know I won't be judged, because Finn wouldn't judge me. I know that.

"Great." He gently kisses the side of my neck, and an involuntary moan leaves my mouth. "You can help by giving me their names."

"No." I turn around to face him, my chest pressing against his. "I want to kill them."

Finn's eyes narrow on mine, flicking back and forth between them. "You're serious?" he asks.

I raise my chin, meeting his gaze confidently. "You know I'm fucking serious."

A groan rises from Finn's throat and he licks his lips. "Okay. On Monday. This weekend you're mine."

———

TAKING A DEEP BREATH, I breathe in the smell of Finn's clean skin. I'm naked and snuggled into his bare chest, his thick arms wrapped around me. He kisses the top of my wet head and I try to remember the last time I felt this relaxed. Before my assault, that's for sure. I haven't felt relaxed for even a second after my attack, because I'm always on the defensive—but not with Finn. With Finn I relax, and he makes me feel safe. He fucked me again in the shower when we got home; slowly, lovingly, perfect. I know it's not him though. I know he needs more, and I want more. I want him to be himself with me. I want all of him. I want to get my life back, and I want to do it with Finn by my side.

17

―

FINN

"Why are you doing this? For revenge, or because they deserve it?" I ask, my hands in my lap and my eyes fixed on the doors of the science building at RSU. It's been three days since I was inside of her for the first time, and I haven't stopped thinking about it for a second. I took her back home with me that night and fucked her again, slowly, never looking away from her eyes, and kissing away the silent tears that fell. I spent the rest of the night holding her and listening to her breathing while she slept. Our weekend together was perfect; we barely left the bed, just cuddling and watching tv all weekend. I've never done this shit, but I don't ever want to stop as long as it's with her. I'd never brought a girl to my house; never had a girl in my bed. Honestly, I was lucky to have had condoms and lube in the bedside table. I kept them there just in case I ever did bring someone home. I'm glad I never let anyone else in there though. It's Huntley's bed; it always has been, I just didn't know it yet.

"Both, but mostly revenge," Huntley says, her focus on her laptop as her short nails tap on the keyboard. She's working on something from school, but when I told her I was going to start tailing the soon-to-be-dead rapists, she wanted to be a part of that too. I tried to convince her to just come along to the final event, but she wanted to be here for it all. Surprising the shit out of me. It's like she was meant for me. Fucking perfect.

"Huntley." I release a breath, thinking about how to say this. I see the pain in her eyes, I saw it the first night I met her. They killed a part of her that night, and she's been trying like hell to find it, to figure out how to make sure nothing like that ever happens again. Fuck, I'm going to rip their fucking heads off with my bare hands. "Revenge isn't going to fix what they did to you, baby." The night I took her to the cabin, I was so furious. I wanted blood right then. But now I've had some time to think about it. She needs to heal.

The typing stops and she turns to look at me. I turn my head and watch her. She's fucking beautiful. She's in my tee shirt that she stole the night we slept together and a pair of black athletic shorts. "I know, but because of Ryan's dad, justice will never be served. I'm just seeing to it that it is." Right, Ryan fucking Kelly. Son of Judge Kelly, one of Merrill Hill's dirtiest judges. Not a fucking surprise that dirtbag covered up a rape he and his two friends committed. His days are fucking numbered now though.

"You gotta work on healing yourself too, baby. Right now you're focusing all of your energy on your vengeance, but once that's gone, you'll be left with nothing but the missing parts of you that they took. That shit will eat you alive, and you need to make sure you're working on it before it comes to that." I take her hand. I'm fucking serious. Right now she has something to live for. Revenge is fucking powerful, and when she doesn't have that anymore, it'll feel as though she doesn't have anything left. But she'll have me, she'll always have me.

"I'm trying, Finn," she whispers. Tears start to form in her eyes. Fuck, that's something else that's changed since we fucked. She lets me inside of her head now; she doesn't lock me out behind the walls and the barbed wire. I love it and hate it in equal measures; I don't want her to hurt, and I know she is.

"I know you are, baby." I bring her hand to my lips and kiss it gently. "You're so fucking strong, Angel, but you don't have to do this alone anymore. I'm right here with you."

She pulls her hand away to wipe at the tears in her eyes, and I look to the doors of the building to give her a little bit of privacy to pull herself together. Students file out of the building and finally, our target makes his way out as well, walking to his Mercedes and sliding inside. It takes everything in me not to ram into the side of his fucking ride and pull him out right here, but I know this shit can't blow back on Huntley. It would look rather odd if the guys she accused of rape end up murdered by her new Outlaw associate. I could get it covered up, but once we start gunning for Kelly, things are going to get a whole lot messier. Huntley did everything she should have; the minute she regained full consciousness, she walked to the student clinic on campus and had a rape kit done. The police were called and she filed a statement. She only had patches of unconsciousness so she knew exactly what had happened to her. The police said they were going to take them in and interrogate them, but Judge Kelly killed the investigation, having the Chief of Police call his men down. the Outlaws have an in with the Chief, so I will definitely be using that to my advantage to make sure Judge Kelly and his fucking demon spawn aren't looked for when we're done. Not that there will be anything left to look for. The other two fuckers should be easy to write off. A reformed druggie and a 5th year senior who refuses to graduate and just wants to party.I switch the car into drive and follow Lucas Denver to the K Gam frat house. When he pulls into the parking lot, I continue on down the road and pull over.

Huntley turns in the passenger seat and watches him through the back window. "We have to make it look like an accident or suicide," I say, watching the rearview mirror as Lucas gets out and walks through the front doors of the limestone estate. "Lucas and Parker are first. We can cover that shit easily. Ryan and his dad are going to take a little more work, but I'll worry about that." I'm going to try to keep Huntley's hands as clean as possible. I know she needs this—or she thinks she needs this—but it's a lot different when you're standing, looking over a bloody body, the life draining from their eyes, knowing you did that.

Huntley turns around and sits back down. "Lucas always goes to Porters for dollar beers on Wednesdays."

Nodding my head, I pull the car away from the curb and drive Huntley back to her apartment. "I guess we got a date for Wednesday then, Angel."

18

HUNTLEY

At the sound of knocking on my door, I leave my closet and walk through my bedroom and living room and to the door. I check the peephole and open it when I see a broad chest in a black tee shirt. Finn is smiling down at me from the other side, his gaze falling down my body before he leans in and kisses me, his arms snaking around me and backing me into my apartment. The door slams closed and I let him lift me and carry me through the room and dump me on the couch. My apartment is small; the kitchen only has enough room for two people to be in it and the only place to eat is at the bar. My living room only has room for my couch, a coffee table, and tv and entertainment stand, but my bedroom is a good size; big enough for my bed, nightstand, and long dresser. The walk-in closet and nice bathroom are what make this apartment worth the price. Well, that and it's across the street from campus, and has a gated parking lot. Finn's body covers mine, and I pull away. "We have to get going, Muscles."

Finn sighs, backing up to sit on the couch. "I don't know what's hotter, you underneath me, or you talking so causally about murder." He stands and grabs my hand, pulling me to stand. "Let's go, Angel."

Porters is packed, it always is on Wednesdays. Dollar beers are a big hit with broke college kids. Finn and I are sitting at a table on the patio. People walk past to hit other bars or restaurants in The District. I didn't want to be noticed, so I'm sitting with my back to Lucas and a black ball cap on my head, with my long ponytail pulled through the gap in the back. It's scary how smooth Finn is, how his eyes track Lucas, but it's not at all obvious. He's trained. He's done this before. I can tell in his relaxed posture and even breathing that this is just another day for him. If I weren't on his side, I'd be terrified. That being said, there's something sexy about knowing you're bedding a monster—a man willing to kill for you.

The pink-haired girl from the club party steps onto the wooden patio and stops by our table.

"The guy at the table by the door, green shirt. Get him drunk and take him home. I'll text you where to stop and we'll take it from there," Finn says quietly.

The girl nods and walks away, her short jean shorts and crop top showing off an absolutely banging fucking body. Big boobs, curves, and a big ass. Lucas won't be able to resist.

And he doesn't. Peyton—Finn finally told me her name—spends the rest of the night with him, supplying drink after drink, shot after shot. About three hours later, they finally stumble through the crowd and onto the sidewalk, taking the turn into the alleyway that leads to the parking lot behind Porters. Lucas has his arm slung over poor, tiny Peyton, but she handles him well, keeping him upright and his feet moving. We follow behind, Finn's footsteps quiet and sure. We're standing at the end of the alleyway, and I peek around his large body to watch Peyton dump Lucas into the passenger seat and then walk around to the driver's side. Looking at Finn over the top of the car, she inclines her head and then gets in, starts the car, and drives out of the lot.

Finn spins around, grabs my hand, and pulls me down another alleyway and back out onto the street. We casually walk hand in hand through The District to the main parking lot and Finn's bike. He gets on and while waiting for me, pulls out his phone. Climbing onto the bike, I settle behind him, my thighs widening to wrap around him. The bike roars beneath us and I rest my chin on his leather-clad back. Finn's hand drops from the handlebar and rests above my knee, his thumb rubbing circles along the bare skin. I squeeze him tighter, holding onto him even though I don't have to with the backrest supporting me. I just want to be near him.

We leave The District and take the road to the University and Greek Row. K Gam is off by itself near a large pond. We take the curving road and Finn pulls off to the shoulder, pulling in right behind Lucas' white Mercedes. Peyton steps out of the Mercedes and gets into a car that was already waiting for her. A blonde woman waves to Finn from the waiting car before pulling onto the road and disappearing, leaving just me, Finn, and one of my rapists.

Finn hands me a small set of leather gloves and I follow him in putting them on. He turns towards the car and we walk through the short grass. Light spills out of the car when Finn opens the passenger side door. Lucas is passed out and almost falls out. Finn hefts Lucas' body out of the car and over his shoulder, and starts walking him to the driver's side. He didn't tell me a plan, so I'm just following his lead, but I open the front door for him and Finn places Lucas behind the wheel and buckles his seatbelt. He kneels in the grass and pulls off Lucas' shoe and then pulls a syringe out of the inside of his cut. He stands and takes a step back.

"You wanna do this part, Angel, or push his car into the lake?" Finn offers me the syringe.

"What is it?" I ask, eyeing the needle.

"Lincomycin. It'll paralyze him so even if he wakes up when he hits the water, he won't be able to do anything about it. His lungs will probably stop working and he'll drown." Finn shrugs, his eyes boring into mine.

"How?" I shake my head. I figured there would be a lot more to murder than this, I mean, there has to be if we don't want to get caught, right? But Finn has thought of everything.

"I got it from a vet. If the family runs a toxicology report, I can get the medical examiner to leave this out as long as the injection sight isn't obvious." Ah... removing his shoe makes sense now.

Taking the syringe from him, I step in between Finn and the car and kneel where he was before. I pull two of Lucas' toes apart and stick the syringe in, plunging the entire dose of the drug into his system. Lucas groans, but he stays asleep, moving his head from one side to the other.

Pulling the syringe out, I stand and take a step back. Finn takes it from me and slips it into his cut again. He sticks his foot inside the car and steps on the brake, trying to fit himself inside to push the gear switch into drive.

My laugh breaks the silence of the night as I watch him shove half of himself in, barely able to reach. He turns back to me with a confused look on his face, which just makes me laugh more. A laugh tumbles out of him too, before he turns back around and grabs a hold of the top of the car. He half sits on Lucas as he slams his foot on the gas and barrels towards the water.

My heart falls into my stomach as I watch the car shoot away from me with Finn half inside of it, steering the car to where we need it to go. Right before the car is about to hurtle off of the small cliff, Finn leaps from the car and rolls onto his side on the ground, watching the car go over the edge as a loud splash sounds below us.

I didn't even have time to think about what I had just done. Murdered someone—one of my rapists. I was too worried about Finn, that he might be hurt. By the time I make it to Finn, he's already pulling himself into a sitting position. I kneel beside him and run my hands along his body and face. He seems fine; nothing feels out of place and I don't find any blood or sore spots. My eyes rise to meet his, which are already watching me, and I get sucked into him like I do every time I look into his eyes.

Before I know what's happening, our lips are crashing together in a rushed sort of way. Our teeth clash and he bites my lips brutally, drawing blood. Finn's hot skin and the rough top of his jeans brush against my knuckles as I fist the hem of his shirt and pull it over his head. His fingers weave into my hair roughly and he grips the back of my head while our tongues assault one another. Finn yanks my head back, pulling my lips from his and his eyes run over my face, taking in every feature. They roam slowly over my bruised and puffy lips, my blushing cheeks, my half-lidded gaze, and my messy hair that his fingers are pulling tightly.

"Can I fuck you?" he rasps. Goosebumps prickle my skin, and it has nothing to do with the chilly night.

Nodding, I rise to my feet and fumble with the button on my jeans. With trembling hands, I finally get it undone and shove my jeans down my legs, stepping out of them and kicking them aside. At the same time, Finn pulls his jeans down to around his knees. The ground is hard as my knees land on either side of his hips, his cock lining up to my entrance. Fuck, I'm so wet, so ready for this. I slide his head in, trying to adjust to his size quickly. I want all of him right now.

"Fuck. You're so tight, baby, always so tight," Finn groans, and a surge of heat rushes through me, allowing me to take another few inches of him.

Sure fingers spread me open and start to circle my clit, the rough pad of Finn's thumb sending tingles all through my body. I lean my hands behind me and raise my hips, making the head of Finn's dick rub against the spot inside of me that has me nearing orgasm quickly. With one hand, I grab Finn's and bring it to my throat. "Choke me," I say in a moan. His eyes widen, and then roll back in his head with a swivel of my hips.

Just when I think he's not going to comply, his hand tightens around my throat, and I keep my hand wrapped around his wrist. I ride him harder, his strong fingers making my vision black as my desire skyrockets. When I think I'm going to either blackout or die of pleasure, Finn moves his hand to the back of my neck and pulls me upright, his hand going back to the front of my throat and tightening again as his hips pump into me brutally. Within seconds, my pussy starts to spasm around Finn and he releases my throat so I can scream through my release. Still trembling, Finn lifts me off of him and turns me around. On my knees, facing the water and the rapidly sinking Mercedes, Finn pushes me down onto my hands and pushes back inside of me. His hand finds my throat again.

"Watch him sink, Huntley. Watch his car sink into this fucking lake and think of him fighting for his last breath while I fuck you so deep no one will ever be able to fill you again." Finn pumps into me so hard, his dick definitely in my cervix this time. "I will end anyone who ever wrongs you, Angel. I am yours to wield as you please." His piercings grate against the sensitive spot inside of me, making my brain short circuit, and all I can do is blink away the buzzing and moan loudly.

It's all too much; the motion of his hips, the last remaining part of the car going under, and Finn's promise. I come apart right then, with Finn's hand loosely wrapped around my throat, his thumb rubbing circles over my thumping vein. Finn isn't far behind me. He fucks me through my orgasm, and then after a few more thrusts he stills, his already fat cock thickening inside of me and sending aftershock jolts through me.

He pulls out of me slowly and I drop my head to my hands, trying to catch my breath. The sound of his zipper reaches me just before the soft thud of his ass hitting the ground. "We didn't use a condom, baby."

"I'm on birth control," I say into the ground, my voice muffled.

"For now," he mumbles. I raise my head to ask him what the fuck that means, when I feel his tongue run up the inside of my thigh. My eyes widen a second before his fingers are thrust to my lips, his cum scooped up on his index finger. I close my mouth around his finger and suck off his cum while his tongue cleans up my thighs and dips into my pussy. I moan while he laps at me, and then he replaces his tongue with his fingers, pumping them inside of me quickly. His mouth moves to my ass cheek where he bites down hard. I yelp, but his mouth is already moving onto my back where he places sweet kisses up the whole way until he's draped over me, his fingers working faster. "Give it to me, Angel," he whispers into my ear, and the strength of my orgasm pushes me forward, my head falling to my arms again. Finn's low chuckle is barely heard over my cries of pleasure.

The moon reflects off of the still water and the sound of Finn's breaths fills my ear as I lay against his broad chest, his arms wrapped around me. We're sitting in the grass, me between his legs and leaning against him, while we watch the water below us. Finn nips at my ear and I laugh, batting him away. This feels natural, like I was always meant to be here with him. "Good thing this is a public park, or else our DNA would be suspicious." Finn chuckles.

I look around the empty area and the lone bench that people

sit on and feed birds at, and then at the dock down below that people sit on and fish off of. "Yeah, maybe we should have used the bench instead."

"Nah, I liked this better," he pauses. "You are so strong, Huntley," he whispers into my ear. "You'll never have to do any of this alone, baby." I turn my head, my hand reaching behind me to cup his strong chin, and I kiss him. I kiss him with so much emotion, I hope he can feel my thanks in it. He's slowly giving me back my life, little pieces at a time. I watch the lake. It looks undisturbed, like there isn't a car sitting at the bottom, a man long having lost his life. A vile monster. A man who took something that was never his to take, nor was it offered. I don't feel a single bit sad for what I helped with tonight; for what Finn and I did. Lucas chose this path when he decided to take part that night at the frat party. The only thing I can feel right now is the warmth seeping into my bones from Finn, and the love he's trying to pour into my body as well. This might make me a monster, just like Lucas was, but I'd rather be a monster who doesn't have to be afraid anymore, than a scared woman who struggles to sleep and never feels at peace. The other two had better count their days, because I found a monster much bigger than they could ever be, and we're coming for them.

19

HUNTLEY

The sun is low, close to setting, but not there yet when I pull into Finn's driveway and park in front of the house. He texted me while I was in class and asked me to come over to hang out. Despite having a paper to finish, I came anyway. I couldn't resist. I wanted to see him again.

Pulling the hood of my cropped hoodie over my head to protect my hair from the light drizzle of rain, I walk around my car to the porch, but music pumping from the shop off to the side halts my movements. I look over, and the large garage door is opened and the lights are on. Finn must be in his shop. "The Walls" by Chase Atlantic becomes clearer as I get closer to the shop.

Stepping inside, I feel like I stepped into a showroom. Cars are lined up on the polished tile flooring. Walking between the cars, I pass them by, looking at each one. A new rhino-lined black Jeep Wrangler without doors or a top; a red, classic Ford Mustang; a white, classic Ford Shelby; and a few bikes parked at the back. Holy shit, my dad would die over the Shelby.

When I get to the end of the line of cars, the brunette and blonde from the club party are standing with their backs to me.

Both shirtless, the brunette's hanging out of the back pocket of his jeans, and the blonde's hung over his shoulder.

"J, come on. Move your hips," the brunette says, standing slightly in front of the guy with shaggy blonde hair. He rolls his hips, moving his hands down his chest, then stops. Turning to the blonde again. "Is that how you fuck? Damn, no wonder your room is always so quiet. Loosen up, Jack." He turns back around. "Come on, again."

"Why do I have to have my shirt off for this?" the blonde groans.

"The views, man, the views." The brunette walks up to his phone that is propped up on a table and presses it. A song starts and the guys do a short dance. The brunette is getting very into it, staring at the camera and running his hands over his body, while the blonde exerts half of the effort and glares at the phone.

The song finishes and the video cuts, and the brunette walks back up to the phone and picks it up, watching it intently. Jack pulls his white shirt on.

"Whatever, this will do," he says, turning around and picking his eyes up. He notices me standing by the Mustang. I stayed next to it with my backpack still hung over my shoulders and watched them—not to be creepy, though now I feel like a creep—but because I was curious and didn't want to interrupt. "Did you enjoy the show, Legs?"

"Is Finn here, Fabio?" I give him a dumb name back, since he gave me one.

A smooth laugh tumbles from his plump lips, his brown eyes sparkling under the bright lights in the shop. "I don't have nearly long enough hair to be Fabio, but you're right, I should be shirtless and on the cover of women's romance novels." He smirks.

"Oh God," I groan and roll my eyes.

Jack clears his throat. "Finn went to pick up his dad's truck, he should be back any minute."

I look over at Jack, his blonde hair hanging in his face. "Thank you. I'll uhh..." I look around the shop, trying to decide what to do until Finn gets here. Should I wait for him here? In his house? In my car?

"You can wait in here, Legs." The brunette motions to a chair by the table his phone was sitting on.

I take a seat on the chair and look at both of them. Not sure what to say. "I'm Huntley, by the way."

"Jack." Jack holds up his hand.

"Leo." The brunette smirks, his arms crossing over his chiseled chest.

Just then, a red pickup pulls into the shop and Finn gets out, his eyes finding mine immediately. His long legs eat up the shop as he walks toward me. His light-washed, worn jeans, black tee shirt, and backward hat make my mouth drool. "I see you met the fuckwits of the Outlaws." Finn towers over me.

"Mmhmm." I nod my head, staring into his deep eyes. A few water droplets cling to the shoulders of his cut.

"I just really wanted to see you." He lets out a heavy breath. "You can go home if you want, but I thought maybe you could hang out while I teach these fools how to change the oil and fix a few dents. Talk to me and keep me from drowning them in the oil?" A small smile plays on his lips.

"I have a paper to finish," I argue lightheartedly. I'm not going anywhere.

Finn grabs my bag from my lap. "The shop has wifi and you can sit and write while we work."

Nodding, I relent. Not that I was leaving anyway, but I had to make him work for it a little bit. Finn takes my hand and leads me to the front of the shop where the red pickup is. "Bring a few chairs for Huntley," Finn calls over his shoulder. "And some beers for everyone."

Jack carries over two tall stools for me to set up on and Leo passes out cans of beer to everyone. I settle onto the stool, resting my feet on the other and propping up my laptop. All three guys roll under the pickup on little boards with wheels, and Finn talks them through whatever they're doing. Occasional grunts leak out from under the car. A little bit later, they all roll out from under the vehicle, Finn coming to lean against the tall workbench behind me and Jack and Leo staying seated on the rolling backboards. Finn cleans off his hands on a shop rag, watching me type.

My laptop clicks closed and I set it on the workbench, turning to face the guys sitting on the ground. "You guys are in the club, right?" I ask Leo and Jack.

Leo nods, swallowing his drink. "Yeah, we're prospects.

"Means they're new." Finn leans over. "Kinda in a probationary period."

Nodding, I take another look around the shop. It's huge in here.

Finn walks back over to the pickup and settles onto the board, rolling back under. Jack follows, but Leo comes over and sits next to me on the second stool Jack brought over.

He holds out his hand for me to shake. "Leo Garcia. Club Prospect and newest Evans Body Shop employee, along with Jack."

I shake his hand, staring at his tanned toned arm. Leo's young; no tattoos, messy dark brown hair, and warm brown eyes. His playful smile is infectious. "How'd you get here, Leo?" I blurt out before I can stop myself. Biting my lip, I look away. That was such an intrusive thing to ask.

Leo shrugs, not phased a bit. "Same as everyone else, I guess. Looking for something."

My eyebrows pull together. "What do you mean?"

Leo leans back on the stool, tossing one arm over the back of it and bringing the other to his lip, running his finger along it. "We're all looking for something when we show up at the club-house. Brotherhood, a connection, a place to belong."

I'm so pulled into him, I can't help but listen to his smooth voice. There's something about him; the determination in his eyes, the want for something that is covered up by his playful attitude. "What were you looking for?"

"Leadership," he almost whispers, his eyes glazing over. Then he clears his throat, his eyes focusing again. "I guess that's what you need when your dad leaves before you were born."

That's what I felt pulling me towards Leo. I felt the same pain in him that's lived deep in my heart my entire life. My mom abandoned me too, though I try not to let it affect me anymore. She chose to leave my dad and me. I won't give her the satisfaction of missing her. I can't say it didn't keep me up at night when I was younger, though. Going over to my friends' houses and watching their moms dote on them or pick them up after school; in middle school when I got my period—God, my dad was not prepared for that, but he handled it like a champ. When I had my heart broken for the first time in high school. I missed her a lot back then, but not anymore.

"Did you find it?" I ask Leo, watching his finger absently run across his lip.

Leo's lips pull into a small smile. "I found so much more. A brotherhood, family. I found my best friends." Leo's eyes fall to the floor where Jack's legs are sticking out from under the pickup.

"Tell me about them," I prod. I can't help myself, I want to keep talking to Leo. I feel a connection with him. Nothing like with Finn, not a chance. A friendly connection, a protective connection over Leo. "Mase isn't here, but he's a computer genius. He can figure anything out if you give him a few minutes and a good internet connection. I think he's lost and trying to find himself. He's shy though, probably because he spends all of his time behind a screen." Finn and Jack slide out from under the pickup.

"Aren't you supposed to be learning shit, asshole?" Finn barks.

Leo smirks, his playful attitude back. "Someone had to keep Legs company."

Finn's eyes widen and he advances toward us. Leo holds up his hands. "Not like that, it's 'cause she's tall. I'm not hurting for pussy bad enough that I need to commit suicide by moving in on your Old Lady." He rolls his eyes.

Finn glares at Leo. "If you make her uncomfortable, I'll drop a car on you next time you're at the shop."

"Noted," Leo says in a bored tone.

Finn looks over at me and I smile. Leo isn't making me uncomfortable. I like talking to him. Finn takes that for what it is and moves to a door that I hadn't realized was there and disappears through it, coming back out a few seconds later with more tools in hand. He points Jack to a spot on the opposite side of the truck and they start to work on whatever it is they're doing.

Leo leans into me. "It's fun to rile him up." He chuckles.

Snorting, I watch Finn and Jack work, both concentrated on what they're doing. "He's going to blow one day."

Leo shrugs, smiling. "That's okay." He watches Jack. "Jack is my other best friend. He's... He keeps to himself a lot."

Jack's square jaw clenches as he bangs on the side of the pickup with a mallet. Pieces of his blonde hair fall into his eyes and his deep brown eyes are almost black. "And he's still your best friend?"

"I get his silence. He's opened up to me a little, but I don't pry and I think he appreciates that. I don't know. I think he came to the club for a safe haven. I think he's running from something and he left someone behind when he did. Or maybe he's running from someone he left behind." Leo trails off, watching his friend. Then his head snaps to mine. "Shit, don't say anything about that okay?" he urgently whispers. "Jack's never said anything, it's just stuff I've pieced together, but I haven't told anyone that before."

"Then why did you tell me?" I whisper back.

Leo shakes his head, looking into my eyes. "I don't know, I was just thinking out loud. You're easy to talk to."

"I promise I won't say anything," I say, speaking low so the others won't hear us.

Leo looks at me, a serious expression on his face. "Pinky promise?" he asks, holding out his pinky.

I take it and we lock our pinkies together. "Pinky promise." I bring my hand to my lips and kiss it. Leo chuckles but does the same to his hand.

20

HUNTLEY

STUDENTS FILE OUT OF THE BUILDING AND INTO THE BREEZY courtyard, but once we step outside, the crowd slows, some even stopping. Looking around, I see them all watching something. That's somewhat normal; there's probably a booth set up with a speaker, food, or performer on campus. It is almost graduation, maybe a company set up a recruiting tent. Not interested, especially in being stuck in a crowd, I shove my way through. But when I get out of the crowd, I see what everyone is staring at.

My monster.

Finn sits on his bike at the edge of the sidewalk. His ocean blue eyes covered behind dark Ray Bans, and his thick, tattooed arms crossed over his chest. A scowl on his face makes him look every bit the club enforcer. But even behind the black lenses, I can feel when his gaze lands on me. The corner of his mouth quirks up and he stands from the bike. He waits for me to walk to him, his stance wide and his arms crossed. And I do. I go to him, because whenever he's around I feel pulled towards him. I have since the first night we saw each other from across the stage at The Second Circle.

My eyes never leave him as I walk across the sidewalk. The

crowd of students, some already leaving, others still staring, all fade away. When I'm in front of Finn, his smile splits his face, his straight white teeth gleaming in the sunshine. "Hey, Angel, come on. I have someone I want you to meet." He grabs my waist and pulls me into him when I'm close enough, his big arms band around me and his lips an inch from mine. I nod, stepping onto my toes to nip at his bottom lip and then place a soft kiss on his plush lips. I can't help it. I feel like a part of me is back, but better. He brings out a side of me I never knew existed; this animalistic, primal kind of need for him. I realized it the night we attacked each other on the grass in front of the lake.

I step onto the bike after Finn is on and starts it up. Wrapping my arms around him, I lean my nose into the leather on his back and breathe him in. The final students disperse as Finn guns it out of the parking lot.

Finn parks the bike beside a white building. The large sign next to the road reads "Big Dawgs." Inside, the lights are low, a real bar and grill type. There's a kitchen on the left, completely open so you can see everything: the grill, the sink, everything. A short, high bar in front of it, and then another long bar on the opposite side of the room with a long wall of refrigerators, the doors clear so you can see all of the beverages in them. There are a few tables on the right and two pool tables behind them, with a modern jukebox on the back wall.

Only a few people occupy the tables, mostly drinking and talking. It's too late for lunch and too early for dinner. A man the size of Finn walks through a door by the kitchen, carrying a big tray of steaming meat. The delicious smell drifts into the restaurant and fills it instantly. Finn pulls me towards the bar in front of the grill, which is where the other man is heading. As we get closer, I can make him out better. Blonde hair and sky-blue eyes, but I can see the resemblance. The wide, sharp jaw; the bulky build; and their smiles are identical. He has to be Finn's father.

"Buddy!" The man smiles, setting the tray of meat down and pulling off his gloves.

"Hi, dad." Finn walks around the bar and hugs his dad. They both thump each other hard on the back and then his dad pulls away, staring into his son's eyes before they break and meet mine. I smile, not sure if I should introduce myself or wait for Finn to do so. Finn takes a step back and holds his hand out for me. Pulling me towards them, he stares at me, catching me in his gaze once more. "Dad, this is the woman I was telling you about."

"Your Old Lady?" His grin grows even wider, if that was even possible, and Finn nods. There's that damn name he called me at the clubhouse. What kind of term is that? Finn's dad holds his hand out to me. "Hi, my name's Randy."

I shake his hand. Strong, a lot like his son's. "Hi Randy, I'm Huntley." Randy is a lot different than his son. Where Finn is intense and mysterious, Randy is calm and light. Finn almost has two different personalities: the Finn he has to be for the club, and the Finn he is with his friends, and me, and his dad. I can see his dad in that version of him. I like both parts of him.

"I know, sweetheart, I've heard a lot about you." His other hand encases the one he was shaking.

"Okay, okay. Go show Huntley your wall of fame while I make you all something." He grabs a menu from the bartop and hands it to me. "Look through and yell out when you see something you want. Your usual, old man?" Finn looks at his father, a smile in his eyes, a lightness that is rarely seen with him.

"Yeah, buddy." Randy has since dropped my hand and he leans in to kiss Finn on the side of the head before motioning me to follow him over to the long wall by the pool tables, with about a hundred picture frames hanging on it.

Randy shows me pictures of Finn and his mom, Olivia, throughout his entire childhood and teen years: Finn's mom laying in a hospital bed, her raven hair twisted into a clip with pieces sticking to her face, and holding a tiny little Finn wrapped up in a handmade quilt; Olivia holding baby Finn at the top of the Space Needle, he couldn't have been older than six months; Baby Finn dressed as a pumpkin and Olivia holding him dressed in overalls with a straw hat; Finn and Olivia sitting in front of a Christmas tree, both in matching pajamas; Finn and his mom at a tee ball game, pee wee football games; Halloween and Christmas photos continue through the years. Finn dressed as a wolf at a school play as a child, middle school football games, middle school band concert, then finally high school football games, and his senior prom. It's like I'm watching Finn grow up, with him growing taller and wider in every picture. His braces, his hair growing longer, and then when he chops it all off. Graduation was the last picture of Finn and Olivia, Finn towering over his mother in his cap and gown. Him holding his diploma with the biggest grin I've ever seen on his face, and his mom staring up at him lovingly, her beautiful black hair cropped short at her shoulders.

"Cancer took her just a few months after Finn's graduation." Randy's voice drops to an almost whisper. "We didn't catch it in time, and she was gone by the time Finn started prospecting for the club in the fall." My heart breaks for Finn and Randy. They loved Olivia more than anything in life, I can tell by the way Finn's face is lit up in every photo. He's not scowling or annoyed by having to take pictures with his mom. He loves her and is proud to be there with her. I can tell by the way Randy stares at the pictures like he's reliving the days in his mind, hearing her voice again, and smelling her perfume. The pictures continue on, so Randy keeps explaining them to me, but I can tell he's thinking of his wife. In the photos now are Finn and Callum. When they started prospecting for the club, holding their brand-new leather cuts with the prospect patch on the back.

Finn and Callum sitting on their bikes, big smiles from both of them. When they patched in, group shots of the entire club, and so many more at club gatherings. In these photos, I get to see Finn turn into the man he is today, the muscles and tattoos. But he still wears that boyish smile in almost all of the photos.

Tattooed hands wrap around my waist and I jump at the contact. Finn's deep laugh vibrates my ear. "Did you decide what you want to eat, Angel?"

"Oh." I laugh and flip through the menu quickly. I hadn't looked at it at all, I was too enthralled with the wall documenting Finn's life. "Popcorn shrimp." I pick the first appetizer that sounds good.

"You got it, baby." He leans down and kisses my cheek softly, then nips at my ear as he pulls away. "Your fries are done, dad," Finn says as he turns to leave.

Randy stops him with a hand on his forearm. "I'll get the shrimp, you sit with your girl."

Finn shrugs and leads me to the bar in front of the grill. Taking a seat next to me, he offers me a beer-battered fry from his plate of two burgers and a giant heaping of fries. The fry is crunchy on the outside and fluffy on the inside, and perfectly seasoned.

I groan as I swallow and Finn leans in to whisper in my ear, "Don't think I won't throw you over my shoulder and fuck you in the bathroom. I don't care who will be able to hear."

My tongue darts out to wet my lips and Finn's eyes zero in on the movement. "That's not a threat to me," I say, boldly.

Finn smirks and turns his head forward to face his dad. "Fucking perfect for me." He shakes his head and mumbles.

Randy fries my shrimp, turning to talk to us and taking bites of some BBQ cheese fries Finn made him. When it's done, we stay at the bar, with Randy pulling a barstool around the opposite side, and we eat like at a normal family meal. We stayed long after our food was done, Randy or Finn leaving occasionally to close someone's tab or make something for a customer. To say I was surprised when a small dinner rush hit was an understatement. It hadn't felt like we'd been here for three hours, but I had a lot of fun getting to know Randy and hearing about Finn's childhood.

The rumbling of Finn's shiny black bike roars louder as we slow to a stop at a red light. I raise my arms and wrap them around Finn's shoulders, leaning down to lightly bite his shoulder. He leans back into my chest, his head turning to place a kiss under my jaw.

"Will you spend the night with me?" He yells over the bike, looking up at me from where his head rests against my chest.

I nod and the light turns green, reflecting off of us. Finn removes one of his hands from the handlebar to cradle my face, pulling me forward into his mouth. He devours me and my hands slide down his chest and over the hard muscles of his stomach. A horn honking behind us startles me and I pull away from him as Finn laughs and guns the motorcycle forward, turning his torso to flip the guy behind us off.

After washing my face and brushing our teeth next to each other at the giant, black marble double sink in the ensuite, I follow Finn into the bedroom. The black silk sheets lay haphazardly around Finn's waist, the blue neon lights making the shadows across Finn's naked muscled chest deeper. I crawl in next to him, and the sheets feel like cool liquid against my bare legs. Finn pulls me into his side, and I rest my head on his chest, admiring all of the tattoos painted across his chest and stomach.

"How long did these take?" I ask, gliding my hand over his warm flesh.

"Saint's been tattooing me since I started prospecting when I was eighteen." I listen to his voice rumbling from deep in his chest.

I turn my head so my chin is resting on his pec and I can look down at him. "Which one is your favorite?"

"My first one," he says, moving his hand to point to a date inked on his ribcage, the back of his fingers brushing against my nipple over one of his tee shirts I'm wearing.

I pull back to look at the scrolling date, more faded than his others. "Do you regret any?"

Finn stares at me, watching me for a few seconds before finally answering. "All of them since I met you."

My eyebrows draw together. "What do you mean?"

He runs his rough finger down my jaw, his eyes still boring into mine. "I wish I would have known I was going to meet you before I got tatted, that way I could have inked parts of you all over my body instead," he breathes. "Your intense fucking eyes." His finger moves next to my right eye. "Your plump fucking lips." His finger grazes my bottom lip, pulling it with the motion. "The dangerous curves of your body." His hand smooths down my back and over my ass. "Even the words you speak. I want you all over me." He grabs my hand and brings it to his lips, kissing the back of it. "You're so fucking beautiful, you mesmerize me every time I look at you. You're more beautiful than anything I've ever put on my body. You're more beautiful than the priceless pieces of art in any museum, and I wish I could have been yours, to show your beauty to everyone who wanted to look." He licks his lips and looks at me. No cocky grin, no kiss, nothing to show this was a line fed to me to get me to do something he wanted, to fall harder for him. Just his truth that rocks me to my core.

I'm speechless. What the fuck does someone say to that? So I do the only thing my mind can think of, I lean down and kiss him. I let all of my emotions pour into the kiss; how thankful I am for him giving me back my life, and my confidence, but also for letting me grow. Finn doesn't shield me from the shit that he does. He doesn't treat me like a broken bird that he has to hide away to nurture back to health. He lets me live and experience and heal myself while he watches and encourages me. He's the missing part that I've been looking for since the night my body was ripped apart and my life was stolen. I'm back, and with Finn, I'm better than I was before.

21

———

FINN

The wind whispers around us, and I watch Huntley as she looks around the outdoor patio. Her eyes catch on everything: the people walking down the sidewalk below and to other wooden tables next to us; the glistening water of the bay in front of us; the snow-capped mountains behind us like a backdrop to the little Alaskan fishing town that Parker Witten moved to after graduating last spring; and lastly, to the small fishing vessels leaving and returning to the bay. Our next mark is on the one that we're waiting on to arrive.

"Are you nervous?" I ask, noticing she's barely touched her breaded fish and fries.

She shakes her head, her eyes still roaming our surroundings. "Just admiring how beautiful it is here."

I agree, it is beautiful. It's a lot different here than in Merrill Hill; less busy, and right on the water. The people are kind, and you have a view of the water and mountains everywhere you look. "Reminds me of Orca Bay, just with all of the fishing boats."

"Yeah, I guess you're right." She finally turns her head towards me and smiles. My heart stops for a brief moment. That smile could make me do a thousand things. All she has to do is flash me one and I'd be on my knees ready to do whatever her beautiful soul wanted. "This has been a nice vacation, but I wish it were longer."

I snort, almost choking on my water. "This is a pretty twisted vacation, Angel."

She shrugs, looking over her shoulder at the small restaurant we decided to wait at. The white paint is peeling in some areas, but the back deck is large and crowded, and the food is good. "Oh shit, did you hear about that Senator's wife that was murdered?" she asks, picking up a fry and dipping it in some ketchup.

My head bobs and I take the fry from her, popping it into my mouth and smiling at her dropped jaw. "Yeah, it's fucking crazy."

"It had to be a robbery, right?" She picks up another fry and puts it in her mouth, chewing slowly while she looks out over the water again.

"Maybe." I take another fry from her plate, narrowly avoiding her swatting hand. Chuckling, I say, "Maybe the Senator was involved in some shady shit."

We both laugh at that, as morbid as it is. Senator Davis was hard as fuck on crime, no way he got caught up in something illegal.

The dark blue fishing boat sails into the bay and docks a ways away from us, but Huntley and I can see it clearly from our table. I toss a few bills on the table, enough to cover our tab two times over, and grab her hand to pull her with me. She follows behind me, her small hand held tight in mine. I pull my black baseball cap off and set it on her head, and she takes my cue and pulls it low, hiding the top of her beautiful face. We stop a few boats away from the one that Parker Witten is on, standing on the sidewalk above the deck leading to the boats. I pull Huntley into my side and tuck her under my arm, raising my other one to take a selfie of us. I snap several photos, looking at the camera for a few, but mostly this was just a cover to watch Parker. Then, because Parker is taking his sweet fucking time getting off of the damn boat, I open up Instagram and upload one of the pictures where we're both looking at the camera and smiling, the snow-covered mountain behind us. Huntley's blue eyes pop against the black of her leather jacket and baseball cap. I type out a quick caption, "Her heart is gold, but her hands are cold." and hit post. Parker hops off of the boat, and I glare as I watch his arrogant swagger as he walks down the deck, staring at the women he passes. Huntley and I stalk him, above him on the sidewalk and several feet back, so he doesn't notice us.

We follow him to his car, conveniently in the same lot as our rental. Not that it mattered. Mason pulled his address for me a week ago after we pushed Lucas' Mercedes into the lake.

The drive to Parker's little cabin is short. He lives on the edge of town so he doesn't have a long commute to work every morning. Can't blame him for that, and it makes this so much easier. No neighbors are a blessing for this kind of work. When we get close to the house, I turn off our headlights and pull up close to the house. Parking behind some trees, we're able to watch Parker through his big bay window.

He's walking into the house, shrugging his heavy coat off and hanging it up by the door, tossing his keys on the kitchen island and grabbing a beer from the fridge. He leans against the counter and takes a long pull from the bottle before setting it down and walking into the bedroom that is off of the kitchen. Popping my door open, I pull on my leather gloves, Huntley following behind me quietly. I take a glance back at her as I stalk through the heavily wooded front yard of Parker Witten. She ditched the ball cap and she's pulling on her gloves as well. Her eyes are bright with adrenaline—they almost sparkle in the low light of the setting sun. At the side door, the one that Parker entered through, I kneel in the damp dirt and pull my lock-picking kit from my back pocket. After fiddling with it for a few tries, the door easily clicks open and I turn the knob silently, standing to my full height and stepping into the warm house. Parker is still in the bedroom, but I know we don't have much time before he comes back in for his dinner. Cocking my head, I signal Huntley to stand on the side of the bedroom door, and I stand on the other, ready to grab Parker when he exits.

We wait only moments before Parker walks through, but his eyes snag on Huntley, and he jerks, stopping in his tracks. Huntley's eyes go wide, and they stare at each other for a second that feels like it drags on for years before Parker lunges for Huntley. She expertly backs away, but before she can even move, I've grabbed Parker by the back of the throat, and I slam the side of his head into the door frame. His head lolls about, clearly dazed, and I drag him to the kitchen island, dropping him into a barstool and jerking my head at Huntley. She rushes over and I pull a syringe from my hoodie pocket and hand it to her.

"You really like syringes, don't you? What's in this one?" she asks, pulling the orange cap from the tip and looking at the needle.

"Heroine with a strong dose of Fentanyl. Parker is ODing tonight." I hold Parker tightly by the back of his neck, forcing his head into the counter. He jerks pathetically. "And don't judge my methods, this is easy." The knock on the head still impairs him, but he's still fighting, so I guess I'll give him that.

I grip his arm with my other hand, squeezing tightly at the top of it to make his vein pop for my girl.

"So you like easy?" Huntley grabs ahold of the flailing limb and squeezes at the wrist, the both of us holding his arm immobile. She spots the vein and stabs the needle into his arm, more forcefully than needed, but really, who can blame her for that one?

"Not even close," I say, watching her empty the syringe into Parker's arm.

She starts to pull the syringe out, but I let go of him to place my hand over hers and pull it away, leaving the syringe in its place. Huntley's hand drops to her side and I raise Parker's head and knock it into the edge of the kitchen counter, in the same place he hit the doorframe, and then let his body crumple to the floor.

The barstool scratches against the wood floor as I pull it further out and take a seat. Sitting over Parker's twitching body, I watch Huntley watching him. Her chest rises quickly but steadily, and she watches Parker seize on his kitchen floor before he finally stops. His wet breathing slows until it finally stops. She watches him the entire time, never taking her eyes off him. She looks like the ruler of Hell standing over her prisoners, ready to set out their judgment and punishment. A fierce look dances in her eyes. Her vengeance is laying at her feet like a fucking offering, and I'm here to worship my queen.

I rise to my feet, pushing the stool back to where Parker had it, and grab Huntley's hand. Only then does she look away from Parker's body.

"Come on, Angel. We have a plane to catch." I tug on her hand to get her moving. We shouldn't linger longer than we need to. The flights and car are booked under fake names, and using fake IDs—one that I already had for myself, and another that I had made quickly for Huntley—but we shouldn't test our luck.

She lets me take her, stepping over Parker's body like it's dog shit, and honestly, after what he did to my girl, I'd treat shit with more respect than I'd treat this thing. "No matter how many times you call me it, I will never be an Angel, Finn. I'm too damaged. I don't think angels dream of bloody revenge. I'm going straight to Hell right beside you," she says, and I stop walking to turn around and look at her.

No matter what she thought, I knew she was going to Heaven. She may think she's damaged but her heart was pure, and if she was convinced she was going to Hell, then I knew she would end up running the whole damn thing with me as her hellhound. Hunting down miserable fucks to please her for the rest of eternity. "Nah, baby. I know evil, I stare at it every day in the mirror. You're not evil." I take her chin in my fingers and make her look at me so she knows I'm not fucking around. "And you're sure as fuck not damaged. You are strong and beautiful, and a fucking warrior. I will not allow anyone to speak about you in that way, even you, Angel." Her teeth sink into her lower lip and tears pool in the bottoms of her eyes, fucking breaking me. "If you're drowning then, baby, I'm right there beside you. You don't ever have to do this shit alone again. You got me. You fucking had me from the first night I ever laid my eyes on you." Huntley nods and I pull her out of the house. Stopping to lock it with my kit and we walk to the car together, hand in hand. "Isn't graduation next month?" I ask, remembering it's about to be April.

"Yeah," Huntley says as we reach the car. "Do you want me to get you a ticket?" I can hear a smile in her voice, even though I can barely see it.

The door slams shut as I slide into the driver's seat, Huntley sliding in next to me. "Hell yeah, baby." The engine starts and I pull onto the road, taking us back to the airport. "The entire club is coming!"

22

FINN

"Hey, man, can you get me in today, I just want something small," I ask into the phone.

Saint sighs and I can hear fingers tapping on a keyboard in the background. "Yeah, I can get you in tonight after my last client, probably around eight."

"Got it, brother. See you tonight." I smile when Saint grunts as a goodbye and hangs up on me. Typical moody bastard. Phone still in hand, I pull up Huntley's messages. It's Tuesday, so she'll have her pole class tonight which ends at eight. Couldn't have planned it better if I tried.

FINN

Meet me at SINdicate at 8.

HUNTLEY

Why?

FINN

Because I said? The fuck?

I roll my eyes lightheartedly, of course she would question me.

HUNTLEY

I don't remember signing up to be at your beck
and call, Muscles.

Fuck, her attitude makes me hard. I mull over my next words. How do I want to play this? Dirty, always dirty.

FINN

You signed your name when I had my hand
around your throat and your pussy squeezed
me tight in response.

HUNTLEY

Mmm, good times.

I'm gonna fuck her. I'm gonna track her fucking phone and drive to her right now and bend her over wherever she's at. Immediately.

HUNTLEY

I'll be there, I suppose. You know, since you
asked so nicely. *eye roll emoji*

I'm pulling up her location on my phone when I'm interrupted by Leo. We both shared them with each other just in case something happened to either of us. We were laying in bed and she grabbed our phones off of the bedside table and turned it on for both phones. She said she wanted to know I was safe and she wanted me to always know where she was. She said it gave her a sense of security, knowing I could always find her. I didn't tell her that I would find her, regardless if she willingly shared her location with me.

"Hey, boss, a guy's out here wanting to order a custom color for his Vett and I need your authorization." Leo stands in my open doorway, his arms holding the top of it and leaning.

"Got it," I say, dropping my phone onto my desk. "I'm coming." Leo turns and leaves and I abandon my naughty plans for Huntley. I got shit to do here at the shop, and none of it has to do with why I opened this place in the first place. I opened Evans Body Shop because I love working on cars. I have my whole life. I didn't want to work for someone else, I wanted to control the projects I took, the guys I worked with, and I wanted something to pass on down to my future kids. Plus, the club sometimes needed me and it just worked better to be in charge of my own shit. I didn't anticipate having to give up all of the fun bodywork and painting to sit on my ass and do admin shit. I fucking hate running the books, making sure bills are getting paid, customers are being charged, parts are ordered, and employees are getting paychecks. I just want to be back in the shop with my guys, but I don't trust anyone to take over the books for me. They're not cooked or anything like that, there's nothing nefarious going on with them, I just don't trust someone to be as diligent as I am with them. This shop is my baby, and I make sure she's running right.

———

THE LIGHT BUZZ of tattoo guns hums through the room, and the smell of vanilla hangs in the air, masking the smell of cleaning products nicely. Saint's shop looks a lot like his home. A lot of black and light wood mixed together. The walls in the shop are exposed brick painted black with light oak open shelves hanging over every station. A giant neon sign hangs on the black brick in the waiting area, a tan leather couch sits under it. The new receptionist—since I had the last one fired after checking out Huntley and making her uncomfortable at the club party—stares at me as I walk in. She's either wondering why I'm not checking in with her or checking me out. I watch her out of the corner of my eye as I walk past, and she rakes her eyes down my body slowly and raises her eyebrows: definitely checking me out. Ignoring her, I walk to the back corner where Saint's bed is. I hear soft footsteps behind me but ignore them, because I know Saint will tell the new tattoo apprentice/receptionist to fuck off. Saint spins around on his little black stool, his blonde hair tied into a bun on the back of his head and sticking his electronic pen behind his ear. The first strums of "E-Girls Are Ruining My Life!" by Bryce Savage starts softly on the speakers wired through the shop. Saint's eyes fall behind me and he raises a hand to shoo away the new girl.

"Where we doing this at?" he asks, his usual bored expression on his handsome face.

I raise my right hand, the palm facing me. "I thought it was about time to finish up the lower fingers."

Saint nods his head and messes with the buttons on his electric bed, maneuvering it into a sitting position. I take a seat when it's done moving and Saint rolls a black table over to my right side, raising it to its level with me and I place my arm on it, splaying out my fingers for him to clean and get to work.

I finish telling him what we're doing when I hear the door open at the front of the shop. My eyes drift over—a force of habit to always be on alert—but at the door, they meet the most beautiful woman I've ever seen. Huntley walks in wearing another one of my shirts that she stole and a pair of short athleisure shorts. The shirt hangs so low on her that you can just barely see the very bottom of the shorts when she takes a step forward, causing the shirt to ride up just a little bit. She looks so fucking beautiful, hair tied in a bun on top of her head, her face flushed and free of makeup. She's a fucking goddess and I can't wait to have her stamped in any place that I can find room on my body. Fuck, maybe I should just go through laser and start completely over. There's a fucking idea. Her eyes lock on mine like we're calling beacons for each other, and she breezes past the front desk, much like myself. I watch her walk to me, loving the way she looks when she watches me; loving knowing that she's mine and I'm not ever letting her go. The rolling of a chair breaks my trance with my Angel, and I look down to see Saint sliding another stool over to the other side of me with his foot.

A small hand grabs my chin forcefully and raises my head, my eyes lock on Huntley's beautiful blue eyes, her pupils blown. "If this woman doesn't stop staring at you I'm going to do to her what you did to Saint's last employee," she whispers over my lips before sinking her teeth into the bottom one.

Without any hesitation, my free hand grips the back of her hair, my fingers sinking into the pulled-up hair and I smash her face into mine.

Devouring her.

Marking her.

Letting every motherfucker in this fucking shop know that she's mine and I'm hers.

She groans and I release her head, letting her pull away. My mouth slides into a smirk, my tongue running over the small indentations from her teeth. I love that she keeps getting rougher and rougher with me and that she wants that from me in return. It feels like she's coming into a new version of herself. One where she's more confident in herself, and I fucking love it. She looks over her shoulder to the girl at the front desk and I follow her line of sight, the girl no longer lurking.

Huntley smiles a very proud fucking smile and takes a seat on the stool Saint rolled over for her.

Saint sighs loudly, and I look over to see him rolling his eyes. "If you two are done pissing on each other, I'd like to go home at some point tonight." A snort bubbles out of my throat, and Huntley smiles viciously at him.

After prepping my fingers, Saint grabs his mint green-wrapped gun and starts the machine. That's an odd color for him. In all the times over the years that I've been in here with him—which has been a fucking lot since almost every inch of my body is covered—he's always had his gun wrapped in black grip tape. The thought leaves my head when I feel the beautiful sting of the needle pushing into the skin of my knuckle, the one closest to the tip of my finger. He pens my name for her into my skin. My first tattoo for her, the first of many as long as I can find the space for them. It doesn't take long, and when he's done, he wipes them down. Before he can wrap them, Huntley grabs my hand.

She holds it gently in hers, maneuvering my big hand with her delicate one, examining the tattoo. "Angel," inked onto my fingers just for her.

Always for her.

I watch her. She purses her lips and sets my hand back down on the small table, allowing Saint to wrap my fingers with small pieces of the wrap. When he's done, Huntley takes my hand in hers again and places a kiss above every letter, then another one to my lips, her hand moving from mine to the back of my neck.

She pulls away before I can turn this gentle peck into something more fun. "My savior," she whispers.

She starts to back away but my hands grasp her face, holding her where she is so she has to look me in my eyes while I say this. "No, baby, you saved yourself. I just made you realize what you were capable of."

"Don't fuck each other in my shop," Saint drawls as he tosses the used paper towels into the trash by his station and dumps the used ink.

Huntley rolls her eyes but a smile is on her lips. "Thanks, brother, I'll see you Saturday," I say, rising from the chair and grabbing Huntley's hand.

"Whatever, just get the fuck out." He turns around and a smile tugs at the corner of his mouth. Saint doesn't have emotions. Not with anyone but us, his club brothers.

I squeeze Huntley's hand and pull her out of the shop. The new receptionist doesn't look our way once.

23

FINN

Shouldering past people, I pull my phone out of the inside pocket of my cut and pull up Huntley's messages. She said she would try to swing by the clubhouse when she was finished with a paper for one of her classes. From the top of my vision, I see Callum's frame spring forward, shoving people out of his way. Pocketing my phone, I watch Callum grab a man by the back of his neck. I rush forward and grab Little Red, turning her around and holding onto her upper arms. My body hovers above hers, watching her back while her man defends whatever the fuck just happened. I know it had to be something though, because Callum doesn't react to anything, ever. He's not afraid of violence, that's not what I mean, I just mean that he doesn't care enough about anything but his brothers to defend anything. Him standing up for Little Red at the bar when they met was a fucking first. He said he was defending her because she was a woman, but I think it was just because it was her. I think he saw something in her that he didn't know he saw yet. He still doesn't know it. He'll realize it though, they both will. They think we don't see the looks they give each other; the looks when one of them isn't looking, the way their bodies gravitate towards one another. We see it. They will too, eventually.

"You okay, Red," Callum says, his grip on the guy's throat tightening. The set of his shoulders is wound tighter than a fucking bow, and he's shaking. Nothing that anyone would notice, but I do. He's enraged.

"Yes. Come here," Reese says softly. I drop my arms from hers, but I stay close behind her, just in case.

Callum shoves the guy away and pushes up from the floor. His eyes are wild when he turns around, but they soften when they land on Reese. He stalks towards her, his nostrils flaring with his heavy breaths. Knowing that Little Red is back in good hands, I turn towards the front door and push past more people. I would have killed the guy if he had laid a hand on Huntley, but I understand why Callum didn't. The guy wasn't wearing a cut, meaning he was with the O'Connells, and right now, with a new business deal fresh on the table, murdering whoever the fuck he was to them wouldn't be the best move on our end. It would piss Ronan the hell off, but he would understand when he came down from his anger. None of us have Old Ladys, but Reese is as close to one as any of us have—Huntley aside—and we have to defend our women.

I'm swinging my leg over my bike when my phone pings with a message.

UNKNOWN

Spot 5. Midnight.

FINN

Will there be any fuck ups this time?

UNKNOWN

No, sir.

Alright, I guess I'm going to need to swing by the house and get the Hellcat.

Pushing open the double doors to Huntley's apartment lobby, the little prick at the front desk raises his head and then looks back down at his phone. Not the most secure. I'll definitely be having a talk with Huntley about that later. Anyone could walk in here, and what's that little fuck going to do? Nothing. Whatever, I punch the elevator button for the third floor and wait for it to come.

Knocking on Huntley's door, I wait and contemplate whether I should pick the lock when she finally opens the door. She's wearing a white crop top with these insanely thin straps and some black jean shorts, her white converse in her hand. Her nipples push against the fabric, and I groan.

She smiles and I forget all about that safety risk in the lobby and focus on her. "Hey, I was just about to leave."

"Change of plans, Angel. Wanna go for a ride?"

Huntley's teeth sink into her full pale pink bottom lip, her mouth curving into a mischievous smile, and she nods slowly.

Fuck me, she's perfect.

Huntley turns and walks into her apartment, leaving the door open for me to follow. She leans against the arm of the couch and starts to pull on her shoes. "What's got you so stressed?" Her delicate fingers twist the shoe strings into a bow.

"What?" I look away from her shoes and back to her face.

She looks at me from below her lashes, her intoxicating eyes pulling me in like a siren's song. "The little line between your brows is your tell." She pauses and looks down at my hands. "And you're playing with your lighter."

Shoving my hands in my pockets, I shuffle my feet. "My brother's girl is having some issues."

Huntley pulls her other shoe onto her foot. "What kind of issues?"

I bite the inside of my lip and watch her. I should tell her. I don't want there to be secrets between us. Not that I'm trying to keep this from her, I just don't want to trigger anything for her. "Stalker issues."

Her hands leave her shoe and her shoulders stiffen. She lets out a long breath before straightening up and meeting my eyes again.

"She's being stalked? Is she in danger?" Huntley's voice is small, withdrawn.

Sighing, I rake my fingers through my hair. "I don't know, I just know my brother is in deep with her and won't admit it, and that's what scares me the most."

Huntley stands, any vulnerability she was showing is gone now. Her shoulders are set, her lips relaxed. "I want to meet her. Maybe I can give her some self-defense tips, talk to her about safety."

I run my eyes over Huntley, thinking. That's not a bad idea; teaching Little Red how to defend herself, the two girls of The Outlaw's meeting. It'd be nice. "Okay. I'll text Cale. You ready for that ride?" My mouth slides into a smirk, the excitement of doing one of my favorite things with my favorite person taking over me.

———

AN HOUR LATER, Huntley and I are pulling into the same parking lot of the last race I brought her to. Fucking Devin walks up to my side of the Hellcat, his confident step pissing me off. Like I didn't threaten his life the last time we were here for putting Huntley in danger by not making sure the roads were blocked off.

Rolling down the window, I hand him my pay in, glaring the

entire time. "If I see one car that's not in this race, I'm coming for your fucking head."

Fucking Devin gulps, his Adam's apple bobbing in his skinny throat. "Understood, Finn."

Huntley giggles in the passenger seat and I pull away from him and join the lineup. We're a little late, but they wait for me. I always win, but people are stupid enough to keep entering, thinking they're going to beat me one day. Maybe they will, but it won't be anytime soon.

Huntley rests her elbow on the center console and leans over it, bringing her lips close to my ear. Her tongue darts out and traces a wet line up my neck before she bites down on my jaw. A growl rolls up my throat that I can't stop, and I feel my girl's smile against my skin. "If you win, I'll let you fuck my mouth when we get home."

Fucking Devin walks to the center of the street, standing in front of the line of cars, all of them revving their engines like they're measuring their dicks. "I don't lose, Angel, so why wait until we get home?" I unbuckle my belt and start undoing the button.

Huntley's eyes go wide, her pupils blown. "While you're racing?"

I shrug, pulling the zipper down and pulling out my half-hard cock. "Why not? This shit has gotten dull after so many races. Make this one interesting again."

The spotlight flashes and I hold an arm in front of Huntley while we all shoot off of the starting line. My arm holds her to the seat so she doesn't go slamming into her seatbelt.

I turn my head and watch Huntley. She licks her bottom lip and moves around on the seat. She leans forward, taking my cock in her delicate hand and running it gently up the length, over my piercings, and her thumb circles the tip. She lowers her mouth onto it, licking a circle around the head before slowly fitting it into her mouth. Her hand grasps the bottom and she hollows out her cheeks. She bobs up and down, sucking my dick tightly into her wet mouth. Every few thrusts, she goes a little deeper, moaning, her hand keeping time with her mouth, and her wrist working me in a delicate motion. I gain on another car, moving around them to pass and moving a hand from the wheel to hold onto Huntley so she doesn't jostle too much. Her tongue starts to flutter over my piercings, and that's the last straw for me. I grab her hair in my hand and pull her off of my dick. "Hop on," I growl.

"What?" she asks, her lips red and plump.

"You heard me. Lose the shorts." I flick a quick glance at her. We're neck and neck with the car in first place, and I'm two seconds from passing him too. The competition tonight was weak. At least last time I had to work for it a little more.

Huntley undoes her shorts and lifts her hips, sliding the shorts and panties down her long legs and leaving them on the floor. I pull into the oncoming traffic lane and reach over with one hand to pull open her smooth legs, lightly running my fingers up her thigh before sliding my fingers up her slit and back down to push two fingers in. She hisses at the intrusion, and I pump my fingers a few times. Her hand covers mine and she uses me to finger fuck her. Stroking her exactly as she directs. Her head falls against the back of the seat and she moans. I suddenly pull out and her head snaps to mine. Fire burns in her eyes, enough to burn down an entire city. That makes me even harder, if that was even possible, and I grab her hand, tugging it so she knows it's time.

After a deep breath, Huntley climbs onto her knees and then gracefully climbs over into my seat, settling herself into my lap. I move her upper body so that she's off to the side of me and I can still see in front of us. Her hand holds the base of my dick as she slowly slides on.

"Oh fuck," I hiss, pressing on the gas to pass the girl in front of us. I sail past her, but she obviously has a booster and presses it, sending her whizzing past us. It's hard to focus on the race when Huntley is squeezing me as tightly as she is, but I know amateur racing, and that was it. She was too soon, too eager; showing her cards and using her only advantage. The race was coming to a close, but it wasn't over. Huntley finally makes it to the bottom of my cock, my dick fully seated inside of her and feeling fucking great, like coming home after being gone and sleeping on shitty hotel beds. She finds a good placement for her feet, her long legs folded up, probably uncomfortably, but she doesn't complain. She just goes to work bouncing on my dick.

"Good girl, Angel," I rasp.

She whimpers in response, her hands holding onto my shoulders, and moves quickly. I flip the switch by my ignition and we shoot forward, Huntley's chest pressing into mine. She moves faster, the speed turning her on, and I feel a rush of liquid coat my balls. Huntley drops her head and grates her teeth along my neck. My dick kicks inside of her just as we're passing the girl who thought she had this race in the bag. I stick a finger in Huntley's mouth and she closes around it, circling her tongue around it much like she did my dick a bit ago. I pull my finger out and drop it to her ass. I gently massage her asshole and Huntley's pussy clenches around me, my piercings groaning along with me. Huntley moves harder, faster, shaking the fucking car.

I see the lights of the end of the race coming up quickly, and I know Huntley's close too. She's going to explode at any moment like a fucking volcano. "Cum, Angel," I bark, and as we're passing the finish line, Huntley cries out, her orgasm hitting us like a ton of fucking bricks, and I can't help but follow her over the edge.

"That's my good girl," I groan. Her pussy flutters around me, pulling every last bit out of my cock. Winning is nothing new to me, but this? This was next fucking level. This shit turned me on like nothing ever has. Huntley turns me on like no one ever has. It's different with her; things feel different, better. She's like nothing I've ever experienced before. I slow the car, and Huntley collapses against me, her breaths fanning out quickly against my neck. I wrap my arms tightly around her back to keep her there. I want to keep her here forever.

I pull up beside fucking Devin and roll my window down just a crack. Huntley jumps, trying to pull away, but my arm keeps her in place, my dick still fully inside of her, never wanting to fucking leave. He shoves my money through the gap and I take it, pulling away before he can say anything.

We drive for a few miles, holding onto each other, driving at a much slower rate than necessary.

I keep a hold of her. I never want her to leave where she is right now. We're perfect here together, joined in a way no one else will ever have from either of us again, because she's it for me and I'm it for her. I know I am. "You're so perfect, Angel. So perfect for me," I whisper into her hair.

Huntley pulls away, placing a kiss on my lips and swinging her legs off of me, she slides off of me and falls back into the passenger seat. My dick leaving her has both of us groaning. Huntley fishes around for her panties and pulls them on before she leans over and takes my cock in her mouth again, cleaning me up as much as she can handle. She pulls off and places me back into my jeans. I leave them unzipped and undone, and drive us back to my house. I have a lot more in mind tonight. Stuff that can't be done in my driver's seat.

24

HUNTLEY

BLOWING OUT A BREATH, I ALMOST FALL INTO THE BACK WALL OF the elevator. Finn and I just left Reese and Cale, after having to get Reese a new phone. When I used her phone to call Finn, I heard the telltale sign that her phone had been cloned. There's no one else who could be responsible for that besides her stalker. Good fucking timing on our end for hanging out with them today so I could offer to show Reese some simple self-defense moves. I could see the fear written all over her face when she heard the little click that her phone made, when she realized what her stalker had been doing right under her nose. She was terrified. That's exactly why I told Finn I wanted to help her; I didn't want her to be terrified anymore. I wanted her to be able to trust in her body that she could defend herself. Being able to hold your own goes a long way in helping your confidence and stuffing out some of the fear. It's never completely gone, but at least it's no longer crippling.

The elevator dings and the doors open to my floor. I'm too focused on my thoughts, my body on autopilot, that I don't even realize someone is standing at my door until it's too late.

"Hey, Lee," a sickly sweet voice says.

My body feels like something slammed into it—probably my attention coming back to me—and bile rises in my throat when I see the smug, evil smile of my ex.

"What are you doing here, Ryan?" I ask. I can hear the tremble in my voice and I pray that he can't. He'd love nothing more than for me to be afraid.

Ryan leans his shoulder against my door frame, his arms crossed over his strong chest. Ryan is a strong man. He played almost every sport you could think of. Not for the college, though. No, he was too focused on his studies and his fraternity. He still kept in good shape, playing on the rec teams that the University gym organized.

"I just wanted to see if you had heard about Parker and Lucas." Ryan cocks his head, his light blue eyes running over my face like he's assessing me.

"I don't keep in touch with rapists." I narrow my eyes, watching his body without making it obvious.

Ryan sighs, "They're dead. They said Lucas drove his car drunk into the lake by K Gam, and Parker overdosed."

"How unfortunate." I see his body tense, and a second before he lunges for me, I turn to run.

He's too fast, too strong. He grabs me by my hair and throws me against the wall, bracing his hands on either side of my head and leaning into my face. He bares his teeth. "Lucas never drove drunk, and Parker hasn't touched anything stronger than weed. I know you're behind this."

"Maybe you don't know your friends as well as you think you do. Just like how I didn't know you," I snap.

Ryan smiles again, his alligator fucking smile that sends chills skittering down my spine. "People have seen you entering the Devil's Outlaws clubhouse. Did you become a club whore? Give up your sweet pussy to exact some revenge?" He laughs, and I feel every ounce of my strength and confidence dwindle away like it was never there to begin with, only a mirage that I let myself believe in. "You always were a good fuck, but not that good." Ryan grabs my throat—nothing like Finn has, the strength difference is worlds apart—but enough to terrify me and make his point. "Listen, you little bitch, you leave me alone or I'll go after your daddy. What do you really think you can do to me anyways? I'm the son of Judge Kelly."

My dad. I never told my dad what happened to me. He would blame himself for it somehow, take it too personally. He wouldn't stop until justice was served, and it never would be; not with the son of a powerful judge as the main aggressor. I couldn't tell him. On top of everything else that I was dealing with, I couldn't take that on too, so I never told him. There's no doubt in my mind that Ryan or his father would find some way to go after my dad, either legally or otherwise, but threatening him? That's my last straw. Suddenly everything I'd learned, the hours of training that this man made me put myself through, came back, and the anger radiates off of my skin. I'm not weak. I'm not alone.

I jam my elbow down into the inside of Ryan's, his nails raking through the skin of my neck as he loses his hold. Then I slam my knee into his sorry excuse for a dick, and when he bends over to clutch at his pelvis, I ram my knee into his face, feeling blood pouring from his nose and spilling onto my shin. I grab his perfectly styled blonde hair and twist his head back so he looks at me as I say this, because this is going to be fucking important.

"Don't you ever threaten my family, and don't you ever come near me again. This was just a warning. I'm not the same girl who you left bleeding in a random person's bed. You come near me again, and you won't walk away from it, got it?" I shove his head away and he falls to the floor, his head bouncing off of the wall behind us.

I run.

I run for the stairs because I'm not waiting for the elevator with him still in the hallway. I sprint down the stairs, grabbing onto the railing when I almost fall a few times. Making it down to the emergency exit, I push it open and shoot out of the building. Sprinting all the way to my car, I unlock it when I'm a few feet away, and slide in. I slam the car into drive and peel out of the lot. I only dial Finn when I'm safely away from my building and already on the way to his house.

When he picks up, I don't even let him answer. "Ryan was waiting for me at my apartment. He knows, Finn, and he threatened my dad!" I yell as soon as I hear the click of Finn picking up the call.

"Where the fuck are you?" he growls into the phone. His voice smooths over me like a safety blanket.

"On the way to your house." I realize I'm crying. I didn't know I was until I finally calmed down enough to take in anything other than where I was going.

"Stay on the phone with me, I'm waiting outside for you." I hear the anger in his voice, the rage. It warms my heart to know he cares so much. Fuck, I can't wait until I'm in his arms, in his house, smelling him and knowing I'm safe. I know I can take care of myself—I proved that tonight—but I also showed my cards. I showed Ryan that I will defend myself and that just means he'll come at me harder next time. I won't feel safe again until I'm with Finn.

My brakes squeal as I slam on them in front of Finn's house, and my door is ripped open before I can even turn the key in the ignition. Finn yanks me out of the driver's seat and lifts me into his arms.

"Fuck, I was so worried, Angel," Finn speaks into my neck, my hair falling wildly behind me and blowing in the light breeze.

"He threatened my dad, Finn!" Tears stream down my face and I wrap my arms around Finn's neck, hanging onto him with everything in me. My legs wrap around his waist so tightly that I think if he let go I would still be hoisted up high, hanging on like a koala.

"What do you want me to do, baby? Do you want me to put a Prospect at your dad's house, follow him everywhere, and make sure Kelly doesn't go near him?" I hear my car turn off and the car door shut, not even realizing he's bent down to do all that.

I try to think about what to do. My dad would never go for that. He'd kick someone's ass if he thought they were following him. "No, he wouldn't go for that." I hear the smack of Finn's feet on his wooden porch, then the door softly opening and closing. I've avoided this for months, never in my life wanting to have to do this. "I have to tell him."

Finn sets me down on his couch, and I fall back into the fluffy pillows that make up the back, my head relaxing back as Finn removes my converse and socks. I place my hands down beside me, wanting to run my hands over the rough linen fabric that's become a kind of comfort I didn't even realize until right now. I move my feet off of his lap and my toes sink into the plush, black, shag rug that takes up the entirety of the living room space. Looking at Finn perched on his low coffee table in front of me, I notice that beside him, in front of the giant floor-to-ceiling window, are two emerald green armchairs. Looking around, I take notice of other added items as well. The large pillows added to the couch in the same shade of green and royal magenta. A large, white ash, circular dining table is sitting off to the side beside the kitchen, with black dining chairs with rattan backs around it. I sit up to better see everything. The kitchen cabinets are painted that same deep green with matte black hardware, and a small bouquet of burgundy peonies sits in the middle of the large black marble island. It's beautiful, the way the colors complement each other but stand out at the same time.

"What is all of this?" I ask, my eyes still landing on all of the changes he's made.

Finn shrugs, his eyes never leaving me. "I added some color."

My head snaps back to face him, my eyes widening. "Because of what I said?" I ask, panicked. I never meant to make him change his house. I was being sarcastic because the only things that weren't black in this house were the floors and the fucking LEDs, which are still placed around the cabinets, but now they're shining a bright magenta to match the throw pillows on the couch.

Finn falls forward, his hands landing on the couch on either side of my legs, his face inches from mine. His perfect, beautiful face. The LEDs in the kitchen reflect in Finn's ocean blue eyes and off of his nose piercing. "I wanted this to feel like home for you. Which it is now, by the way. You're not going back to your apartment until that fucking prick, Kelly, is taken care of."

I just nod, too distracted by his beauty to argue. Not that I would anyway, I don't ever want to leave Finn's side.

Lust and possession pass through me, the need to claim Finn and have him claim me. I place my hands on his shoulders and push him back. He falls onto his ass on the coffee table where he was before, and I follow him, spreading my legs over his and straddling him. My hands run through his slicked-back hair and bury in it, holding his head so I can explore his mouth and claim it with my own. He lifts me up, his hands on the backs of my thighs, and carries me through the house and into the bedroom, our mouths never leaving each others'.

Finn drops me on the bed, my body bouncing. I watch him take off his shirt in one fluid movement and drop his jeans and boxers, stepping out of them and standing in front of me, stroking his thick length. My mouth waters watching him, and he stares at me expectantly. Oh, right! I sit up and hurriedly pull my clothes off, tossing them all onto the floor, but my mind halts all lustful thoughts and I remember that this is the first time I'm fully naked in front of him. My arm bands around my breasts, hiding them. My eyes fall to the bed; I don't want to look at Finn.

His hand lifts my chin, forcing me to look him in the eyes. "What just happened?" he asks softly.

"Can I please wear your shirt?" I whisper.

Finn pulls away and I feel a chill where his body was. My heart wants to believe this will be the time that he rejects me; finally throws me away, finally realizes that I'm too much work. I place my hands down on the bed beside me, intending to stand up and grab my clothes to leave, but before I can, Finn lays his shirt in my lap and turns to dig into the bedside drawer. "Put it on, Angel. I'll teach you to love your body again. I'll remind you every day that I love it."

I pull his shirt on and lay down, tears pooling in my eyes at the emotion in his voice.

The bed dips where his knees land beside me, and he takes my mouth again. His fingers slide down my body and caress my opening, rubbing the wetness around and up to my clit. His fingers slip in at the same time that his tongue enters my mouth, and he drags two fingers over my g spot roughly. Moaning into his mouth, he swallows them and fucks me in unison with his tongue, both rubbing roughly inside of me. A gentle vibration sound barely whispers into the room before I feel it press against my clit. I jerk at the surprise, but Finn's body above me holds me in place. He clicks the speed up, his fingers piston inside of me quickly, and I feel a gush of liquid rush out of me, running down my thighs and over my ass.

Stunned, I pull away. "Um... Did I just..." I trail off

Finn smirks, his tongue gliding along his lower lip. "Squirt?" Oh yeah, baby." He has an evil grin as he slowly massages the inside of my pussy. My head lulls back, a moan slipping from my lips.

"I've never done that," I say, moving my hips to get him to pick up speed again.

Finn pulls out and climbs over top of me. Fisting his dick, he pushes inside of me slowly. "You're about to do it again on my dick." He pulls out and pushes back in. "I want these sheets ruined."

I moan loudly, his words doing just as much to me as his dick. He moves inside of me before pulling out and reaching for a pillow, placing it under my butt, and pushing back inside. The head of his dick rubs against my g spot and rushes at it. Fucking me quickly, he picks the vibrator up again and presses it against my clit on medium speed. His tattooed hand holds my hip, my legs resting over his thighs, and he fucks me with shallow thrusts. Before long, my body tenses and pulses all over.

"That's right, baby. Squirt on my cock. Soak me." Finn growls. Not stopping for even a second, he tosses the vibrator away and comes down to cover me, pushing deeper into me. He holds my head in his hands and fucks me into the bed, his hips merciless as they pound into me. My arms wrap around Finn's shoulders and I hold on. It's all I can do with the speed of Finn's motion. My screams and our bodies slapping together fill the room—the most perfect sound.

Finn bites down where my shoulder and neck connect. The pain sends jolts all the way to my pussy and triggers an orgasm. Finn groans as I spasm around him, but neither of us stops. His hips pick up more speed and my orgasm keeps crashing over me, wave after wave of pleasure.

"Oh my God, I can't stop cumming!" I groan, my head lulling to the side.

Finn watches my face, never stopping his motion. "I know. You're so fucking beautiful." He slams into me a few more times, shoving all the way in and releasing. My orgasm finally subsides, and I can feel the hot ropes of Finn's cum hitting my walls.

My body feels numb, and I drop my hands onto the bed. Finn rises up, pulling out of me, and bringing another moan out of my throat. He pulls the pillow out from underneath me and tosses it aside. Pulling at the hem of his shirt, he pulls it off of me, but I don't care that I'm naked in front of him. My brain is in a lust haze, and I don't have the energy to move right now.

Finn lays next to me, staring at my body and gently dragging his finger along my arm, down my stomach, over my hip, and back up. "I love your body, Angel. It's not shameful to be naked for me, or for you. Embrace your body. It gives you life, lets you do cool tricks on the pole, kick the shit out of bags, and it'll bring life into this world one day. Worship your body, don't be ashamed of it." He places a kiss on my shoulder, the same place he bit me earlier. "I want to take a picture and blow it up and hang it over our bed."

He continues to watch me. My body, my face, my breathing, everything. "Take the picture, Finny, it'll last longer."

"Don't tempt me, Angel," he says in a serious voice.

I reach out for him and he picks me up, carrying me up the bed and laying us under the sheets. "Whatever. Do what you want, as long as you let me sleep."

Finn's deep chuckle is all I hear before the sheets are ripped off of me and his shirt lands over my face. I raise my hand to grab the shirt, but Finn takes it and places it on the bed. "Lay still, I'm getting my picture," he says, moving my body in the way that he wants.

I lay there, a little stunned that he actually took me up on it, but not upset. I like the thought of him having pictures of me in his phone. I like the thought of a picture of me hanging in our room, though a picture of us would be much hotter.

The camera flashes through the black material covering my

face, and Finn moves my hands again, covering my breasts and bending one of my legs. The flash lights up again and Finn continues to position me in different ways.

When he's finally had enough, he locks his phone and pulls the shirt off of my face. "Can I see them?" I ask, a little hesitant now that I actually have to look at them.

"Not yet. I'll show them to you soon." Finn slides into bed beside me and covers us up, wrapping me in his arms. "Goodnight, Angel."

"Goodnight, Finny," I whisper, nuzzling my face into his warm chest.

25

HUNTLEY

The next day, Finn takes me to my dad's house on his bike. I tried to convince him to take one of his cars. It's going to be hard enough to explain to my dad everything that happened that night at the frat house, but to also tell him that I'm dating a member of the Devil's Outlaws? That is going to rock him. My dad isn't a very traditional man, he just wants the best for me, and a criminal isn't that. But Finn and I... He's it for me. I couldn't shake him even if I wanted to.

Finn cuts the bike's engine in the driveway of my childhood home. A modest two-story house; nothing really special, but it's home. My dad keeps the house looking nice; repainting the white siding when it's needed, keeping the lawn looking nice, and even taking care of the few potted plants he's managed to not kill that sit on the steps to the porch. I climb off of the bike, followed by Finn. My distressed boyfriend jeans, white crop top, and black leather jacket match his light-washed jeans, soft black tee shirt, and leather cut. Taking one last deep breath, I lead him to the door, knocking a few times and then walking in.

"Daddy?" I yell into the house.

The living room on my left is empty, and the staircase in

front of me is quiet. "In here, Princess," my dad hollers from the kitchen on my right.

My hand is sweaty as I grab Finn's and lead him into the kitchen. We walk by the small, round dining table sitting in front of the window and I see my dad standing behind the kitchen peninsula, placing a few pots on the counter.

At my arrival, he abandons the cookware and opens his arms for me. I walk right into them, always comforted by my dad. Finn and my dad have that in common. They both make me feel safe, but when I'm around my dad, I still feel like a little girl. Not because he treats me like I'm a child, but because of how he dotes on me when I'm around. I guess my dad and Finn are a lot alike in that regard. When my mom left, my dad took on every role to care for me. He was there when I got my first period, buying me pads and tampons. He was there for my first boyfriend and break up, taking me to the movies and letting me pick every kind of chocolate they had from concessions. He's always been my best friend, my protector. Just not when it came to Ryan. That would have broken him, and I couldn't do that to him.

"Hi, daddy." My voice is muffled by his big chest. His gray shirt smells like him, his soap mixed with the fresh scent of the outside and a hint of gasoline. My dad was always working on something on the weekends, mowing, trimming trees, watering the yard. We had a lot of elderly neighbors and he helped with things they needed often: fixing things around their houses, shoveling their snow, salting their sidewalks when ice was going to hit, mowing their yards, or cleaning out their gutters.

"Hey, Princess," he coos in his deep, familiar voice.

I pull away and we both turn to Finn, still standing on the other side of the peninsula with his arms hanging at his side and his legs spread. A small smile adorns his face, but my dad's gaze is solely focused on Finn's cut.

Finn steps forward, his big hand extended to my dad. "Finn Evans," he says, confidence in his tone. My stomach is in knots. I knew this was a bad idea to bring Finn, but I also knew I couldn't do this without him, and I wanted my dad to meet him.

My dad pauses, then finally grabs Finn's hand, hesitantly. His eyes roam over Finn's tattoos. "Nik Novikoff. Who are you?" His voice is gruff, his jaw set. I knew he would judge Finn.

"My boyfriend."

"Huntley's man," Finn and I say at the same time.

My dad's head turns toward me, his eyes wide. I give him a small smile. I feel terrible springing this on him, but I have to tell him about Ryan.

He drops Finn's hand. "You didn't mention a boyfriend when you were over for dinner last."

"It's new," I answer, my gaze finding Finn's. He watches me. My dad grunts, pulling my attention to him. "Here, daddy, let me help." I pick up the deep pot and take it to the stove. "What were you going to make?" Finn pulls a barstool out from the peninsula and sits down. My dad stays on the other side, watching him, his arms crossing across his big chest. "Dad," I say when he doesn't answer me.

"Lasagna soup," he finally grunts.

I head to the fridge and take out the meats for the soup. "It's a little warm for that, isn't it?" I dump the meat into the pan to fry.

My dad turns around and leans against the counter, his back on Finn. "I wanted it." Nodding, I continue stirring the meat.

I cook the rest of the meal mostly in silence. My dad asks about my classes and work. I tell him about my scholarship and how my classes are going. I tell him about Finn, his shop, his beautiful home, his dad and his restaurant, and Finn's collection of cars. The cars pique my dad's interest slightly, and he and Finn carry on about that for a while while we eat, but for the most part, my dad ignores Finn. It's not like him to be so rude. I've brought home a few boyfriends before, and he's always tried to get to know them.

After Finn and I picked up the dishes, my dad leans back in the dining room chair with a beer. I decide I need to get this over with.

"Daddy, I actually came over because I needed to talk to you," I say, sitting down next to him at the round table. The sun is setting outside of the window. The beautiful pinks and purples shine behind the trees that tower over all of the houses in the neighborhood. My dad's eyes bore into mine, unblinking. I take a deep breath. This is going to break his heart. "I was assaulted a while ago, and now he's threatening to come after you." I watch as emotions pass over my dad's handsome face; the face of the first person I ever loved. My first protector and best friend. His entire face bunches together, almost falling into itself. Hurt and grief. Then his nostrils flare and his brows set into a hard line. His gaze swings to Finn, whose tattooed hand was squeezing my thigh under the table. "I'm taking care of it, but I need you to be aware of it. Finn wanted to put a club protection detail on you, but I knew you wouldn't accept it."

My dad stands so quickly that his chair crashes to the floor with a loud thud. His fist smashes onto the table, and I jerk back in surprise. "You," he snarls at Finn, leaning over the table and pointing at him. "Your gang caused this. You hurt my daughter!"

My eyes fly between the two of them. Finn stays seated, his jaw clenching, and the hand on my thigh twitches. "No." He forces through clenched teeth. "My *club* had nothing to do with this. I've been taking care of the fucking scumbags who hurt Huntley." Finn stares at my dad out of the top of his vision. His ocean blue eyes turn into a stormy blue.

"It happened months before I met Finn, daddy. Almost a year ago." I place my hand on my dad's fist that's balled on the table. He looks down at me, his gaze softening. "It was Ryan and his friends."

My dad falls into his chair like the air was let out of him. "Why didn't you tell me before now, Princess?"

"I needed to deal with it alone. I'm sorry." I couldn't handle his grief or sadness on top of my own. I would have broken. All of his features sag, his slight wrinkles deepening. I know he wishes I would have confided in him, and I'm feeling his hurt of not doing so, but I just couldn't. "I'm okay now. Finn has helped me a lot in the last few months."

He swallows, his Adam's apple working in his throat, and roughly rubs at the blonde stubble, a few gray hairs dotted through. "I'm gonna kill him," my dad seethes, shaking his head. "And he's threatening me now?" My dad stares at me, waiting for an answer, so I nod my head. "You don't need to worry about me, baby girl, I'll take care of him. You won't ever have to see him again."

I take his hands in mine on the table, and he squeezes me like a lifeline. "I'm taking care of it, daddy. I'm making sure he will never be able to hurt anyone else."

Dad shakes his head. "You don't have to do that, Huntley. I'm the one who's supposed to protect you."

"I need to do it, daddy." I squeeze his big hands back. The rough skin of his working hands comforting under my touch.

He nods, finally, and looks to Finn, his gaze hardening again. "I still don't trust you, or the Outlaws," he says to Finn.

Finn nods slowly, pursing his lips. "I hope one day you'll see how important your daughter and her safety are to me, Mr. Novikoff." Finn stands from the table. "If you'll excuse me, I have to make a phone call before it gets too late." He bends his big body and speaks over my head, quiet, but loud enough for everyone to hear. "I'll be right back, I'll just be on the porch, Angel." Then he kisses my head softly and walks out of the dining room. The front door opens and closes, and my dad watches me.

"Why a criminal, Huntley? That's not the life I wanted for you." My dad shakes his head, his lips pressed into a tight line.

Scoffing, I shake my head. "What did you want for me, dad? A white picket fence with an accountant husband who played golf on the weekends?" My fingers rake through my blonde hair, the same color as my dad's. "Because I always wanted someone who would love me more than himself and protect me like you do. Someone who works hard and takes care of his family and friends. Someone who never gives up." My eyes watch Finn pacing the porch through the window, his phone held to his ear and one hand twirling a lighter between his fingers. "That's Finn, daddy. He's a great man, and the club are not bad people."

"They're criminals, Huntley," he protests. His voice is strong with conviction, but soft for me.

I stand and walk to my dad. Bending down, I wrap him in my arms, my cheek resting on his shoulder. "I love you, but you're wrong about him, daddy." Then I stand and grab my jacket off of the back of my chair.

Before I walk out of the room, he grabs my hand and squeezes it. "I really hope I am, for your sake, Princess." I nod and walk out of the room and through the front door.

Finn is sliding his phone into his pocket, his eyes watching me on the dim porch. The sun is almost completely down now, and the streetlights slowly turn on along the street. I reach for his hand and feel the warmth of him when he grabs it. His strength flows through me; his love, his warmth. I can do anything with him at my side. I pull him towards the steps, but he stays put. Turning around, I follow his gaze to the door, his eyebrows drawn in and his eyes narrowed. "You shouldn't say goodbye, just let him absorb tonight."

"Yeah, I wasn't sure," Finn admits with a small laugh. "I've never met the parents." Finn and I walk down the steps and to his bike in the driveway. "Why didn't you tell him all of what happened?" Finn's head is cocked to the side.

"It would have destroyed him to know what they did to me. This hurt enough without the details," I say, looking down at my feet. I don't want to look into his eyes.

Finn's fingers lift my chin and he kisses the corner of my lips. "Let's go, Angel. I have a surprise for you at home."

He swings his strong leg over his bike and kicks the stand back. The motor turns over, the deep rumble settles in my soul like an old lullaby, and brings me a new comfort I didn't realize I needed until I met Finn.

FINN LEADS me through the house after parking the bike in the shop. I flip on the lights and lean against the kitchen island as Finn goes to the back door. I watch him, wondering what he's doing. In the times I've been here, we've never been in his backyard. He slides the door open and steps onto the dim back porch. The light in the back is on, but it's not helping a whole lot.

Sighing and thinking about my dad, my eyes catch on an envelope from RSU's Financial Aid office.

I pick it up as Finn walks back into the house, leaving the door open behind him. "Are you enrolling at RSU?" I ask, showing him the envelope.

Finn stares at it for a moment before answering. "No. I'm a benefactor for a new scholarship. That's just the confirmation of it." Wow. Of course, he's giving money to someone for schooling. His selflessness never ceases to amaze me.

"That's really great, Finn." I smile, so proud of him.

Dropping the letter back to the counter, a small ball of black fur rushes into the kitchen, Leo sauntering in behind it. The little puppy runs circles around the large, open living area, running laps around all of our feet before Finn lifts the little fur ball up. It lavishes his face with licks, its little fluffy tail wagging so fast it looks like it's going to either break off or lift the pup up in flight.

Leo laughs at the end of the island, watching Finn be attacked by tiny kisses from the sweet puppy.

"Shut up, Leo," Finn snaps, moving around the island to me.

"Did you get a puppy?" I ask Leo.

Leo shakes his head, and I turn to Finn where he stands next to me.

"She's yours," he says, the puppy twisting in his hands to try to lick my face. I take her from him, holding her under her fuzzy little arms and looking into her sweet face. She's a completely black German Shepherd with little tan legs, like she's wearing socks.

"Why?" I ask, looking up at him while the soft puppy licks my neck, where I cuddle her against me.

Finn licks his lips, watching the puppy snuggle into my arms. "There will be times when I can't always be with you, and I want you to still have someone watching over you." He reaches out, his scarred, newly tattooed knuckles brushing over the little puppy's head. "Noctem will be trained to protect. It'll take a little bit of time for her to connect with us, but after that, she's supposed to be incredibly protective over her owners."

"Noctem?" I ask, scratching under the little puppy's chin.

"It means darkness in Latin, sometimes it refers to Hell," Finn says while Leo starts making his way to the front door.

"Well, see ya guys later! Let me know if you need me to puppy-sit little Noxy again!" he says over his shoulder as he walks through the door.

I bring Noctem up to my lips and press a kiss to her soft head. "Thank you, Finny. She's adorable."

Finn wraps his arm around me and pulls me towards the side door again. "Let's go get our girl a whole buncha shit from the pet store."

I bite my lip to hold in my smile. That sounds like the perfect way to end a stressful day.

26

FINN

I'm sitting behind Cale and Little Red at a stoplight on my bike. We have our first real lead into Reese's stalker, and are finally going to go end this shit. I got the call from Cale and left my house immediately, leaving Huntley chasing Noctem around in the backyard. I need to call and get someone out there to fence the yard. I don't want Noctem wandering off into the woods and getting picked off by a bear or something. We've had our baby girl for a week now, and she's been perfect. She's taken to her kennel at night perfectly, and she comes to the shop with me while Huntley is in class. Noctem will be Huntley's guard dog, but she's just a puppy right now. Instead, either me or Leo have been going and escorting her to her classes. Occasionally, she'll let one of us sit in class with her. Other times she sends us back to the shop and I FaceTime her while she's in class; just watching her beautiful face as she types notes on her laptop, both of our sounds turned off so we don't disrupt each other. That's what I'm thinking of when the light turns green and Cale starts to move into the intersection: Huntley barefoot, in one of my shirts and some little shorts, chasing around a little black fur ball. Noctem's little high-pitched barks and Huntley's laughter carrying around to the side of the house when I was leaving. I didn't see the van until it was too late; until it was slamming into Cale's truck and sending it flipping onto its side a few times before finally landing on its top in the middle of the road.

I sit there, watching the Raptor tumble over itself and then see the taillights of the van speeding away down the street. I check the intersection and gun my bike toward the Raptor. Everyone stopped, watching the truck rock back and forth as it settled on its top. Luckily there weren't any cars in the lanes that the Raptor toppled into, or else this could have had a lot more injuries.

My boot shoves my kickstand down on the sidewalk, engine still running. I sprint towards the truck. I check Little Red first—it's what I would want, and what Cale would do for me if this were reversed. Reese is yelling Cale's name, so I know she's alive. Her voice sounds constricted and she coughs a few times. The dust from the airbags must be getting into her throat. I pull her door open easily and tell her to put her hands on the roof so I can cut her seatbelt. It likely won't unbuckle with her weight pressed against it. She does and I watch Callum as I cut through the belt. He's still. So fucking still. I pull Reese out of the truck and carry her to the curb. Tears pool in the bottom of her eyes and I know mine look panicked, because I am. I'm so fucking scared right now, and I can only think of one other time I've felt like this: when my mom was dying and there wasn't anything I could do to save her.

Reese blinks rapidly, but I can tell she's lost. Maybe it's panic, maybe it's a fucking concussion, but I yell at her anyways so maybe my voice will break through. "I'm going to sit you down next to my bike, okay, Little Red? I'm going to get Callum out, he's going to be alright, okay? Hold on." I set her down on the sidewalk and I run back to the wreck.

Reaching Cale's side, I bend down to watch him through the

window. He's bleeding pretty badly from his head and his shoulder is definitely out of place with the way it's hanging.

I yank open the door, but it doesn't even budge. I yank harder, and harder, and harder.

It doesn't open.

The panic sets in deeper. My mind runs a million miles an hour, everything passing through it. Huntley, Cale, Reese, the club, his business, even his piece of shit parents. What the fuck am I going to do?

"Call a fucking ambulance!" I yell at the people standing wide-eyed on the sidewalk. "Call for fucking help!" A few people pick up their phones and put them to their ears. I pull on the handle again, but it still doesn't give. I bang my fists on the bottom of the truck, on the side by the door, anywhere I can either take my aggression out on or maybe knock something loose so I can open this fucking door and get to my brother. When I'm about to try to pull him out through the windshield, I see Reese crouching down on the ground by the broken window, her hands and knees hitting the ground hard. The glass has got to be cutting into her skin, I can hear it crunching with every step I take. Reese cries, yelling at Cale to stay awake and telling him she loves him.

About fucking time one of them admits their feelings to the other. I just wish it hadn't taken this for one of them to come clean.

The sirens in the distance feel like a huge weight being lifted from my shoulders. Help is coming. My head falls backward and I look up at the sky, the oranges and pinks splashing across it like a watercolor painting. I'm not sure if I believe in a God, but I thank whoever the fuck sent help so quickly.

Two ambulances and a firetruck screech to a halt behind us. Several paramedics rush forward, one lifting Reese from around her stomach and two more grabbing my arm to pull me away from Cale.

My arm snatches out and squeezes the male's throat. "Get him the fuck out of there, do you hear me?" I roar into the man's face. "Get my brother out of that fucking wreck and get him to the fucking hospital!"

The man's eyes are wide and he's still in my grip, barely able to nod, but he does while removing his hand from my arm and holding them up next to his head in surrender.

I push away from him and go back to my bike, taking the key out and then joining Little Red in the back of one of the ambulances. I'm not leaving her. Not without Cale to watch over her.

The ambulance rocks with my weight when I sit down on the bench beside Reese. After trying the door handle like I had been doing, Firefighters pry open Callum's driver's door with the jaws of life tool, and it takes almost four guys to pull his completely still body from the car and place him on a gurney. A scream rips through my throat that I thought I was keeping contained, until I realize it came from Reese. She's lunging for the door, crawling across the gurney on her hands and knees with tears streaming down her face. I grab her by the hips and hold her to the bed, trying my best to keep my hands from shaking too bad and the tears I feel in my eyes to not fall over. I stare out of the back doors; even as Callum is wheeled into the other ambulance, even as the driver of ours comes over to close the doors and get into the front seat.

"Is he dead?" Reese asks softly, like she doesn't want the answer because she's too afraid of what it might be.

Dead.

The one word I refused to think about the entire time I watched him stuck in that truck, because I don't know what the fuck I would do if I lost him. Callum has been my best friend for the last seven years. He's been my other half, my platonic soulmate, my fucking brother. Losing him would be like losing Huntley, my dad, losing my mom again. I love all of my brothers and I'd fucking die for any of them. I'd be just as broken up about losing any of them, but Callum is more than just a brother to me. I met Callum when he was recovering from a broken heart, when he still carried around that fucking engagement ring, and kept it in the bedside table in his room at the clubhouse. I watched him shut himself off from a lot of people. I drove by his parents' house with him to make sure they were okay when there were threats to the club. I watched him almost fucking cry the first time my dad called him "son," and made his favorite dishes at holidays because he spent those with us now. I watched him watch Little Red from across the rooftop of Mickey's, and I watched him slowly, without knowing it himself, let her in and fall in love with her. I saw the look in her eyes when she saw him. They were it for each other, and if this is the way they fucking ended, then I had no hope with Huntley. Callum and Reese were pure fucking hearts. They deserved a lifetime of love together. Not this. They didn't deserve this.

"I don't know, ma'am." The paramedic, the same one who probably has bruises on his throat from my hand, says as he puts the truck in drive and follows the one with Callum.

Reese, now having settled in the gurney, takes my hand from my lap and holds it between both of hers. Holding tightly to each other, I watch our hands, praying to anyone that will listen that they keep my brother on this earth.

27

HUNTLEY

F LIPPING THE LIGHT OFF IN THE KITCHEN, THE ENTIRE HOUSE TURNS dark, with the exception of the LEDs lining the kitchen counters and the back of the TV in the living room. Noctem follows behind me, trotting happily with her tail wagging. She chugged her entire water bowl when we came in from playing, so I know she'll have to go back out again soon, but after that, she should hopefully sleep for a few hours before waking up again. The smell of buttery popcorn fills the house and Noctem almost face dives into the bowl when I set it on the arm of the couch to grab a blanket for us to wrap up in.

Finn left a while ago to check out a lead with Cale about Reese's stalker, and after I grew tired of chasing Little Noxy around the backyard, I knew I was going to need something else to distract me from worrying about Finn. We had no idea what they were walking into, and although I trust my man to be able to take care of anything that was thrown at him, I don't trust him not to sacrifice himself for the people he loves. After settling on the couch with a huge soft blanket wrapped around me and Noctem sleeping in my lap, I click through the movies on the streaming service. A scary movie should do the trick.

I don't even get through the opening credits before my phone buzzes on the arm of the couch next to my giant bowl of popcorn. Seeing Finn's name, I'm sure he's going to tell me that he's on his way home.

Instead, when I answer the phone I'm met with Finn sobbing. "There was an accident," he manages to say through sobs. "I don't think Cale's gonna make it. They took him back for surgery but I can't find anyone to tell me anything."

I shoot up from my seat. Noctem rolls to the side, but stays snoring softly in my lap. "Finn, calm down. Tell me what happened."

He breathes in a ragged breath before answering. "We were on our way to the address Miles gave Cale, and someone blew a stoplight and ran right into them. Reese is okay, I left her to get examined and I tried to find someone who knew something about Cale, but no one is saying anything." He makes a roaring sound. "Heads are about to roll if I don't find out some information about my fucking brother!" Finn yells, not so much to me it sounds like, but to the people he's standing around.

"Sir, please, we don't know anything yet, can I please escort you to the lobby? I promise someone will be out shortly to speak with you, but right now the doctors and nurses are doing everything they can to help your brother." I hear a sweet-sounding woman say on the other end.

"He's my best friend, Huntley. I can't lose him. Not him too," Finn cries on the other end of the phone.

I click off the tv and pick Noxy up. "I'm coming, babe."

"No." Finn quickly snaps. "No, Angel, please stay home. The guy who hit Cale and Red fled and the club is looking for him. I don't want you on the road when we haven't found him. Please, baby, please stay at the house with Noctem." Finn sounds defeated and scared, and it takes all of the strength from my body. I've never heard him sound anything but confident and sure.

I snuggle Noctem closer to my face. "Okay, babe. Please call me if you need anything. I will be there in a heartbeat."

Finn sniffs and lets out a huge breath. "I know, Angel. I'm going to try to find something out." He pauses so long that I check to see if he hung up. "Fuck. I love you, Huntley. I know this is the worst fucking time to say this, but I fucking love you and today made me realize that I needed to say that to you before I don't have the chance to." I sit there speechless. Do I say it back? Do I feel that strongly for Finn? "Fuck, I shouldn't have said that over the phone," Finn says.

"I love you too." I rush, and I mean it. He changed my life, and I will always be grateful to him. I love him and I think I knew I would love him from the moment I saw him. There's no other way to explain our magnetism, other than that we knew we would come to mean a lot to one another.

"Fuck. Say it again, just one more time. I need it," he sighs.

Grinning, I say, "I love you, Finn."

"I love you too, Angel, forever." I hear buzzing and then a door slams shut. "Okay, I'm going to try to get some answers and find Reese."

We say goodbye and end the call, and I turn the movie back on.

It's not long before a number flashes on my screen, a number that I don't have saved to my contacts. "Hello?" I answer slowly.

"Huntley, it's Leo," Leo says quickly.

I pause the movie and absently pet Noctem's head. "Hey. Why are you calling me?"

Leo pauses for a long time, and with a rush of breath he finally speaks. "I'm coming to get you."

"Is Cale okay?" I ask, sitting up again and laying Noctem next to me on the couch.

Leo sucks in a breath. "Finn didn't call you?"

I take the blanket off of me and lay it over the arm of the couch, turning the TV off. "Yeah, he said Cale was in an accident, but I haven't heard anything else."

"Finn texted Saint a few minutes ago. Cale didn't make it," Leo says slowly, softly.

"No," I croak.

Leo clears his throat. "The rest of the club is already on their way to the hospital to be with Reese and Finn. I think he'll want you there."

My heart breaks, for Finn, for Reese, for... "Randy. Did Finn call his dad?"

"I don't think so, Finn only texted Saint a few words and hasn't answered his phone since." I hear a door slam on Leo's end and the sound of a deep motor starting.

"I'll call him," I say, dread pooling through me. I don't know what to say to him. He lost a son tonight.

Leo agrees and hangs up and I rush to get dressed. A pair of black sweatpants and Finn's shirt that I was already wearing. I carry Noctem to her kennel and I call Randy.

Randy cried when I told him the news. Broke down on the phone and cried. His tears made me cry too. I met Callum and I really liked him, but I didn't know him that well. I felt for Finn though, and for Randy. When I saw another call from Leo, I told Randy that I needed to call him back. Randy said he would come get me and I couldn't argue with him, not right now. I just decided to call Leo back and tell him to go to the hospital and we would be right behind him.

"Fuck, Huntley, I'm so sorry, but Cale's alive. There was a fucking mix up and he's fucking alive!" Leo yells as a greeting, a bit of excitement and awe in his voice.

"Oh thank fuck," I sigh. "Randy said he would come get me. Oh my God, I need to call him back!"

"Okay, yeah. That's a good idea. Be careful though, okay? We couldn't find the piece of shit that hit Cale," he says.

"I'll be careful," I promise him.

"No. You know what you guys, wait at the house and I'll come get you." He rushes out.

I shake my head even though he can't see. "Leo, we'll be okay. Go to the hospital with the club. I'll call if I see something."

Leo sighs. "Pinky promise?" he asks.

I smile, remembering the first time we pinky promised. "I pinky promise," I say before hanging up.

Finn calls me again as headlights flash through the living room windows.

"Hey, Angel. You talked to Leo?" he asks.

I watch Randy step out of the red pickup that Finn was working on in his garage when I met Leo and Jack. "Yeah, how are you?"

Finn sighs, and it sounds like the entire world is sitting on his shoulders. "A lot better now. I'm sorry I didn't call I—"

"You were grieving and in shock, I'm not upset." I interrupt him and Randy gets to the porch and knocks on the door.

"Okay, Angel. Can you bring us some stuff? I think I might stay here with Cale tonight if that's okay?" Finn sounds so small, like a child asking his parents for something and it breaks my heart. I need to be his strength right now. I open the door and let Randy inside. We hover in front of the open door while I hold the phone to my ear.

"Of course, babe. What do you need? Randy and I can bring it to you. He came to get me after Leo called."

"Hey, buddy," Randy's deep voice rumbles and I pull my phone away and switch it to speakerphone. "How are my boys doing?" Randy's eyes are red-rimmed, but he has a watery smile on his face. I called him back after I got off the phone with Leo.

Randy was still sniffling from the first call and he broke down all over again when I told him Cale was alive.

"We're okay, dad," Finn answers.

———

THE SOUND of deep laughter echoes down the white hallway as Randy and my footsteps thump against the tile floors. Pushing open the door to Callum's room, Finn is slouched in a tiny padded chair, his thick legs resting on the bed in front of him next to Cale's. Callum is laying in the bed, the thin cream blanket is pulled up to his waist and his arm is in a sling. He has a gash on his head and throat, but he's alive.

Randy rushes to Cale's side, setting Finn's duffle bag on the floor beside the bed so he can bend and place his weathered hands on both sides of Callum's face. "You scared the shit out of me, son." He shakes his head, his lips pursed. "I don't know what I would have done without one of my boys."

Finn pulls me onto his lap, one warm hand resting on my waist. Callum grabs Randy's wrist, squeezing it while looking into his eyes. "I'm sorry, old man." Randy lets go, but not before bending down and placing a kiss on Cale's blonde hair. He sits down in the chair on the other side of the bed and Callum turns his gaze to us. "Hey, Huntley," he says softly.

"I'm so glad to see you" I say back, just as soft.

Callum nods and Finn pulls me closer into his chest while Cale and Randy talk.

"Thank you so much for being here for me, Huntley," Finn whispers in my ear.

I turn my head so I can see him. "I'd do anything for you, Finn," I say quietly.

Finn's eyes darken and his voice drops into a deep husky tone. "I'll hold you to that, Angel."

Leaning in, I nip his lower lip in answer. Finn's hand moves to my neck, pulling me to his lips. He kisses me hard, claiming me with his tongue before he quickly pulls away. My face heats. His dad is in the room, less than ten feet away from us, but with the way the conversation never stalled, I'm hoping they didn't pay us any attention.

"I love you so fucking much, Huntley." He squeezes my throat—not enough to cut off air, just enough to show power—and looks into my eyes.

"I love you too, Finny," I whisper before placing a quick kiss on his plush lips.

28

———

HUNTLEY

THE SUN IS SETTING OFF TO THE SIDE OF THE SHOP WHEN I PULL into the parking lot. I pull right up to the open garage door and step out of the car. Noctem jumps out after me and sprints into the garage in search of Finn. It's been a few days since Cale was released from the hospital, and I've barely seen much of Finn since then. When Finn called me at closing time and said he was staying late to catch up on payroll before the end of the week, I decided that I'd bring him dinner. I'm tired of sitting at Finn's house with just Noctem, and Finn not getting in until late.

I'm several paces behind Noctem, her little nails tapping against the concrete floors as she bounds into the carpeted office at the back of the shop and barks at Finn. He picks her up and stands from the large, brown, leather office chair. His old tee shirt, worn jeans, and backwards hat look great on him. Walking around the large wooden desk, he meets me out in the garage, grabbing the brown paper bags from the Chinese restaurant we went to on our impromptu first date.

"Hi, Angel. Thank you for bringing dinner." Finn takes the bags from me and kisses me gently. Of course, the heavy bags

177

that I was struggling to wrangle, he grasps just fine in his fist; taking them back to his office.

I land in the chair on the other side of his desk while Finn pulls the styrofoam boxes out of the bags and opens them, handing me mine. He sets Noctem down to get some of her food that he keeps in little light pink dog bowls behind his desk, and he leans against the desk, holding the container in one hand and shoveling the noodles in with the other.

We eat in silence, mostly because Finn is shoving the food into his mouth so quickly that he can't talk, but he groans every few bites and closes his eyes.

He finishes in what seems like three bites, grabbing the container of egg rolls and finishing one in two bites. "How's work?" I ask, finishing my food much slower.

Between egg rolls, he says, "Busy and boring." He sighs heavily. "I didn't realize when I started working for myself that I wouldn't actually be doing the shit that I started this company to do."

"What do you mean?" I ask as Finn finishes another egg roll and picks Noctem up again, holding her in his other arm.

"I started this shop so that I could work on the shit I wanted to work on, make my own hours, work with guys I liked, but really I'm always doing paperwork back here and my guys are the ones working on the projects I wanted to take."

My brows pull together in confusion. This seems like a pretty simple fix. "Then hire someone to deal with your accounts."

He shakes his head, pulling another egg roll from the container. "The only people I trust with that shit are my brothers, and all the ones smart enough to do it are running their own shit."

Standing, I walk around to the back of the desk and take a seat in the rolling leather chair, setting my food next to the keyboard. I click around on the screen to see what programs he's using and what he's working with. "I'm familiar with these programs, why don't you take a break with Noxy and I'll finish up your payroll?"

Finn's mouth drops open. "That's fucking it!" Finn shouts.

He stands facing me on the other side of the desk, egg roll half eaten. "What?" I ask, picking up where he left off.

"What are your job plans for after graduation?" He takes a seat in the one I vacated, Noctem climbing up his stomach to rest her head on his neck.

My fingers halt over the keyboard and I bite my lip. "Well, I don't know. I haven't really thought about it yet." I drag my eyes up Finn's hard body, slowly making my way up to his eyes. He has manic glee shining in his eyes and is grinning. "Janet offered me a part-time job coaching pole, but other than that, I thought maybe CPA." I don't know why I'm nervous, like I want Finn's approval. I know he would approve of anything I do, but the truth is, I don't know what I want to do. I know I like the subject of numbers and doing the stuff that I'm helping him with right now, I just don't know exactly where or how I want to use my degree.

"What about working for me?" Finn watches me closely, his eyes roaming my face and down to my shoulders and hands. When I don't answer, he continues, "You could set your own hours, decorate this office, hell I'll even add on to it to make it bigger for you. You could bring Noctem to work and you'd get to see me all day." He's smiling by the end of his proposal, like a kid who wants something but doesn't want to look too excited. He always looks so pure when he smiles, like he *is* still a kid.

"And what would I be doing?" I ask.

Finn scratches the bottom of Noctem's chin, her nose shoved into his neck. "All of the backend stuff. Payroll, invoices, ordering inventory, transactions. All the computer shit." He continues to watch me. "You can say no, Angel." He gives me a small smile.

"I don't think I want to say no," I say, a slow grin pulling at my lips.

Finn sighs, "Hell yeah! You're hired. After you graduate, you can start whenever you want."

Laughing, I finish his payroll and close out of the program. "Oh? No interview? I was really hoping to show you how much I wanted the job, how *hard* I was willing to work for it."

Finn sets Noctem down in the seat next to him and stands, slowly making his way behind the desk to me. He pushes the chair out from under the desk and leans down to my eye level. His hands hold onto the armrests, caging me in. "How hard, Angel?" he whispers, his voice dropping to a husky tone that sends goosebumps skittering down my bare legs.

Glancing down at Finn's hands braced against the armrests, I notice a fresh tattoo on his finger. My brain stutters, the flirty banter forgotten as I focus on the single "H" tattooed onto his left-hand ring finger. His hand burns in mine when I lift it to examine it. "What's this?"

"I got it the morning after I told you I loved you. Before everything went to shit with Cale and Little Red." Finn pulls his hand from my grip and uses it to raise my chin to look at him. "You're my fucking soulmate, Angel, and I'm going to marry you one day. I just got my ring early."

Oh my God.

Yes.

The loud crash of something metal falling onto the concrete floor of the shop pulls our attention away from one another. Noctem's head perks up and she lets out a high-pitched bark. She jumps down from the chair and runs over to us to sit in front of my feet.

Finn pulls open the top drawer of the desk and pulls a black handgun from it. Cocking it, he quietly walks to the door that we left open and peers around the corner.

He lets out a breath and drops the gun to his side, flicking the safety on and taking a step back over to the desk, and setting it down. Callum stumbles through the door of the office as Finn does so.

"What are you doing, brother?" Finn asks, watching Callum lean against the doorframe, a large, almost empty bottle of whiskey in his grip.

"Just wanted to see you." Callum smiles. His eyes are glassy. He's drunk. This is the reason Finn hasn't been home until really late the last few days. He, Saint, and Ronan have been taking turns making sure Callum doesn't drink himself to death or choke on his tongue after he finally passes out. He's gone off the deep end, drinking all night, sleeping all day, not going to work, and barely showering, by the looks of his greasy hair and short beard. Reese breaking up with him the day after he got out of the hospital has taken him to rock bottom.

"How'd you get here? Did you drive?" Finn moves around him to look out into the garage.

Cale rolls his eyes and stumbles to the chair in front of the desk, falling into the chair and almost missing it. "No. Someone hid my keys so I walked."

Finn and I both look at Callum with confusion clear on our faces. I blink slowly, watching Callum. "That's like seven miles," I say.

Cale grins. A cocky grin that he shares with every single one of the brothers. "Luckily I had someone to keep me company." He holds up the bottle of Jack.

Finn snorts as he lands in the seat next to Callum. My gaze snaps to him, warning him. We talked about this the night that the club threw that party to cheer Cale up. Drinking and fucking everything isn't going to fix this. Though apparently, Callum hasn't touched anyone. Finn says he's gone back to his room every night alone. He's drowning in his pain. I know how that feels. He needs to embrace it.

"You gotta talk sometime, Cale." I lean back, picking Noctem up and holding her against my chest.

He watches me from the bottom of his vision, slouched so far in the chair that his head is resting on the back of it. He brings the bottle to his lips and tips it up, pouring the rest of the liquor down his throat and using the back of his hand to wipe at his mouth. "What do you want me to say, Huntley? She fucking left."

"So what? You think she was the one?" Finn watches us quietly, but my gaze is focused on Callum. We're getting through this shit tonight.

Cale's eyes leave me and he stares at the ceiling. "Yeah, I do." Every muscle in Callum's body just seems to give up in that moment, like any anger or fight he had just left with that confession. "And she just fucking left me. Everybody always leaves me."

Tears pool in the bottom of my eyes, but I hold them in. He doesn't need me crying for him. He needs strength. "Well, she wasn't." *Yes, she was, but maybe there will be another one.* His eyes snap to mine, one tear rolling down his cheek. "Your family hasn't ever left you, Callum. Your real family. Your brothers. They're here for you, find strength in them." Cale turns his head and looks up at Finn. "I'm not telling you to get over it, but you have to get through it."

Finn gently takes the bottle from Callum's loose hold. "You've gotten through this before, Cale. We'll help you get through it again." Finn pushes his fingers through Callum's messy hair and shakes his head playfully. "You're never alone, brother."

HUNTLEY

After weeks of planning, it's finally here. Ryan dies today. I wish I could say I felt something. Anything. Scared, relieved, nervous, excited. It's scary not feeling anything, knowing that you're going to take someone's life. The same someone who has been visiting me almost every night in my dreams for close to a year, still tormenting me long after the attack.

It ends tonight.

I won't allow a ghost to terrorize me.

Leo drops deftly onto the couch, lifting his legs to rest on the low coffee table in front of him. I'm pouring Noctem's food into her bowl while Finn and Mason mess around on Mason's computer in Finn's home office. Mase is sending all of the dirty documents he found on Judge Kelly to the Chief of Police. He's doing it anonymously, of course, so no one in the club is suspected, even though the Chief is in with the Outlaws. If this goes above the local police, we don't want a paper trail leading to us. Especially since after tonight, Judge Kelly and his son will be on the run, so Judge Kelly doesn't have to answer for his crimes.

Crimes that include accepting sex for lessening sentences and swaying rulings, accepting bribes from the ones he didn't want to sleep with, a few prison hits he paid for, having a seven-teen-year-old girlfriend, and of course, intimidating me into not pressing charges against his son and friends.

Oh, yeah.

When I filed the police report and was sitting in the hospital after getting a rape kit done, Judge Kelly came in and laughed in my face. He told me that no one would ever believe me against three highly respected men in one of the wealthiest fraternities on campus. Boyfriends can't rape their girlfriends, I must have asked for it and then regretted it, crying rape when all was said and done.

Completely alone in a room with a man the age of my father who was much bigger than me, and still naked under the hospital gown, I didn't fight him. I thought he was right. He told me I would embarrass myself by trying to ruin their lives and end up only gaining a negative reputation for myself.

So I never pressed charges.

I waited, and I found my own devil.

Now I'm serving my own justice.

I'm wearing black leggings and a tight-fitting, black, long-sleeve shirt, with black sneakers. I figure all black will hide the signs of blood, and athletic wear is easy to move in, right?

Leaving Noctem to eat her dinner, I join Finn and Mason in the office. The sound of keyboard taps greets me as I enter the room. Finn is towering behind Mase with his thick arms crossed over his chest, and Mason is staring intently at the large desktop screen in front of him.

Finn's eyes snap to mine as soon as I walk through the door, our bodies always aware of one another. He watches me walk to him, his chin raised; always so strong and confident. I draw my strength from him. Like a queen and her king.

A lost soul and her devil.

"Are you ready, Angel?" Finn asks. I appreciate that he never asks me if I'm sure, or if I want to back out. He doesn't treat me like porcelain, instead letting me determine how far I want to go, and what I can handle. He's always there to catch me if I fall, though. He holds out a small flip phone.

Nodding, I take the burner phone from him and pull up the contacts. There are only a few names, and I don't recognize any but one. I click on his number and put the phone to my ear. I turn around and lean my back against Finn's chest, wanting to wrap myself in his scent and forget about who I have to call now.

"Hello?" Ryan answers, a small question in his tone.

"Ryan." It's all I'm able to say, hearing his voice sends shivers down my spine, fear rising in my gut. I don't know how to start this conversation. Finn told me what I needed to say to get him out of his house, but I didn't ask how to start a conversation like that.

He chuckles. "I knew you'd come crawling back, Lee." Ryan's voice bleeds down the line. Bile rises in my throat at his greeting, picturing his gloating smirk.

"I'm leaving town and I need money. I figured you'd want to trade cash for my silence." Exactly what Finn and I practiced, but this was as far as we got. We didn't know how he'd react, so anything after this is on me. I have to read him and rely on the hope that I know him well enough to pull this off. With Finn's information, I think I have something that he can't afford to pass up.

He laughs, this time so loud that I have to pull the phone away from my ear to avoid going deaf. "Did your biker boyfriend knock you up and now you have to leave town to get away from him? What, did he threaten to beat the baby out of you?" I can feel Finn's body stiffen behind me, telling me that he can hear everything Ryan is saying. Finally, Ryan's laughter has died down and he's speaking normally, still a few notes of laughter in his tone. "Why the fuck would I negotiate with you anyways, whore? You broke my fucking nose when I last saw you. If you were going to talk, you would have already done so. Nobody is going to believe a biker slut." Pride mixed with anger swells inside of me. I love that I caused him some amount of pain, that I disfigured his pretty boy fucking face, even if it wasn't that serious. But I'm enraged at the way he's talking about Finn, about the club.

Finn's chest rises and falls, the heavy, slow breaths fanning out over my head as I lean back into him. His hand runs up the side of my body and encloses around my throat. The heavy presence of his hand is enough to calm my nerves, and his breathing evens out.

"I know about Mckenzie, and I know that even though your mom hates your fucking guts, along with your scummy ass dad, she wouldn't stand to be made to look like a fool. Especially while she's away saving lives." Ryan is completely silent on the other end. "I'll tell everyone that your dad has been sleeping with a minor, and he forced her to get an abortion."

"She never got an abortion. She was never pregnant." He snaps.

"I'm not sure that's going to reassure your mom. All she's going to hear is that your dad is having an affair with a seventeen-year-old."

"How much do you want?" Ryan sneers down the phone. I got him. He knows I've got him.

I breathe a sigh of relief. This is going perfectly. "Twenty thousand. You have an hour to get it or I'll tell anyone who will listen. Police, media, anyone. I'll text you where to meet me." I end the call without letting him answer me. Giving him the chance to answer will give him a false sense of power. He doesn't have that anymore.

Finn turns me around, taking the closed phone from my clenched hand and sliding it into his pocket. "You are the strongest person I've ever met, and you're going to do fine tonight." His hand wraps around my throat, high enough so my head has to tilt back and I have no choice but to look into his beautiful eyes. "I'm here with you every step of tonight, whatever you want to do or don't want to do, I support you all the way." I sharply nod my head, as much as I can with his hand holding my head mostly immobile. His lips press into mine and I devour him. My hands wrap in his shirt and pull him closer to me. He lets me control him and the kiss, but he eventually pulls away, placing one last kiss on my forehead and turning his attention to Mason. "Watch our locations and wipe any traces of us." Mase nods and I follow Finn out of the room. We walk through the living area, and I pick up Noctem and pet her behind her ears. Handing her to Finn, he kisses her head and places her in Leo's lap on the couch. "Be ready if I need you," he says, and then pulls me towards the front door. He leads me to my car and opens the driver's side door for me. It's dark out; it's the last week of April and warm. The gas station at the edge of town should be deserted on a Friday. "I'll be right behind you in the van." He pulls me into his chest with a hand buried in my hair. "I love you, Angel."

"I love you too, Finny." I kiss him and pull away quickly, sliding into the car. He shuts the door for me and I watch his large form stalk to the van that's parked behind me. He's supposed to text Ryan the address to the gas station and we'll meet him there.

My mind is free of thought on the drive to the gas station. I'm not worried about Ryan, and I'm not worried about our plan falling through. I know Finn will have done everything to make sure this is a success. I don't want to think about how I'll feel when this is over; if I'm a good person or not.

I don't care.

I was a good person, and I was taken advantage of. I was

kind, I helped people, I believed in people. In goodness. I don't care anymore. If being a bad person, if being a monster, means that I stand up for myself and I defend myself, then fuck it. I'll be whatever I need to be to protect myself and those that I love.

The gas station is empty and dark. There aren't any lights on anywhere; not in the building, not under the old roof over the gas pumps, and there aren't any street lights for miles. I park under the awning and get out of my car, leaving it running and leaving the headlights on. Taking a seat on the hood, I watch Finn pull over and park the van behind a large covering of trees.

We wait.

Me on the hood of my car, and Finn hiding somewhere in the trees or behind the building. I'm not sure. I'm not sure how many times I check my phone, but finally, a car pulls into the gas station, parking in front of mine.

Ryan and Judge Kelly step out of Ryan's silver BMW with five minutes to spare. I guess Finn told them in the text that both of them had to be present for this. Ryan grabs a small bag from the backseat and they walk over to me.

They both stare at me, Ryan glaring, and the older Kelly watching me like he's assessing me.

Ryan throws the bag of what I'm assuming is money at me, and opens his mouth to say something that looks spiteful from the acidic look on his face. But before he can, Judge Kelly collapses to the ground with a loud smack. Ryan and I both turn to him and see Finn standing in his place holding the barrel of his gun, having just pistol-whipped the man. Ryan lunges at me, his hand holding my throat, and crushes me onto the hood of my car.

Pulling my knife from the holster that was strapped to my thigh, I jam it into his side. He yelps above me and slams his head into my nose, causing me to pull the knife out with the sudden impact. Blood rushes out of my nose, covering the lower half of my face, but I don't give him the satisfaction of seeing my pain. His grip tightens and his eyes turn wild, his pupils blown wide and making his eyes appear completely black. He's squeezing hard enough to cut off air, but I'm not afraid, it's only a matter of time before...

Ryan's rageful eyes turn to fear almost as quickly as the sound of a gun cocking echoes through the silence. I look beyond Ryan to see Finn standing behind him, holding his gun to the back of Ryan's head. My eyes switch back to Ryan's again, and I smile a wide, manic smile, blood covering my teeth. "Let. The fuck. Go." Finn growls, sounding completely animal and not at all human. Ryan lets go of me and stands up. Finn steps back to allow him room to move away from me. "It's hard as fuck not to come to your rescue, Angel."

Spitting the blood out of my mouth I watch my man stare at me, not at all concerned with the disgusting people that we are about to abduct. "I know, Pretty Boy," I say, smiling at him.

Ryan's laughter breaks our connection, and I want to kill him just for that. "Do you know who we are, asshole? Are you really going to let her pussy cause you to end up in jail?"

"I know exactly who you are." Finn shoves the gun into the side of Ryan's throat, pushing it in painfully. "I'm the one that's going to rip your heart from your chest, just so you know how it feels."

I step forward, taking the syringe that Finn gave me earlier tonight from my pocket. Taking off the orange casing, I take another step toward Ryan and Finn. Finn grabs Ryan's arms and holds them behind his back, his hold strong enough that even with Ryan thrashing violently, he still has no chance against Finn.

"You stupid whore, you're not going to get away with this!" Ryan fights.

Placing my hand on Ryan's head, Finn gets the message and

kicks his knee out, causing Ryan to crash to the concrete on his knees before me.

"That's where you're wrong. I'm going to get away with everything. You, on the other hand, are going to die tonight. By the hands of a stupid whore." Then I shove the needle painfully into the wildly throbbing vein in his neck.

He fights against us, but wedged between the two of us with his hands held immobile and Finn standing on one of his calves, he isn't going anywhere. He eventually stops fighting, losing consciousness. He falls into me, but I step away before he can touch me and Finn lets go too, letting him fall face first onto the ground.

Finn grabs my jaw and raises it to his, turning my face side to side to look at my nose. "Are you okay?" he asks, his eyes hard, brows set in a hard line.

I nod. "Yeah. Thank you for letting me take care of it. Mostly." I smile at him.

Finn takes a black bandana from his back pocket and gently daps at my nose, cleaning up the blood that poured out, but has slowed down significantly. "It was hard not to grab him when he lunged at you or shoot him in the back of the head when I had a hold of him." Finn sneers.

"I know. Thank you." I rise onto my toes and place a kiss on the corner of his lips.

Finn squeezes my jaw, holding me to him. He runs his tongue over my lips and pulls away before I can take his tongue in between my teeth. "Let's go." He pulls away and bends down to throw Judge Kelly over his shoulder. I pick up Ryan's feet and try to drag him, but Finn stops me. "As much as I would love to give him road rash on his face, I don't want to leave any blood behind. Yours is going to be enough to clean up."

Rolling my eyes, I nod, agreeing with Finn. We flip Ryan over

—not so gently—and Finn helps me drag him to the van on his back, picking up the bag of cash on the way.

I follow Finn to the murder cabin and park out front while Finn pulls into the garage. Finn carries both men into the basement through a hole in the floor of the garage, and he shows me how to chain them to the chair so they aren't able to break free.

Both men are still unconscious and tied up, and we step back. Finn starts to pull out the tools that I found last time I was here. "Do you want to torture him, or just kill him?" Finn asks, his back to me while he sorts through the cabinet next to the sink.

I watch Ryan, mulling over what I want. "I want him to hurt, but mostly, I just want him dead." I finally decide. I don't know if I have a stomach for bloody murder. The last two have just been me injecting them with something. No blood, no screams. Just them fading away.

"He's not going out easy. I need to watch him suffer, so it's either by your hand or mine, but he's not leaving this basement whole." Finn lays sharp knives and a cattle prod on the metal table I'm standing by.

"Go ahead." I gesture towards Ryan.

Finn stops and turns to look at me. We watch each other, completely silent. "You can go upstairs, and I'll come get you when he's ready." Taking another look at the tools laid out, I decide he's right. I turn to walk to the stairs, but Finn's voice stops me. "What about the judge?" he asks.

I cast a quick glance at the corrupt judge hunched over on the metal chair. "I don't care about him," I say, and then take the stairs to the living room in the cabin.

I wait for hours upstairs, while Finn does whatever he's doing downstairs. Not one sound makes it upstairs though; the cabin is completely quiet while I sit on the couch and read and play games on my phone.

Eventually, the panel in the wall pushes open and Finn steps through, wiping his hands on an old rag, rust coloring covering the entire thing. He walks into the kitchen and pulls a water bottle from the fridge, downing the entire thing before tossing it into a recycling bin and coming back into the living room. "You ready, Angel?" He stands at the secret door, watching me.

Standing, I slide my phone into the waistband of my leggings and follow him back down the concrete stairwell.

I was not prepared for what I would walk into.

Judge Kelly is sitting motionless in his chair, a giant pool of blood around his feet. His torso is chained to the back of the chair, keeping his chest sitting up straight with his arms chained to the side of the chair, holding them straight down. Both of his wrists are slashed open, and he's facing Ryan's chair.

Ryan, on the other hand, is naked and slightly hunched over, with his hands chained behind his back. His back rises slightly as he cries quietly, blood dripping into a pool under his chair. Finn steps behind Ryan and yanks his head up by his hair, pulling his body up with the motion. Ryan whimpers and squeezes his eyes shut.

I can't hold in the gasp when I see Ryan's body. His face is mottled with bruises, swelling, and small cuts. Both eyes are almost swollen shut and already a deep purple. His nose is crooked and his jaw is hanging a little slack and off-center. Blood spills from his mouth and pours down his chest. I take a deep breath when I see bloody holes where his nipples should be, and the word "rapist" carved into his stomach in sharp, bloody letters.

A sick chuckle works its way up my throat and out of my mouth when I reach his blood-drenched pelvic area, the biggest source of the blood pooling on the floor. Ryan's limp dick lay on the floor, the sawed-off edges of skin making me want to vomit, but also giving me bone-deep satisfaction.

Ryan and Finn watch me walk toward them slowly. Finn pulls a rolling metal table next to Ryan, with two items on it. A jagged, scary-looking knife, and a gun with a silencer on it. The same gun that Finn offered me at the clubhouse the first night we had our first real conversation. I bend down to Ryan's level, speaking directly into his ear. I want this to be the last thing he ever hears, the last thing that absorbs into his vile fucking mind. Other than the fact that he's dying, of course. "I hope Hell fucks you as terribly as you fucked me."

I pick up the gun and place it to Ryan's forehead. Finn steps away, and Ryan whimpers, more blood spilling from his mouth.

I pull the trigger.

Blood splashes onto my stomach and Ryan's head slumps forward. With a shaking hand, I set the gun on the table and collapse to the floor.

Finn catches me inches from the concrete, and lowers me the rest of the way, his body coming down next to mine. Finn sits on the ground with his legs extended in front of him and holding me in between them. I stare at Ryan's beaten face, tears forming in my eyes.

Not for him. Fuck him. For me.

For the me that was a good person before this. The me that doesn't feel any different now that he's dead. Now that they're all dead.

I thought that I would feel a weight lift from my shoulders, and my vision would become clearer. My head not feel like it's in a fog, or my heart feel like chains are wrapped around it constantly. I thought I would feel how I feel when I'm wrapped in Finn's arms.

But I don't.

I don't feel anything but pure rage, wishing I could kill Ryan over again. My breathing picks up, coming out in short, sharp breaths. My heart beats wildly in my chest.

"Talk to me, Huntley," Finn snaps. His voice pulls me out of my panic attack.

"What do I do now, Finn? It's done. They're dead, they're all dead." The tears flow from my eyes.

He rests his forehead against my temple, speaking into my ear. "You live now. You spent the last year in Purgatory, you weren't living. Now you live."

I turn to look at him. His eyes pulling me in and anchoring me. "I live for you now," I whisper, not meaning to say it aloud.

Finn shakes his head. "No, Angel. You live for yourself. You deserve the fucking world, and you deserve to live for yourself. To do all of the things that you always wanted to do." His eyes sparkle like the sun reflecting off of the ocean. "Graduate, build your dream house, get married, have babies." He takes a big breath, but I keep holding onto his gaze like a lifeline. "Or don't do any of that, but now you live for yourself."

I place my shaking hands on his cheeks, feeling his warm skin under mine. "How do you know all of this?" I ask.

Finn wipes the last few tears. "Because at one point, I didn't want to live at all, and Ronan made me realize that I needed to live my life for myself. A life that I loved, and a life that I wanted to live." My mouth drops open, sad that Finn ever felt that way; scared that I may not have ever met him. He changed my life. "Don't be sad for me, Angel. I got everything I ever wanted when you walked into my life."

"Did you tell anyone how you felt?" Talking about him takes my mind off of the dead bodies sitting next to us, though the strong iron smell filling my nostrils is still keeping me aware.

Finn purses his lips and shakes his head. "People don't pay attention when a man is struggling mentally. I knew that, so I tried to deal with it on my own." His thumb swipes at more tears that slide down my cheeks. "Ronan could tell though, and he helped me through it. I owe him my life." I break down and throw myself into him, sobbing into his chest. He holds onto me equally as tight as I'm holding onto him. Running one of his hands down the back of my head, he rests his chin on my head. "I'm okay now, Angel. I'm okay."

Pulling away, I turn and tuck my legs underneath me, looking into Finn's eyes. We watch each other, the moment stretching on as the metallic smell of blood hangs in the air. Finn's chest starts to rise quickly and his nostrils flare. I know he wants me, his worried gaze quickly turning into lust.

I quickly pull the long-sleeve shirt over my head, leaving me in my bra and leggings, and Finn springs at me, pushing my back onto the cold concrete. He lowers himself over me, his mouth feverishly finding mine. Our teeth and tongues clash in a fight for power. My hands slide down his sides until I reach the bottom of his shirt, and I pull it up and over his torso and head. Finn sits up on his knees, and with one hand, he reaches behind his head and pulls his shirt the rest of the way off. His arm and stomach muscles ripple. I groan at the sight of him, and he smirks.

Leaning back down to kiss me again, I place my hands on his head and push him down. He takes the cue and kisses his way down my neck and chest, stopping at my bra to reach behind me and unhook it, pulling the garment off of my body and replacing the cups with his mouth. He sucks my nipple into his mouth, flicking the bud with his tongue and then nipping it. Moving to the other, he does the same thing, but this time he bites much harder, pulling a yelp from my lips.

Grinning, he kisses down my stomach until he reaches the waistband of my leggings. He pulls them down my legs, taking my panties with them, and tosses them away from us, leaving me shivering against the cold concrete. Lukewarm liquid brushes my arm, but I ignore it.

Finn slides down my body, settling down between my legs.

He slides his hands under me and lifts my hips right up to his face, and he dives in. I cry out when his teeth graze my clit and he licks a long line down my slit, then back to my clit. He turns his face sideways, his tongue licking across my clit before sucking it roughly into his mouth. He moves two thick fingers inside of me, turning them palm up, and roughly glides his fingers against the upper wall of my pussy. His movements become faster and faster, picking up speed as well as intensity. My moans fill the air and my body stiffens and turns slack when my orgasm spreads through my body, liquid spraying out of me.

Finn pulls back, a smug grin on his face as he watches my chest heave with my heavy breaths. "I love when you do that," he says, his hand coming up to wipe the liquid from his chin.

"Shut up." I sit up and reach for his belt, undoing it and his button. He helps with the zipper and stands to remove his jeans. He kicks them off with the rest of his clothes, and drops to his knees and settles between my legs again.

He lifts my hips and rests me on top of his thighs as he slides me over him, with no warning, no getting used to his large size. He fully settles himself inside of me and starts fucking me; pulling and pushing my hips, his fingers digging in painfully to my hip bone. The stretch of his cock inside of me and his biting fingertips bring me to life. I play with my breasts, pinching and rolling my nipple between my fingers. Finn watches, his face scrunching together as his movements pick up.

He slows, pulling almost all the way out and letting his piercings glide through my opening. I clench my muscles around him and he groans, closing his eyes briefly. "Don't freak out," he rasps, but before I can ask about what, he's pulling out of me and flipping me over.

My eyes widen when I see blood covering the floor beneath me, the giant puddle surrounding me. I feel a cool breeze across my back and know that my back is covered in Ryan's blood. Finn groans again and pushes inside of me violently. I moan, the intrusion welcomed now. I stare at the blood on the floor. My mind is confused, being repulsed and extremely turned on simultaneously; knowing that Finn is taking what I willingly gave him in the blood of my tormentor.

Finn's hands hold where my hips meet my thighs, and he pulls me back onto him while he also thrusts, burying himself in much deeper. His piercings graze that spot inside of me and trigger an orgasm. I raise onto my forearms, not caring about the blood anymore, and try to calm my breathing. "You're not done yet, Angel. I'm gonna fuck you so dirty, God will never take you." His chest pushes into my back as his fingers reach above my head and swipe through the blood. His fingers disappear from my vision, and I feel the cold liquid being spread over my asshole. Clenching at the surprise, Finn leans over me again, and his chest brushes my back. "Use your words. Yes or no?" he asks into my ear.

"Yes," I breathe.

Chuckling darkly, he leans back and continues rubbing the blood over my ass. His hand leaves me before I feel the head of his dick slide into my pussy again. Confused, I start to turn my head back around, but then I feel his finger pushing into my ass. He fucks me slowly at first, his finger and cock sliding in simultaneously. Another orgasm builds slowly, softly, and when I relax around him and start moving my hips with him, he picks up his speed, fucking me violently. His hips slam against my butt, his finger pushes in deeper, and his piercings drag against my g-spot. My orgasm explodes so hard that I have no chance of hanging on, and I let go, shocks spreading through my body and my vision blacking out. I don't come to until Finn's pulling out of me.

I push up onto my knees, looking at Finn over my shoulder. He's sitting on the floor with his hands behind him, trying to slow his breathing, watching me. "Did I lose consciousness?" I ask.

Finn nods. "I think so," he says, his throat sounding dry.

My mouth drops and I turn to face him. "And you just kept fucking me?" I'm trying to pretend to be mad, but honestly, the thought of him taking advantage of my body is pretty fucking hot. In a consensual way of course.

He shakes his head. "No, I saw my opportunity and I finished in your ass."

"What?" I squeak. Finn's laughter fills the room, so loud it almost echoes. Based on his laugh and his cum spilling from my pussy, I'm pretty sure he didn't. Finn is so big, I'm pretty sure I'd without a doubt know if he did stick it in my ass. I reach out to shove his shoulder playfully, and he catches my hand, pulling me into his lips.

He kisses me gently, pulling my bottom lip with him when he pulls away. "Go upstairs and take a shower, Angel. I have one last thing to take care of." Finn stands and pulls me up with him. I leave the room, leaving my clothes on the floor, and walk up the stairs and into the cabin. Finding the bathroom isn't hard, the cabin isn't very big. When I'm about to step out, Finn steps into the tub. His hands and forearms are bloody and when I just stare at them, he finally speaks. "I told him I was going to take his heart." With that, he rinses the blood and cleans the rest of his body.

After showering and changing into fresh clothes that I didn't know Finn packed, he leads me out back and to a firepit. I sit on a chair and watch as Finn starts a small fire. Taking a seat next to me, he slowly adds wood to it and builds it up.

He pulls his burner phone from his pocket and puts it to his ear. "I got two bodies, they need to disappear completely," he says into the phone. "The cabin. I need them gone immediately." He listens some more, his expression neutral. "Great, I'll wait for you." Finn ends the call and slides the phone into his pocket. Placing another log on the fire, he adds a few pieces of our clothes to it.

"Who was that?" I ask, watching the fire burn our bloody clothes.

"A doctor. He's gonna come get the bodies and sell the organs on the Red Market, and then do whatever he does with the bodies." Finn adds another piece of clothing. My head turns to his. What the fuck? He can sense my mood, he always can. "It's the cleanest way to get rid of them. No trace."

Nodding, I accept it. I trust Finn to take care of this. I watch as he adds more logs and the rest of our clothing, and we wait for the doctor to come and get Judge Kelly and Ryan's bodies.

30

HUNTLEY

THE LOCK ON THE DOOR CLICKS AS I LOCK UP THE YOGA ROOM AT the University gym. The halls are quiet; only quiet hums of cardio machines whirling or the loud thump when someone drops their weights on the mats in the weight room.

Finn's Hellcat tears out of the parking lot, he and Reese on the way to Cale's house to wait for a Prospect. Mason called while I was showing Reese some self-defense moves, to say that he finally found Reese's stalker. Good thing we met up for a self-defense lesson today.

Hopefully, she doesn't have to use anything I just taught her.

I watch them leave through the glass doors at the front of the University gym, and then I walk out to my Camaro. We drove separately today because I wanted to go to the boxing gym before this.

Finn's house is quiet when I let myself in, as expected. I walk into his bedroom and open Noctem's kennel. Her eyes snap open and she rolls onto her belly, stretching her little body before standing up and trotting out of the kennel. Picking her up, I take her to the back door and take her outside to run around and relieve herself.

We make our trip short, me being paranoid and wanting to be locked inside with Finn's alarm system active.

I figure it's going to be a long and stressful evening as the club goes to end Reese's stalking problem, so I sort through the refrigerator and find something to make dinner out of. Stuffed chicken with a side of vegetables and mashed potatoes should be enough for Finn when he gets home.

I feed Noctem and then sit at the table and eat, scrolling through TikTok. Of course one of the first videos I see is a thirst trap of Leo standing in a plain, white, v-neck shirt, and when the beat drops, the video cuts to Leo shirtless with his cut on and the lights dimmed, making his abs look even more cut. Rolling my eyes, I click on the comments and leave a few puking emojis before scrolling on. He's been able to amass an impressive following, which has resulted in several guys saying they wanted to join the Outlaws, and a couple hundred thousand girls realizing how sexy a man on a bike can be.

My phone vibrates in my hand, a message notification appearing at the top.

FARRYN

I miss you. I feel like I only see you in class anymore.

HUNTLEY

I know, I'm sorry. Things have gotten… intense.

FARRYN

With your hot alpha biker from the party?

HUNTLEY

Yeah. I've been staying at his house a lot.

Or you know, all the time. A slight lie doesn't hurt.

> **FARRYN**
> I'm happy that you're happy. I'll kill him though if he hurts you.

> **HUNTLEY**
> Hang out soon?

> **FARRYN**
> Yeah, babe. Just text me!

Putting my phone on the counter, I transfer all of the food into containers and leave them to cool on the counter. Noctem and I move into the living room and we settle on the couch with a blanket and the remote. My phone has been silent, and I know that means that everything is going to plan, but not being there is driving me insane.

Pulling up Netflix, I searched for the *365 Days Trilogy*. Reese was telling me today how the last movie just came out and she's pissed. That should keep my mind busy for a few hours.

31

FINN

I'M STANDING IN THE DOWNSTAIRS BATHROOM OF CALE'S townhouse, zipper down, cock out, and just finished pissing when I hear a faint creek behind me. It could be Reese, she's the only other one in the house, but my gut says otherwise. It's confirmed not even a second later when I feel the cold metal of a gun barrel pressed to the back of my head.

Unless Little Red has been playing us this entire time, this isn't good.

Turning my head slightly, I find a tall man with brown hair and brown eyes. He's indeed got a gun, but with the motion of my head, it's now digging into my fucking temple. His face is twisted into an ugly scowl, and I have no fucking clue who he is.

Something tells me he ain't here to suck my dick, though.

I have a suspicion this is Little Red's stalker.

"You gonna kill me with my cock out, or could I at least put it away?" I ask casually. I'm not afraid of dying, I never have been. I'm a little bit more hesitant now that Huntley's in my life though. A man with nothing to live for is always going to be the bravest in the room. That's why I haven't headbutted this moth-erfucker and turned his gun on himself. No man with any sort of sense would come into an Outlaw's home and hold their enforcer at gunpoint.

I left my gun in my cut, which is still in my car, and since I didn't hear any gunshots or screams, I'm going to assume that Reese is still upstairs. I have to get this guy out of the cramped bathroom and take him out. I've given up hope that Red's gun will still be on the counter in the kitchen. If this man was worth anything, he would have spotted it and disassembled it or picked it up.

The man moves to my side, the gun sliding around to my forehead. He's shorter than me by a few inches and much smaller. I can take him with no problem if the gun to my head wasn't a factor.

"Zip up and walk into the kitchen, slowly," he spats.

Rolling my eyes, because fuck him, I do as he says. Not being able to wash my hands is pretty fucking gross, but I'll just consider us even when I'm using those same unwashed hands to strangle the life out of him.

I step into the kitchen and subtly scan the counter for Little Red's gun. It's gone, but I expected that.

"Out the door." He nudges my back with the barrel of the gun.

I walk to the small bar cart by the back door with the man following behind me and stop, causing him to step close to my back and block his view of what is in front of me. This might be a terrible fucking idea, but nothing is happening to Little Red with me here.

I grab the two thousand dollar bottle of Japanese Whiskey that Sebastian Segreto gave Cale and me—sorry, brother—and I turn around, smashing the bottle across his head. He stumbles to the side, dropping the gun and catching himself against the kitchen island. Immediately I'm on him, picking him up by the collar of his black henley and turning and throwing him into the bar cart.

The entire thing smashes beneath his weight, bottles of liquor shattering on the floor, and a hole the size of him in the wall where I threw him.

Bending down, I pick up the gun that he dropped. I click off the safety—fucking noob could have ended me had he not had that shit on—and aim the gun at his head.

He sits up laughing, fucking cackling. "I wouldn't do that if you want Huntley to continue to be safe."

I pause in cocking the gun and blink at him. "What?" I ask, my voice so low it would make most men shit their pants.

"If I don't check in with my partners, they've been instructed to storm your house and do exactly what her ex-boyfriend and his friends did to her in that fraternity bedroom last year." He brushes his brown hair out of his eyes, pushing the hair back.

"How do you..." I trail off, trying to think of something, anything, but my brain fucking quit when he said Huntley's name.

The delusional fuck—correction, dead delusional fuck— smiles wide. "I know everything, Finn. Just like I know that your alarms have been deactivated and my guys are waiting for my word to move in, shoot your new puppy in the head, and pass your girlfriend around."

"I'll fucking kill you," I snarl, baring my teeth.

"Go ahead, check your alarms. See if I'm lying." He's not phased one bit, and the smile never leaves his face.

I pull my phone out of my back pocket and click open my home security app. He was right, the alarm was on before I went to the bathroom, and it's off now. I raise my head to say something, threaten something, I don't know, but he's already barreling at me.

My back collides with the barstools and we fall to the floor, the thin metal legs stabbing me in the back and sending pain exploding through my entire spine. I don't think it broke the skin, but fuck that hurt.

I kept a hold of the gun in the fall, and I point it at his forehead at the same time that he presses a knife to my throat.

"One of us is dying today," I say, my voice calm. It won't be me.

The blade presses in harder, the small bite of skin splitting makes me narrow my eyes on him. "You're right, Finn, but it'll either be me and your girlfriend, or you. What's your choice?"

I look into his deep brown eyes, insanity swirling like fucking poison, and I come to peace with the only option I have.

The gun makes a thunk noise when it hits the floor. The man picks it up, training it on me, and stands up. He motions for me to rise and I do. He twirls the gun around in an indication for me to turn around and again, I do. I'm about to die execution-style in Cale's kitchen, leaving both of our girls defenseless, and I have no other option. My heart seizes in my chest and I feel nothing but rage and extreme disappointment in myself.

I failed everyone that I love.

How could I have finally come so close to having everything that I ever wanted and it'll all be torn away like this? Huntley was right, fate is shit and people are cruel.

Fate wouldn't give me the most amazing woman I've ever met, only for me to die like a coward in my brother's kitchen

Fate wouldn't have Huntley assaulted only to find someone to trust and have him murdered.

Fate wouldn't bring back two people who were meant to be, only for her stalker to come in and steal her away, causing my brother to lose both the love of his life and his best friend all in one night.

There's no telling where I might go when I die, but if I have to go to a God that allows this to happen, I hope He sends me away. How can someone be so cruel to do this to people?

The man places his hand on my shoulder and pushes down. I drop to my knees before him and I feel the gun press into the back of my head. He leans down to my ear and whispers, "Did you know they recorded the entire thing? I wonder how many times they jacked off to your girlfriend's cries and pleas. Don't worry, I wiped it, but I did keep a copy for you." Tears prick my eyes, but I refuse to give them to him.

Hurried footsteps pound down the stairs and pull his attention from me. Reese runs around the railing of the stairs and stops dead in her tracks.

"What are you doing, Eli?"

32

FINN

THE LAST THING I REMEMBER BEFORE IT ALL WENT BLACK WAS yelling at Reese to run. That was it, and then I fell into complete blackness.

"Finn." A voice slithers through my brain, coaxing me back to consciousness. "Finn," the voice hisses again.

Guess I'm not dead.

I recognize that voice though, and I'm not sure if I feel relieved that Reese is alive or worried that she's wherever I ended up. "You should have run, Princess." I rasp out, the pulsing pain at the back of my head increasing with my consciousness.

"He would have shot you!" Reese snaps back, irritation laced through her voice. Good. I need her angry for when we escape.

I pick my head up from where I was hunched over and rest it against a wooden pole behind me. The pole I'm handcuffed around, I notice, as I try to move my arms and they don't budge. "Still." I open my eyes and look at our surroundings. "Why the fuck are we here?" I look around at the open space of Cale's warehouse, the roofing supplies laid out on the other side of the warehouse, and two of Cale's work pickups parked at the back of the warehouse to my left.

"You know where we are? Where are we?" Reese whispers again.

My eyes blink involuntarily, trying to clear my vision but also from the pain in my head. "The warehouse." So I guess the guy at Cale's wasn't Little Red's stalker? Right? Because why would he bring us here? This has to do with the club. But how did Reese know his name?

Speaking of the dead motherfucker, he steps out of Cale's office, which is where the secret door to our ammo room is. Fuck. He steps around in front of us, his stupid Sperry shoes tapping against the concrete floor. What did Little Red call him? Eli?

"Where's Huntley?" I growl, glaring at the man standing in front of us.

"Who?" Eli asks, his face splitting into an infuriating smile. "Oh, your girlfriend, she's fine. I only told you I had her so you would surrender." *Thank fucking God.*

His eyes rake over Reese and I try to pull his attention away from her. "Why are we here?"

Eli walks back and forth between Reese and I, his hands clasped behind his back and smiling to himself. "Well, I knew your club of criminals would never let Reesey and I go easily, so I brought you both here to see what your club is doing in the basement. I know you make bullets. With that and trading you, the club would be wise to allow us to calmly leave town." So this *is* about Reese. This *is* her stalker. Fuck me, how did he figure out what we were doing in the basement? Fuck, the spy we found and that I tortured in the basement of the cabin. Eli must have hired him.

"Why are you doing this?" Little Red squeaks beside me.

Eli abruptly turns toward Reese and walks to her, bending

down in front of her and gently cupping her cheek. She pulls as far away as she can, her nose scrunching. "Isn't it obvious? I love you, Reesey, and we can finally be together." Little Red tries to pull away again. "You were too good for my stupid best friend, and way too good for a criminal." He pushes away from her and stands back up.

I scoff. "You really think Callum is going to let you kidnap Reese?"

"He will if he doesn't want your little operation to be turned over to ATF and for you to make it out of this alive," Eli snaps, his collected exterior cracking.

I shake my head, a laugh tumbling out. "You chose the wrong club to fuck with and the wrong woman to stalk."

His manic smile slides back into place. "We'll see." Eli walks toward Reese and she backs herself into the pole, her shoes sliding against the floor in her attempt. "Now if you'd be so kind as to pass my message along to your little club, Reesey and I will just be on our way."

He walks around the back of Reese and messes with her cuffs, quickly closing them around one of her wrists and one of his. Smart move. He yanks her up, using his hand that's cuffed next to hers, and I want to punch his fucking teeth in.

Reese picks up her little fist, cocking it back, and I'm leaning forward as much as I can so I can really see when she fucking delivers this blow that he so fucking deserves. It's great to see Little Red grow a backbone and stick up for herself. But then, he presses the barrel of a gun to her forehead and my lungs seize in my chest. He wouldn't. He's getting what he wanted; he wouldn't kill her now. I look closer at the gun with the red trigger. It's Red's gun. The gun that Callum had a tracker installed in.

They're already on their way. I know it.

"I wouldn't," he says, pulling me back into the moment. "In

fact, just to make sure you comply." He slides the gun off of her forehead and aims it at me.

He fires and I feel the shot burn its way into my shoulder. I fall forward, my arms trying to grasp it, but the handcuffs don't move. I growl low in my throat, trying to take away from the pain.

"Finn!" Reese yells.

"Let's go. Or else the next one is more serious," Eli barks.

"Don't move those fucking feet, Reese," I grit out through clenched teeth.

Reese shakes her head, her eyes shining with tears while Eli drags her past me and out of the back of the warehouse.

I watch them run through the warehouse doors, Eli pulling Reese behind him, her sneakers squeaking on the concrete floor. The low rumbles of bikes perk my ears, and I turn my head to watch the front door and large garage door.

A few seconds later, the front door bursts open and my club storms in; Callum at the front, Leo behind him, with Mason and Saint bringing up the rear. Their guns are raised and their heads swivel around, taking everything in.

"Get me out of these fucking cuffs!" I yell, yanking the cuffs against the pole for added effect, then regretting it because it rocked my shoulder.

Mason and Leo quickly walk off to hopefully find something to cut the cuffs.

"Where's Reese?" Callum asks, bending over in front of me while Saint kneels down next to my shoulder and shines his phone flashlight over my shoulder.

"He went out the back with her. Some fucker named Eli," I say, and then growl in my throat when Saint presses his discarded shirt into my shoulder, sending a slicing pain through my entire arm and up into my neck.

Callum straightens and a shot rings off behind the warehouse. Callum darts for the back door, leaving Saint pressing his formally gray shirt into my shoulder, the blood eating up the light fabric.

"He has a gun!" I try to yell out to Callum, but he's already through the door and out of earshot.

"No shit," Saint deadpans, and I want to smack him.

I glare at him and watch his stupid smirk kick up. I swear he fucking jacks off at night to all of the times he irritates someone. "I was trying to be helpful."

Saint motions for Leo to come over with the bolt cutters he and Mason found. "Be helpful by walking your ass to the truck, I can't carry your big ass."

Saint helps me stand, sliding under my uninjured arm, and together we walk to Cale's pickup, still running in front of the shop. It's quiet out here, and that worries me. Are they standing over Reese's dead body? I think I'd hear Cale if he was, or I'd hear another few shots. One for Eli and one for himself. I don't think he could lose her again.

I don't need Saint to walk, but it's nice to have the extra support. Mason and Leo run around the side of the building to check on the guys, and when we get to the truck, Saint opens the backdoor, raises my arm off of him and gets into the truck, motioning me in after him.

I step into the pickup, hunching down and finally clutching my shoulder.

Saint bats my hand away. "Lay down, let me take a better look at it."

I do as he says and lay my head in his lap, my knees bent on the seats.

He makes a cut in my shirt near the wound so he can just pull it apart without me having to try to take it off, shining the flash light on it again and feeling around on my back.

"What do you think?" I ask, watching his eyes narrow as he

examines. Saint went to EMT training when he was a Prospect, so he's not a doctor, but he's as close as we got, and he always patches us up as best as he can. "No exit wound. You need a hospital to make sure nothing is damaged. Might as well let them take it out instead of me. At least there you'll get painkillers."

"True," I grunt, and the doors to the pickup open. Callum and Reese slide into the front seats and Ronan lifts my legs to sit under them in the backseat.

33

HUNTLEY

The credits roll over the screen, and the second movie pops up at the bottom in the "Suggested For You" section. I pick up the remote and click on the picture of the second movie. Noctem has long since fallen asleep, and I even laid down across the couch.

My phone lights up on the coffee table and I pull my body up to answer it. Leo's name shines on my screen and I immediately pick it up, my stomach twisting into knots. I know something is wrong.

"Huntley, you have to get to the hospital. Finn was shot," Leo yells over the sounds of bikes in the background.

"What happened? How bad is it?" I stand, immediately picking up Noctem and running to her kennel.

A bike revs in the background. "Reese's stalker ambushed them at Cale's house. Took them to his warehouse and shot Finn in the shoulder. I think he's fine, but we gotta go to the hospital."

Panic floods my system. "Is Reese okay?"

"Yes, she's fine. We have her, but I have to go!" Leo says quickly.

"Okay, go! I'm on my way!" I shove my feet into some sandals and run out of the front door and to my car.

I break every speed limit restriction on the way to the hospital, passing people in non-passing zones, and getting several honks and glares. I don't care. The only thing I care about right now is on his way to the hospital, and I don't know how bad it is.

Finn was shot.

I slam on my brakes in front of the hospital doors. Fuck a parking spot, I don't have time. I rip my keys from the ignition and run inside the emergency entrance. I run to the first person I see, a tall, blonde man.

Cale.

I grip his shoulders, my nails biting into his skin—not on purpose but out of fear. "Where is he?" My head feels like it's swimming, and I feel disoriented.

Strong hands pull mine from Cale and lead me away. Ronan's sweet blue eyes look down into mine. "We just brought him in." He pulls me towards the row of gray chairs that face the front desk and the doors that lead back to the ER. "Saint went back with him and he'll be out soon with an update."

Saint. That was the only word that registered in my head at that point. I look around for him, but my eyes land on someone else instead. Reese stands there, staring at me with wide eyes, a few flecks of blood splattered on her neck and a few on her cheek. She looks afraid. Of me.

Standing, I walk over to her. She was captured just like Finn, and she must have been terrified. I'm so glad to see her alive. Almost as glad as I'd be to see Finn right now. I didn't see her when I came in because she was slightly behind Cale, but when I walk over, she stands tall, though her eyes give her away.

Bending down, I gently wrap my hands around her upper arms. "I'm so glad to see you, Reese. I was so worried when Leo called and said you were taken."

The swinging doors of the ER pull my attention from Reese. Saint walks through the door, a red-tinged disinfectant wipe clutched in his hands. My knees feel weak, and I think they might give out. We make eye contact immediately, and he stops a few steps in front of me. "He's fine, the bullet didn't hit anything major, just lodged itself into his obnoxious amount of muscle. I guess being a giant fucker finally paid off for him. They're removing the bullet now, and will transfer him to a room so they can continue to replenish some blood."

Relief washes over me like a wave. I let out a deep breath. "He's okay," I half ask, half state.

A while later, Saint and I are sitting in the waiting room chairs. Ronan is on one side, holding my hand tightly. A young nurse walks through the ER doors that Saint came through not too long ago. "Are you the group waiting for Mr. Evans?" I stand and start to walk toward the nurse, everyone else following behind me. "I can take you all back to him now."

We follow him through a few hallways before he finally stops, opens a door, and motions us in. We all step into the room, and although it's a normal-sized room, it seems tiny with all of us crowded in it.

Finn smiles at all of us, and my eyes fill with tears. I'm so fucking happy to see him. "Thank fuck, beautiful. I fucking missed you." His voice is raspy; rough.

I run to the bed and grab the hand on Finn's uninjured side. "I was so scared. Don't ever leave me behind again." Shaking my head, I stare at his bandaged shoulder. "I don't know what I would ever do without you," I whisper.

Finn pulls me onto the bed, my knees hitting the firm mattress on either side of his hips and my hands land on his body to steady myself. Without thought, one hand lands on his cheek and the other rests on his chest over his heart. He leans back against the pillows and runs his hand gently up and down my spine, taking a slow deep breath. Letting it out he reaches up to cover my hand cupping his face. "The only way I'm ever leaving you is in a body bag, and even then, it's only physically. I told you we're fucking soulmates babe, and my soul will continue to look for yours until we're together again, spending eternity together wherever the fuck we end up."

"You could have ended up in a body bag tonight," I growl.

Finn shakes his head with a small smile on his face. Squeezing my hand, he says, "I ain't going out that easy, Angel, and I'm not leaving you without telling you I love you one last time."

———

I SHIFT on Finn's lap, my knees on both sides of his thighs and my face pressed into his chest while we're reclined in the hospital bed. Everyone has left and gone home, leaving us alone. Finn gets released tomorrow and I decided to stay with him. Leo was sent to the house to get Noctem and watch her for the night.

Finn's hand runs through my hair, sweeping it away from my face. "What are you thinking about, Angel?" His voice rumbles through his chest where my ear rests.

"When Leo called, I thought that was it. I couldn't think, I just had to get to you." My finger traces lazy patterns over his good arm and he groans.

"I thought about a lot tonight. A lot about regret." The seriousness in his voice makes me sit up to look into his face. "I love you, Huntley, and I don't want to have any more regrets." He takes my hand that was hanging at my side. "My entire life I've been waiting for something. I didn't know exactly what I was waiting for, but when I saw you, I knew I was waiting for you," he sighs. "I keep doing this shit to you, life making me realize that our time is short and I'm not invincible. You deserve so much better than this. I don't even have a fucking ring, but," Finn looks into my eyes, his hand holding onto mine tightly. "Huntley, will you marry me?"

Tears slide down my cheeks and I don't try to brush them away. They're tears of happiness and I don't want to be rid of them. Nodding frantically, I pull his face to mine and smash my lips to his. His teeth pull on my bottom lip, opening my mouth for him to explore with his tongue.

Finn's hands slide under the waistband of my sweatpants and he starts to push them down.

I place my hands over his, stopping him. "We can't. You were shot." I pull away from him.

"Then you can ride me. I'm sitting here in a fucking gown, make me feel like a man again." He reaches for me again with his mouth, biting my jaw. I groan and let go of his hands, letting him slide the fabric over my butt.

I climb off of the bed and take my sweats and panties the rest of the way off, while Finn pulls up his hospital gown and kicks the blanket off of him. Climbing back on top, I hover over him, but he holds me still, dipping his fingers into my wet pussy and sloppily pumping them inside of me. He pulls his fingers out and uses my wetness to lube his dick. His hands grasp my waist again and he pulls me down over him, slowly, letting me adjust with every inch that enters me.

Placing my hands behind me, I lean back and wave my hips. Finn's tip grinds against my g spot and makes me moan. Finn's rough thumb starts to circle my clit, pressing lightly, but getting harder with every circle of my hips.

"Gotta be quiet, Angel." Finn rasps.

Nodding, I go faster, my eyes closing with pleasure. With time, I'm able to put more of Finn inside of me, my pussy almost dripping by the time I've made it to the bottom of his shaft. Finn starts to pump up into me, our hips meeting each other in a team effort.

"I'm gonna cum," I whine, moving my hips faster.

Finn removes his thumb from my clit and reaches forward with his good arm. Grabbing me by the throat, he pulls me forward and into his chest. I bite down on his shoulder to keep myself from screaming through my release. Finn's hand tightens around my throat, not allowing any noise to leak from it.

"You're gonna be my wife and I'm going to fuck you every fucking night, making you cum so many times you're going to forget your fucking name, and only remember my last name. *Your* last name," Finn hisses in my ear. I cum harder.

When my pussy stops convulsing around him, he lets go of me. I stare down at the deep teeth marks on his shoulder. "Turn around," he demands, his voice low and rough. It sends chills down my spine.

I do as he says and ride him in reverse. Sliding back down his cock, I place my hands on the bed in front of me and lower down onto my forearms. I bounce my ass over his dick and Finn thrusts up to meet me. We get progressively rougher; the sounds of our bodies hitting against each other have to be heard from the hallway, but Finn's close, so I don't stop. I can tell in the pace of his breathing and the small groans that leave his throat. He slaps my ass hard. Once, twice, and then he places his big hand on my tailbone and shoves me down, lifting his hips to push himself as far in as he can. His thickening cock triggers a small orgasm, and I have to bury my face into the bed to stay somewhat quiet. I can feel Finn's cum hitting my walls, and it makes my pussy flutter again just at the thought.

Finn leans forward and kisses where his hand was, then moves a little lower and bites my ass cheek. I lurch forward and he laughs darkly.

Ignoring him, I slide myself off of him and step into the

attached bathroom, cleaning myself up and grabbing a wet washcloth for Finn. Stepping around the doorframe, I launch the wet cloth at Finn's face, smacking him in the cheek. We both erupt in laughter and Finn cleans himself up while I redress.

The room is a little chilly, but cuddled up next to Finn, I don't even feel the chill, just the warmth of his body next to mine. He clicks through movies on Netflix, finding something for us to watch, and I snuggle in closer to him, hating that he smells like a hospital and not his usual spicy cologne or his fresh body wash.

"Tomorrow I have to go pick out a ring. I can't tell your dad I'm marrying you without a ring on your finger," he whispers into the top of my head, placing a kiss there.

I still, my eyes widening. Oh shit, my dad.

34

———

FINN

Huntley steps out of the master bathroom, her face buried in her phone while I'm buttoning the last button of my white shirt. I left the top few undone, and hold my thin gold chains in my hand. The sun shines in through the open window on the opposite side of the room, bathing the entire room in more light than it's probably ever seen. I'm not sure if I've ever opened the blackout curtains before. Huntley is wearing a flowing black skirt that hits her about mid-thigh, and a black lace see-through top that doesn't have any sleeves and covers her collarbones. I can see her black bra through the shirt, and I love it. Sexy and classy, perfect for her. Not that anybody would see it under her graduation gown anyways. She finally looks up from her phone and smiles at me, slipping her feet into her nude heels and fastening the buckle. I watch her long legs—even longer in the tall heels—as she walks over to me. Taking the chains from my hands, she steps behind me to drape them around my neck. When she's done, she smooths her hands down my shoulders, and I turn my head to watch her. She picks up my cut from the bench at the end of the bed and pulls it over my arms and onto my shoulders. Turning around quickly, I grip her waist before she can move away from me.

My Fiancée.

My eyes roam over her beautiful face; sharp jaw, high cheek-bones, plump red lips, big blue eyes, thick eyeliner, and long lashes. She's so fucking stunning.

The most beautiful woman I've ever seen. The strongest woman I've ever met.

Mine.

Forever.

I slide the engagement ring off of her finger and grab the thin silver chain from the bedside table, running the chain through the ring. Huntley turns around so I can fasten it around her thin neck. We decided to wait to tell her dad. Me asking his permission to marry his only child with a gunshot wound in my shoulder and my arm set in a sling probably wouldn't reassure him that I was going to keep Huntley safe for the rest of our lives.

I'm asking him tonight though, at the graduation party at his house. It's been two weeks since I was shot, and I was able to ditch the sling this week. That week with it was brutal, though. Now I know why Cale was always so grumpy when he was wearing one. Well, that and he was nursing a broken heart.

After snapping the clasp together, my hands slide over Huntley's shoulders. One hand circles her throat, applying slight pressure, and the other tilts her head back to rest against my chest. "I'm so fucking proud of you, Angel." I stare into her intoxicating eyes. "Despite everything that you've been through, you owned your shit and are graduating Summa Cum Laude." A smile stretches her lips, I know she's proud of herself too, and she fucking should be! "I'm gonna show you just how proud I am of you tonight, but right now we have to get you to that school so everyone can watch my smart fiancée walk the stage." Leaning down, I kiss her gently to not mess with her lipstick. "I love you, Huntley," I say when I pull away.

She turns around and wipes the red from my lips, then she turns back around and looks at Noctem. "Can she go, Finny?" she begs, and my dick twitches, realizing I might have just discovered a new kink.

I grin, thinking about how I now have to make Huntley beg me the next time I'm about to fuck her. She swats my stomach with the back of her hand, and I startle, zoning back into the conversation. "What?" I ask.

"I asked if she could come and you had some dumb grin on your face." Huntley glares at me.

"Of course she's coming, didn't you notice her little bow? She dressed up for you!" I point to Noctem, laying on the bed with her collar with the purple bow attached to it. The same color purple as Huntley's cap and gown.

Huntley lets out a shriek like a child, and turns to leave the room. "Come on, Noxy!" she yells over her shoulder. Noctem hops off of the bed to run after her mother, and I follow along behind my girls.

Everyone is already waiting for us when we pull into the parking lot of the football stadium, and I mean everyone. Huntley's dad, my dad, Cale, Little Red, Saint, Ro, Mase, Leo, Jack, Wyatt, Nate, Tobi, and whatever girls from Huntley's pole class that aren't graduating as well.

Putting the car in park, I look over at Huntley looking at everyone waiting for her. She blinks tears away as she pets Noctem's head. We get out, Huntley making her way down the long line of loved ones, and me holding onto Noctem's leash.

Finally, we all make it into the stadium and find seats. I'm sitting between my dad and Huntley's, and Cale is sitting on the other side of my dad with the rest of the club stretching out beside us or around us. The girls from class found other seats, and Farryn is graduating too, so she's with Huntley now.

We sit and wait for over an hour, watching everyone walk the stage, but finally, they get to the N's.

"Huntley Novikoff. Summa Cum Laude," the announcer calls.

We all stand, with me cradling Noctem, screaming Huntley's name, and whooping and hollering. Leo even brought a blow horn and blows it a few times. Tears well in my eyes, but I brush them away before anyone could notice. Well, before I thought anyone could notice.

When we sit back down after Huntley had shaken the University President's hand, my dad leans over. "She's quite a woman, Finn, you better not let her go."

I turn my head so I can look at him. His blue eyes nothing like mine, but the most familiar eyes I've ever known, other than Huntley's. "I don't ever plan to," I say honestly. I watch the photographers take pictures of her with the President and coming down from the stage. Even from here I can see her wide smile. My heart swells in my chest with pride. She didn't smile like that when I met her. Shit, she didn't smile at all, and self-ishly, I hope that I'm part of the reason she's smiling again.

———

A NICE BREEZE blows through Huntley's long, curled hair. She switched her heels for converse when we got here and I rolled my sleeves up to my elbows. We're in her dad's backyard for her graduation party; her dad and mine at the grill, and everyone else spread out around the large backyard, either at the two large tables set up or sitting around on outdoor chairs scattered around. Jack and Leo are playing fetch with Noctem, and I'm sitting with Cale and Saint while Huntley stands off to the side talking to Ro and Little Red. I look over at Callum, his eyes on his woman as well. Cale and I are kicked back in the chairs, my legs hanging open wide and Cale's arms resting behind his head.

"Who would have thought that I would be the first one to get engaged?" I ask. I called Cale the minute Huntley climbed off of my dick to go to the restroom after she said yes. I was giddy like a fucking girl, and couldn't wait to tell my brother. He, of course, told everyone else, because bikers are worse than old ladies when it comes to gossip. That's okay though, I want everyone to know Huntley's going to be my wife.

"Me." Cale laughs, his eyes still on Reese.

My brows pull together. "Really?"

He finally looks over at me out of the corner of his eyes. "You've been trying to find a love like your mom and dad's ever since I've known you."

I think about that for a moment. "No, I haven't. I haven't dated anyone since I've known you."

Cale smirks. "Exactly. Your heart was searching, but you could immediately tell when someone wasn't worth your time. None of them were Huntley."

I watch him, then look over at Huntley and Reese again. Reese is leaning in and whispering something into Huntley's ear and in response, Huntley throws her head back laughing. Cale never said shit like this before he met Little Red. I'm glad they're finally getting what they deserve. "When are you gonna make her your Old Lady?" I know he's going to, there's no way he's letting Red walk away now.

"Soon, brother, just waiting on the rings." His mouth breaks into a wide smile.

After dinner, when people have taken off or are sitting around quietly talking and drinking, I decide it's time to talk to Huntley's dad.

Squeezing Huntley's thigh, I address her dad, "Mr. Novikoff, could I speak to you for a minute?"

He pauses the conversation he was having with Cale about his roofing company and looks at me. More like glares at me, but I'm trying to ignore that. His eyes pass between me and Huntley. "I suppose." I stand and he follows me inside the house.

The back door leads to the kitchen, so we stop in there. I turn around and lean against the kitchen counter, listening. No one is in here. He stops in front of me, several feet away, and crosses his arms over his wide chest. He does not like me.

Sighing, I get on with it. "I want to marry your daughter, Mr. Novikoff," I start. "I love Huntley, and I know that we haven't been together long, but I know that she's the one for me. I will protect her and love her for the rest of my life, and after that, my brothers will protect her and love her too." His face turns from glaring to surprised, back to glaring, but I finish up. "Huntley loves you and I respect you too much to not ask for your permission. So here I am, coming to you to ask for your blessing to marry her."

Nik rubs at the white and blonde scruff on his chin. "Be honest with yourself, Finn. What kind of life are you going to give my daughter?" Aw, fuck, this isn't going to go well.

A little offended—okay a lot offended—I cock my head. "A good life. I own my body shop, my house, and several cars, I have different streams of income, and a damn great family. Your daughter will never want for anything. Not materialistic or otherwise. She will be surrounded by all of the love in the world, and I will do whatever I can to give her the life that she's always dreamed of."

"What about when you get carted off to jail? I don't think she wants to be a prison wife. I like your brothers, Finn, I think they're fine men, but not for my daughter." He stares at me with the same eyes that Huntley has, but right now, his are making me see red.

"My brothers are great men, and so am I. I wouldn't put Huntley through me going to prison." My fingers flex at my side, the only thing I can do to not ball my fists. I wouldn't hit Nik, it's just something to help the anger.

"I don't believe you have any say when it comes down to that. So no, Finn, I don't give you my blessing." He crosses his arms again, watching me. "I think we're done here."

I look to the floor and nod, feeling like I did when my dad would ground me for sneaking out when I was in high school. I walk past him and back into the yard. Huntley catches my eye and I subtly shake my head and walk to the back gate. I need a fucking smoke.

Huntley finds me leaning against the Shelby, holding the joint between my lips while I light the end. She wraps her arms around my waist and leans into my chest. I drape one arm around her back and hold her to me, resting my chin on her head. Holding her calms my erratic fucking heart, and I think she was listening for that because when it finally slows down, she pulls away.

Grabbing my chin in her delicate hand, she brings it down so I'm looking at her and not the houses in the neighborhood. "Talk to me," she says.

Blowing out the smoke, I tell her. "He said no." Her eyes widen, but we should have expected this. I don't know why we thought he would support us. "My brothers are good enough to fix his roof, to eat his food. I'm good enough to talk cars with, but not to marry you."

Her entire face falls, and it breaks my fucking heart, more than her dad denying me did. "Finn, I don't think like he does." Her hand rubs my chin.

"I know, Angel." I nod. "I wanted his blessing, but the only thing that matters is what you want. Do you want to marry me, Huntley?"

"Yes," she breathes, nodding her head.

I shrug, dropping my other hand to rest on her waist, but keeping the joint away from her. "Then we're getting married."

She smiles, biting her lip. "When?"

I chuckle, her excitement is exactly how I feel. I'm giddy like a fucking girl at the thought of making her my wife. "I'd marry you right now. Just tell me what you want, how you want it, and where, and I'll make it happen."

She looks off to the side for a minute before looking at me again. "I don't want anything big, just you, me, our dads, and the club at the courthouse, and then maybe a small reception at Big Dawgs."

My heart clenches. "Don't sacrifice what you want for me, Angel. I'll wait for you for however long you want. Don't choose the courthouse because of time or money, just plan what you want."

Huntley shakes her head, putting her hands on my chest. "That is what I want, Finn. I don't want anything big and I want to marry you as soon as possible."

"What about at the house?" I put the joint to my lips and inhale, taking a second to think. "We can have the ceremony in the backyard and the reception in the shop?" Huntley narrows her eyes. "I want to give you more than a courthouse wedding. I want everyone to see you in your dress and walking down the aisle to promise to spend the rest of your life with me. I don't want anyone, not your father, or our future kids to think we rushed this."

"Okay," Huntley agrees softly. "You'd clear your cars out of the shop for this?"

I'm a little caught off guard, I thought she already knew this. "I'd do anything for you, Angel."

Huntley smiles and raises to her toes to give me a quick kiss. "Okay. When?"

"As soon as you get a dress and we get a license." I shake my head, smiling. "Dad's gonna be so excited to cater the reception."

Huntley bites her lip again and I pull it out with my thumb, staring at her perfect lips. "What about decorations?"

My eyes move to hers. "What do you want, baby?"

"Flowers." She smiles shyly.

I continue to stare into her eyes; the eyes that have pulled me into her since I saw her in a dingy strip club. "Then we'll call every florist in Seattle and fill the entire damn shop with flowers."

Huntley's face breaks out into a huge grin. "What about being your Old Lady? Isn't that what you called me at the club-house and what your dad called me?"

Cocking my head, I take a drag from the joint. "You already are my Old Lady. I claimed you the night at the clubhouse party, you just didn't know it." My smirk spreads as her eyes widen and her mouth drops open.

Everything finally clicks together for her. I've been all in since the moment I laid my eyes on her.

Her mouth closes and she sucks her teeth between her lips, nodding. "Come on, let's go back in and say goodbye. I want you to show me what it feels like to be your Old Lady." She turns on her heel and walks back toward the backyard.

Hurriedly, I drop the remainder of the joint and stub it out with my boot. Jogging, I catch up with her when she's at the gate, and we go back in together.

35

FINN

THE CHAPEL SMELLS LIKE SMOKE AND MY BROTHERS' COLOGNES. Cale's sitting next to me, smiling like a fucking loon because he finally proposed to Little Red, asked her to be his Old Lady, and bought them a damn beautiful lot outside of town. It's only been one month since I was shot and two weeks since I asked Huntley's dad for his blessing and he said no. That hasn't stopped us though, and he eventually gave in. He's not happy, but he's accepting it. The light overhead casts a warm glow over the long, wood table. We don't have any windows in the Chapel. The shit we've been dealing with is far from over, but at least we finally have a fucking win under our belt. A loud bang echoes through the clubhouse—the sound of the front door being kicked in. All ten of my brothers and I are out of our seats and running through the chapel doors, pulling our guns from our waistbands or holsters within seconds, but when we round the corner into the main room, we all stop in our tracks.

"FBI! Put down your weapons!" A woman with short, dark brown hair yells, and all the other agents raise their handguns and rifles.

We all pause, looking back and forth between us, waiting for

Ronan to speak. Ronan starts to slowly bend and place his gun on the floor and we all follow, kicking them away from us.

"On your knees, hands behind your head!" The woman yells again, and of course, my fucking apprentice, Leo, is the one to defy orders. Always so fucking hot-headed, it's one reason I took him in. One of the agents forces him down to his knees and then kicks him square in the back so he falls to his stomach, while they handcuff all of us. Two agents hold rifles pointed directly at mine and Ronan's heads, while the others trash the clubhouse.

They toss all of the liquor off of the shelves, letting them shatter on the floor, flip tables, cut open pillows on the couches, and stomp upstairs into the adjoining rooms. They destroy everything.

"I hope you have a fucking warrant, because I'm gonna wring you fucking dry for throwing my prospect to the floor and holding a gun to mine and my brothers' heads," Ronan growls to the brunette who seems to be in charge and is watching her agents tear everything apart.

"Oh, I assure you we do, Mr. McKenna." The agent's face slides into a smug grin.

"For fucking what?!" Saint yells, trying to stand before being kicked down onto the floor by the same agent who kicked Leo down. "Fuck!" Saint yells when he smacks his face on the wood floor. I'd laugh if this wasn't so fucking serious.

"For the murder of Michelle Davis." The agent who kicked Saint and Leo spits out, kicking Saint in the side.

Why does that name sound so familiar?

Oh fuck. The senator's wife.

I look between Ro, Cale, and Saint. What does he mean for Mrs. Davis' murder? We didn't have anything to do with that. We talked about her murder a while ago at Cale's, but all we knew was that she had been murdered and gang violence was suspected. We thought we were in the clear.

We should have been in the clear.

I wrack my brain for any explanation. We didn't have any dealings with Senator Davis, he was as clean as they come. He would rather see us in prison before dealing with any of us. Mrs. Davis was just as squeaky, the stereotypical housewife and arm candy. Their marriage looked strong from the outside. Impenetrable. But looks can be deceiving.

None of us were fucking her. Ro's strictly on a cut slut diet, always has been. I can't remember the last time Saint hooked up with anybody, but that's nothing new, he's incredibly picky. Cale and I are happily engaged. Mase has been cyberstalking some chick. Leo is trying to see if his dick will fall off from too much use. Jack is a lot like Saint, but I think he has a girlfriend in his hometown. He sneaks off a lot when he thinks none of us are watching, but I'm always watching. Maybe it is Jack. I could see him being into an older woman. I don't know what's up with Wyatt, he sticks to himself a lot. It's not Tobi or Nate, they're in the same boat as Ro, trying not to knock anybody up.

We stay there on our knees or stomachs with guns to our heads, while the other agents rip, tear, break, and open our entire clubhouse. Every room. All we can do is kneel here, watching, incapable of doing anything. Pictures are smashed, furniture destroyed, all for what? For them being fucking wrong?

Finally, all the agents make their way back into the main room of the clubhouse. Each one scowling. They didn't find shit.

"Well?" The woman in charge snaps.

A few shake their heads, but one speaks up. "We looked everywhere, but we didn't find anything."

She smacks her lips, her eyes slowly going down the line of my brothers and me, taking in every one of us slowly. "We're going to find out who murdered Mrs. Davis," she promised.

"I hope you fucking do," Ronan growls. "And when you do,

I'd like a fucking apology for what you did to my brothers and our clubhouse today."

Two agents work their way down our line, removing our handcuffs, and when they're done the entire team leaves without a word. Leaving us to fix the mess they made. Well, leaving the club sluts to fix it.

Ronan helps Saint to his feet and Saint holds his hand to his side where the douchebag agent kicked him. "Chapel. Now!" Saint yells.

"I'll call Miles and have him bring his bug detector." Cale pulls his phone from his pocket.

36

HUNTLEY

The light hum of conversation and laughter fills the warm, silent night on Allie's back patio. Reese called me and invited me to her surprise engagement party after she found out about it. I'm sitting on Allie and Sophie's outdoor sectional. The patio lights cast a romantic glow over everyone, and the firepit in the center of the sectional keeps us all warm.

Sipping my champagne out of the plastic flute, my phone vibrates on the couch next to me. Seeing Finn's name, I immediately pick it up and move away from the group to answer it.

"Hey, Old Man. You miss me already?" I purr into the phone.

"Are you still at Allie's?" Finn snaps. His tone sets me on edge, every muscle in my body tightening and panic starting to swirl in my lower belly.

I turn around and look at the girls behind me, talking and laughing without any care in the world. "Yes," I finally answer.

I can hear wood smashing on Finn's end. "The clubhouse was raided by the FBI. My dad's on his way to get you and take you back to the house in case they go there next."

"Okay," I say, walking back over to the couch to get my purse and shoes that I had kicked off on the outdoor rug.

"Tell Little Red that Mase is on his way to get her. I'll be home as soon as I can, Angel."

"Okay," I answer again, not sure what else to say.

"I love you, Huntley." Finn's voice is rough and it wraps my heart in warmth and calms my nerves instantly.

"I love you too," I say, hanging up.

Leaning over, I whisper into Reese's ear what Finn told me. Her green eyes grow about five sizes and she downs the remainder of her champagne, then leans over and whispers into Allie's ear before kissing her on the cheek.

Allie lets out a long breath and picks up her phone from the couch, her soft, mint eyes wide. Taking the steps down into the grass, she puts her phone to her ear and calls someone.

I follow Reese inside the house and through the front door to wait for our rides on the porch.

"Why do you think the FBI raided the clubhouse? Because of the ammo?" Reese asks. It's bright outside with the street lights lining the road in front of us and the porch light shining behind us.

Ammo? "What ammo?" My head snaps to the side to look at Reese.

She quickly looks away from me, shuffling on the porch step that we're sitting on. "I'm sorry, I thought you knew. The club makes illegal ammo."

Well, that's a much better thought than the FBI looking into what Finn and I had done. "I'm not sure." I shake my head. "But if they were looking into the ammo then I think it would have been ATF, not the FBI."

"Oh, right." Reese's voice is soft while she stares at her hands. Her new engagement ring sparkles even under the low lights.

"Your ring is beautiful," I say, trying to cheer her up a bit.

She looks up at me, tears pooling in her eyes. "Thank you, yours is too. I love the color."

I move my hand around, staring at my emerald-cut Ruby engagement ring and the black Property Band with the light blue stone on the bottom. Property of Finn Evans is inscribed on the inside of the band.

Randy's old pickup pulls into the driveway, Noctem's growing body sitting in his lap and looking out of the driver's side window. I stand and take the last step off of the front porch when a bike speeds down the road and stops by the curb, the roar of the engine eating up the silence of the night. Mason swings his leg over his bike and takes his helmet off, waiting for Reese. The front door opens and Allie steps out, watching Reese and I walk to our rides. Mason hands the helmet to Reese, but he watches Allie the entire time, and she watches him. Interesting. I get into Randy's pickup, Noctem jumping from his lap to mine and we back out of the driveway, leaving all of them behind us.

"Did Finn tell you what was going on?" I ask when we're on the road.

"Only that the clubhouse was raided and he asked me to take you home and stay with you in case they came there next." He sucks his teeth between his lips.

"Yeah, that's all he told me too." I pet Noctem's head and watch the trees blur together through the window.

37

FINN

My boots crunch over the broken glass in the Chapel. Shadow boxes that were hanging on the wall with club memorabilia are laying on the floor, and the bandanas, pictures, and random shit from over the years are laying scattered on the floor with the shards of glass from the boxes being smashed. Chairs are laying on their sides, some with armrests broken off, and the heavy wooden table is laying on its side. Jack and Leo tip it back over, and Cale and I pick up the chairs and place them around the table again. Wyatt drags the broken chairs into the hallway and Ronan and Saint step into the Chapel.

Miles walks around the debris with a little device, running it over every piece of furniture, over the light fixtures and vents. He scans every inch of the room. He turns to look at all of us gathering in the room or outside of the double doors. "It's all clear." He walks to the door and shakes Ronan's hand before leaving to scan the rest of the clubhouse.

Ronan looks around the small room shaking his head. "What a fucking mess," he says under his breath. Saint collapses into his seat, hunching over a little and nursing the side he got kicked in. "Mason went to get the Princess?" he asks.

Cale nods, falling into his seat next to mine. "Yeah. I figured I was needed here, and she wouldn't mind seeing him."

Ronan nods, his eyes scanning the room again. Mason and Little Red became pretty close while we looked for her stalker. "And Huntley is taken care of?" Ronan looks at me.

I stop twirling my lighter when Huntley's name catches my attention. "Yeah." I cough to clear my throat. "My dad went to pick her up and take her home."

Ronan nods again then looks around the table with a serious expression. "I need to know now if anyone has anything to do with Michelle Davis' murder." Everyone is quiet, looking between each other. "Nate? Tobi?" he asks, looking at our older guys.

"No," Tobi says.

"Not me, Ro," Nate echos.

Ronan looks at Jack, Leo, and Wyatt at the back of the room. "Prospects?"

"No, sir," Wyatt says, his deep voice rough.

"Not us, Prez," Leo says and Jack shakes his head silently. Which surprises me. I expected some sort of dumbass comment from him. "Damn shame though. She was hot, even for an uppity bitch." And there it is.

Ronan rolls his eyes but I caught him coughing to cover up a small laugh. "What about Mase?" He's still talking to Leo.

He shakes his head. "Nah, he's hung up on some blonde bitch he met at a bar."

"Call Robinson and see if he can figure out why the FBI is looking at us for the murder," Ronan says to Saint.

Nodding, Saint pulls his phone out of his cut pocket. His lips pull into a small smile when the screen unlocks, illuminating his face. Narrowing my eyes, I watch him, looking over to see if Callum caught it too, but he's staring down at his phone as well, missing the weirdness that Saint is exhibiting. He's been doing that a lot lately; glued to his phone, smiling at it a lot, and being extra bitchy some days. Moody as fuck, to say the least.

"Last thing before I let you all go. Did anyone decide to take it upon themselves to dispose of Eli's body?" Every head in the room snaps to Ronan. Cale's phone clatters on the wood floor.

"What?" he asks.

Ronan rubs at his blue eyes. This is turning into a shitty fucking day. "The Doctor called me a few days ago. I guess he was in Europe and couldn't update me sooner, but he said when he got to the warehouse, there wasn't a body. Drag marks were leading into the woods that he thinks are from an animal, but I wanted to make sure no one here went back to the body." Again, no one says anything, just exchanging glances around the table. Ronan looks at each of us individually. "Okay, have Mason keep an eye on his accounts and see if he can do a facial recognition thing to look for him, but the Doctor is sure it was from an animal taking his body," he says to Saint again.

Saint nods quietly and Ronan raises the gavel. He holds it in the air, looking at the closed doors leading into the clubhouse. The room is silent. He brings the gavel down onto the wooden table, the loud crack followed by the scraping of chairs against the floor as we all rise to leave. There's a lot to think about today. Eli's missing body and the FBI on our tails for something we had no part in. Fuck.

I follow Cale out of the clubhouse. His footsteps stomp his way to his bike. "You okay, brother?" I ask as he swings his leg over his bike.

"Nope." He pulls on his helmet, staring straight ahead.

Placing my hand on his shoulder so he doesn't just take off with me right next to him, his head finally turns to me. "You going home?"

He shakes his head. "To the warehouse to watch security footage from that night."

I remove my hand and swing my leg over my bike. "I'm coming with you."

He nods once, sharply, and we both start our bikes and ride out to his warehouse.

38

HUNTLEY

THE BOYS ARE HIDING SOMETHING; SNEAKING AROUND THE clubhouse and whispering. Finn left me at the bar for the millionth time, saying he had to go take care of something. Reese slides onto the barstool next to me, trying to look over the bodies packed into the clubhouse.

"Did Cale ditch you too?" I lift my water bottle to my lips.

Reese sighs. "Yeah, but I'm looking for Allie. Do you know what's happening tonight?"

I shake my head, watching the bartender mixing drinks for some guys a few seats away from us. "Not a clue, just that Finn said it was a big deal." Reese nods and searches the crowd again. A club party on a Tuesday is a little weird, but it's not like I have to worry about being punctual for work tomorrow since my fiancé is my boss.

The front door opening catches my eye. Allie steps through, and several eyes stop to watch her. She's beautiful, yes, in a girl-next-door kind of way; innocent, soft, and blonde. But she's also a little out of place. Her shiny blonde hair is twisted into an updo on the back of her head, with curled pieces loose and framing her face, and she's wearing a silk terracotta-colored slip dress with a draping neckline and thin straps. Her dress ends high on her tan thighs, the color bringing out the beautiful tones of her suntanned skin, and the thin, strappy, black heels make her feet look delicate—making all of her look delicate.

She sees Reese and me at the bar and makes her way over to us. Reese reaches up from her barstool to wrap her arms around Allie. Allie's eyes close at the contact and a small smile pulls at her soft pink lips. She pulls away, her mint green eyes opening and landing on me. Smiling, she pulls out the seat next to Reese and sits down, ordering a vodka sprite when the bartender comes over.

Finn, Cale, Saint, and Ronan step up to the bar and surround us. Ronan standing to my left, Finn behind me, Cale to my right behind Reese's chair, and Saint between Reese and Allie with his back turned towards us. Swiveling around, I place my legs on either side of Finn and cross my arms under my chest.

Finn rests his hands on the bar behind me and leans down closer to me. "Don't give me that attitude, Angel."

"Then tell me what's going on. You've been ditching me all night," I snap.

He grins, bending further and running his nose along my jaw before biting down on it hard. "You're about to find out."

Pushing him away, I turn back around to face the bar. Ending our conversation.

Jack, Leo, Mason, and a man I've never seen before walk into the clubhouse, and Ronan hops onto the bar next to me. The music cuts and everyone falls silent, turning to look at the President of the Devil's Outlaws. It hits me then what kind of men these guys are. Dangerous and respected, but kind and loyal as well. I was in a viper's den without ever realizing it. I never really gave the club much thought; I've always separated Finn and the guys from the club. But it's sinking in now that this will be the rest of my life; coming to club events, becoming a family with these men. It's not a negative thought, I just realized that I haven't been very active in Finn's club affairs—not like Reese. She knows all of the guys well and has spent a lot of time with the Prospects. I only know Leo well.

"Tonight is a very special occasion," Ronan starts. "Around a year ago, we welcomed four new prospects into the Outlaws."

"Hell yeah!" A voice yells from the crowd, that I'm pretty sure was Leo.

"Hot ones, too!" A woman also yells.

Chuckles pop up here and there from people, including Ronan on the bar. "Anyways, after proving themselves on many different occasions," The entire clubhouse goes quiet. Like they're all expecting something big to happen. "Tonight, we welcome four new brothers to the Devil's Outlaws!" Ronan yells.

Cheers erupt from everyone in the building; screaming and hollering—celebrating.

Mason, Leo, Jack, and Wyatt come to the bar and Ronan points to a box behind the bar that Peyton hands him. All of the new members climb onto the bar, making Reese, Allie, and I have to pick up our drinks to avoid them being stepped on. Ronan passes out the curved patches that the guys have on the back of their cuts to all of the men on the bar, and then he passes out the large skull with snakes surrounding it. He hugs every guy when he gives them the skull patch and he pulls away, adopting a serious expression again. The crowd goes silent again and Ronan speaks. "Do you all agree to represent the Outlaws for the rest of your life? To put your brothers above all else and to live and die by the Devil?"

A chorus of yesses leave the men's mouths, smiles on everybody's faces.

"Welcome to the Devil's Outlaws," Ronan says.

"Outlaws never die and the Devil always wins!" Every man with a cut yells. Finn's shout almost busts my ear drum.

The men hop off of the bartop, their shoes landing hard on the wood floor next to me.

"Crank that shit up and let's get fucking drunk!" Ronan bellows, and the music is turned back on again, thumping louder than before.

"OUT THE ROOF" by Chase Atlantic drowns out the conversation of all of the people in the clubhouse. Finn pulls Leo into a hug and slaps his back hard. Pulling away, he says something to him and Leo smiles widely. Finn lets go of him and hugs the other guys, all of the brothers hugging each one, I can hear a few yell "congratulations," and "welcome brother." Finn breaks away from the crowd and comes back to me.

"I'm sorry for being absent tonight, Angel, we had to do our final vote on the Prospects and get their patches together. What can I do to make it up to you?" Finn watches me out of the bottom of his vision.

Placing my hand on his wide chest, I push him backward so I can slide off of the barstool. I take his hand in mine and lead him upstairs. We walk hand in hand to the last room on the left. I can hear the lock slide out before Finn pushes the door open and steps aside so I can walk through. With my back to the door, I hear the door shut and the lock engage. Turning back around, I push Finn into the door and step into his body. He stands with his back against the door and watches me from above.

"I don't like being ignored, Finn." I cock my head and look up at him.

"I'm sorry, Angel. I had club business to take care of." He gently runs his fingers over my jaw.

"Is the club more important than me?" I ask. I don't want him to choose, but I do want to know the answer. I'd never make him choose between me and his brothers.

"Nothing is more important than you," Finn whispers.

"Good." I drop to my knees and unbuckle his belt, pulling it from the loops and tossing it over my shoulder.

Finn spreads his legs, his arms hanging by his side. I make fast work of his button and zipper and pull his jeans down enough to pull his rising erection from his boxers. I run my hand over the length, slowly increasing in grip and speed. My thumb runs over the piercings on the bottom, and Finn groans as he watches.

Leaning forward, I kiss the head and open my lips to take him in. I stop just after the tip and suck gently, sliding my tongue across the seam where the head meets the shaft. Staring at him, I pull off and lick up the side from base to tip and swirl my tongue around the head. "Do you want to fuck my mouth?"

"Mmhmm," Finn moans, moving his hands to cradle my head. I take him into my mouth, about halfway, and play with his piercings. Moving my tongue in an "S" movement, causing the piercings to slide with my tongue. "Don't tease me, Huntley. There are more ways to choke you than just with my hands." Backing away, I raise one eyebrow defiantly. Finn smirks, running his tongue over between his teeth and shaking his head slightly. "My dirty fucking girl. Open up, Angel." I move forward and open my mouth, gently licking the slit on his head, collecting the precum on my tongue. "Wider, baby."

I open my mouth wider and Finn slowly feeds me his dick, our eyes locked on each other. He starts to enter my throat and I lock up, not able to breathe and gagging. "Swallow it, Angel." Finn rasps. I obey his command and attempt to swallow around his girth breaching my throat. He works with my movement, pushing in deeper. We repeat it a few more times until he's all the way in, and my nose brushes the soft skin above his dick. Looking up, I can see the Outlaw tattoo that sits between his hips. "Hold on, Angel, and tap out if you need to." His hands weave through the hair on the side of my head and grip tightly into the hair at the back, and my hands rest on his thighs. His hips start to move quickly. He pulls out only slightly before rushing back in. I try to breathe through my nose, but I can't get enough air in. I keep my eyes on Finn, his eyes slowly lowering the faster he gets. Finn moves even faster, if that is even possible, and tears form in my eyes, running over the edge and down my cheeks. His piercings drag across my tongue and scrape my throat, but it doesn't hurt. "Make yourself cum," Finn growls, his grip on my hair tightening.

Quickly unbuttoning my shorts, I slide my hand inside and right into my panties. I'm soaked. I didn't even realize how turned on I was because I was too focused on Finn. I easily slip two fingers inside and press the heel of my hand against my clit, pressing into it with every thrust of my fingers. I set my pace to match Finn's and I watch his eyes dart between my hand in my shorts and his cock in my mouth. My moans make my throat vibrate around his dick, and Finn moans loudly, dropping his head against the door briefly, before picking it back up to watch us. "You. Are. So. Fucking. Beautiful." Finn groans, puncturing each word with a hard thrust into the back of my throat. I cum around my fingers, my eyes closing as Finn's cum shoots down my throat. I swallow around him, my throat massaging his thick cock, until he slowly pulls out. I pull my hand out of my shorts and stand up.

Finn grabs my hand at the wrist and brings my fingers to his mouth, sucking my orgasm off of them. Pulling my fingers from his lips, he brings his thumb to my face and wipes the lipstick from the corner of my mouth and under my bottom lip.

"Thank you." I smile up at him.

"I love you," he says, pulling a black bandana from his back pocket and handing it to me. Gesturing to my eyes after I take it from him.

"I love you too," I whisper, before turning around and walking to the bathroom to clean up my makeup in the mirror.

When I step out, Finn pulls me under his arm and we walk out of the room and back down into the party, which has now turned into a full rager.

People are everywhere. Topless girls dance on the bar, guys are playing pool, LEDs flash from under the doors of a room down the hall, and shouts are coming from outside. Mason, Leo, Jack, and Wyatt are sitting around a table, Cale and Nate standing behind them, watching. A blonde woman is sitting in Mason's lap, leaning over the table and sewing the MC emblem onto his cut, but he's focused on Reese and Allie at the bar. A girl with a long brunette balayage sits on Leo's lap, topless, facing him and sewing some patches onto the front chest of his vest. Jack sits alone, hunched over the table, sewing his patches on quietly, and Wyatt is sewing on his top patch while taking direction from a girl sitting next to him.

Finn places a hand on Cale's shoulder, getting his attention. Placing my hand on Finn's cheek, I turn his head toward me and rise on my toes so I don't have to yell at him.

"I'm going over to talk with Reese and Allie," I say.

He nods. "Okay, I just have to talk to Cale for a minute and then we'll go pick up our baby and go home."

"Okay. If I catch you looking at anyone's tits, tonight will be the last night you have a dick." I raise my eyebrow and watch him.

Finn's mouth spreads into a smile. "You don't have to worry, Angel." Rolling my eyes, I turn around and walk to the bar.

39

FINN

"I'D LIKE TO START CHURCH BY WELCOMING OUR NEW BROTHERS," Ronan starts.

A few guys clap softly, while others knock their knuckles on the table. Everyone is way too hungover from the initiation party last night to be more excited. Leo is sitting next to me with his head buried in his hands. Mason, across the table, slouches in his chair with his hood covering half of his face. Jack is next to Leo and is resting his head on the back of his chair. And Wyatt is beside Tobi, sipping some cloudy drink. Our new brothers. Pulling the joint from behind my ear, I light it up and set my lighter on the table in front of me.

The club whores were able to get the clubhouse and the Chapel into normal order the day after the raid, and the Feds never went by our homes or our businesses. I don't know why they only got a warrant for the clubhouse. If it were me, I would have checked everywhere. It feels off, like they came at us half-cocked, but with this magnitude of the crime, it doesn't make sense for them to do this half-assed. We looked into the murder of Michelle Davis. Her husband is calling for heads, which explains the Fed's involvement. Her brother is somewhere high up in the Bureau. This is personal.

"Alright, before we get to the main reason I called Church. Cale, you got some info about Eli?" Ronan asks, steepling his fingers and leaning back in his chair.

"Yeah." Callum shifts in his seat. "Finn and I watched the footage from the warehouse. It's a little hard to see because of the distance and the dark, but a cougar drug his body into the woods, and then we lost sight." I hold in the first toke, letting the sweet smoke sit in my lungs before letting it out.

"You're sure?" Saint speaks up, his head resting against the back and his eyes closed. Not gonna lie, I thought he was asleep when I glanced over at him before. Shoulda known he wasn't though, fucking control freak would never miss Church.

Ronan watches Saint and then returns to Cale. "It *is* odd for a cougar to have found a dead human."

"Is it possible he wasn't dead?" I look from Ro to Cale, taking another hit.

All eyes turn to Jack. The quiet gets his attention and he picks his head up. "I definitely hit him, but I can't guarantee death. A double tap had the risk of hitting Reese, and we left so quickly."

"So it's possible that a cougar sniffed him out and took him back to his cache to finish him," Ronan supplies.

No one says anything, agreeing with him. It's odd that a cougar was around the warehouse, but that late at night, with no one around, it's not impossible. We've seen tracks in the woods surrounding it before, just never this close.

"Okay, moving on. I had someone approach me last night about prospecting for the club." Ronan pulls out a lighter and a pack of smokes and lights one up. "I know we don't usually take on so many prospects in a year, but he was really excited about wanting to join."

"Who?" Saint asks, looking at Ro out of the corner of his eye.

Ronan looks at our new brothers. "Nox. The guy you all brought." He gestures to Leo, Mason, and Jack. "Any of you want to vouch for him?"

"Remember, you'll be responsible for him and will have to answer for the things he does along with him," Saint cuts in.

The guys look around at each other. "We just met him last night before we came to the clubhouse."

"So no one vouches for him?" Ronan asks, but when the guys stay silent, he finally says, "Okay, we'll see how he does as a hang around for a few weeks, and then we can see about him prospecting." He smiles like he's remembering something. "I respect his courage to come up to me last night."

"That usually means they're unhinged," Saint says, his eyes closed again, but now he's massaging the bridge of his nose.

Ronan shrugs. "We could use some excitement in the club." Saint snorts, but doesn't say anything else. "Alright, last thing. Stay out of trouble while we figure out why the FBI is looking into us. I don't want to give them a reason to bust in here again." He bangs the gavel down on the table and everyone groans at different sound levels from the loud crack of wood on wood. Ronan laughs while we all lazily stand from our chairs. "Oh, Mason, I need you to run a check on the hang around. Name is Lennox Price, and he goes by Nox." I pull the ashtray from the center of the table and stub out my half smoked joint, leaving it.

"Got it, Prez. I'll get it to you by tonight." Mase salutes Ronan before walking through the Chapel doors and up the stairs to his room.

Saint stomps through the door and to the bar. He walks behind it and grabs a water bottle from one of the refrigerators and grabs a bottle of aspirin from under the bar.

Leaning over the bar, I take the bottle from him and swallow a few myself. "Where are you going?" I say when I notice he has his keys in his hand.

"To talk to Robinson and see what he's got about the raid." Saint takes another gulp of the water.

"Want some company?" I ask.

Saint shrugs. "Sure."

I follow him out to our bikes and we ride side by side to go meet our pocket cop.

40

FINN

WE PULL UP TO THE BEST ICE CREAM SHOP IN TOWN IN SAINT'S Audi. He insisted that we take this instead of our bikes, so we stopped by his house and switched them out.

"Leave your cut." Saint slides his cut off of his shoulders and folds it before getting out. I do the same and follow him to the trunk, where he lays the cut down. Placing mine next to his, he closes the trunk and starts towards the ice cream shop, which we parked a few shops down from. I pull on a baseball cap and pull it low to help shield my face.

We ordered inside and then found a lone table outside that was farther from everyone else.

I put a heaping spoonful of ice cream into my mouth. "I took you for more of a plain vanilla kind of man."

Saint glares at me, his plastic spoon halfway to his mouth. "I am, normally. Strawberry shortcake is only a summer flavor." He holds his small cup of vanilla ice cream with strawberries and cake pieces, leaning back in the wrought iron chair. "Sorry, not everyone is interested in the 'Chocolate Explosion.'" Saint eyes my chocolate ice cream with brownie bits and fudge in a waffle cone bowl with a chocolate-dipped rim.

I shrug, looking around for Robinson. "Simple tastes for a simple man, I get it."

Saint's eyes narrow even more and he releases a very dramatic and long breath.

"I hate you," Saint mumbles. I open my mouth to say something, but Robinson steps out of his restored 1973 Ford Bronco in civilian clothes. I know it well; I'm the one who restored it for him.

I incline my head toward him, letting Saint know that he's here.

Robinson sits down between Saint and me, and Saint passes him a milkshake that he bought inside. "Thank you," he says and then clears his throat. "You're on the FBI's radar because of a tip. I don't know if it was from an informant or if someone called it in. I don't even know if the source is reliable, but Mrs. Davis' brother and husband don't care. They're coming down on anyone they even suspect is connected to this."

Saint drags his hand down his face. "Fuck."

"Yeah." Robinson takes a drink of his milkshake. "But they went easy on you guys compared to the other people they've hit."

"Who else are they looking into?" I ask, my eyes scanning the crowd for anyone that might pay attention to us.

"No other organizations, only a few individuals. Mostly political figures who've had issues with Senator Davis."

"Something's off. First the word going around is that it was gang-related, then someone name-drops us, and the Feds only look into us and political figures? Why aren't they checking other gangs in the area?"

Robinson rubs his hand over his short cropped black hair. "I don't know. I haven't heard of any other clubs or gangs being investigated. Did you guys piss anyone off?"

Saint shakes his head. "No. We've had a peace pact with the

only other club in the state, and Los Lobos aren't even on our radar; we have no business in the bay."

"Do they have anything solid on anyone?" I ask.

"They're keeping things pretty quiet, but the only solid lead I've heard of them having was you guys."

Saint sighs, dropping his bowl of ice cream on the table. "Alright, well keep us updated."

Saint stands and I follow him, but Robinson speaks before we can leave. "I will, but keep things low-key in the meantime, okay?"

"Yeah," Saint says as he turns and walks away.

I throw up two fingers in goodbye and walk with Saint back to his car.

41

FINN

Approaching headlights shine over the logs of the lumber yard, announcing the O'Connells' arrival. Ronan angles his head toward Nox, our brand new Prospect, and I nod, letting him know that I'm on it. Nox was eager and he fit in with the club, so his hang-around period only ended up being a few days long. Plus, this drop came up with the O'Connells and we figured it was a good time for Nox to get his feet wet. We're putting a lot on the line trusting him with this connection so soon, and it makes me nervous. He didn't go down into the basement of Cale's warehouse, and he didn't look in the boxes, but what the fuck else do biker clubs do in the middle of the night when exchanging black duffle bags with someone else? Everyone knows something illegal is going down. One whisper to the right person is all it could take to cost us something.

Either our operation or our lives.

Dropping my joint to the gravel, I snuff it out with my boot and pull Nox by the back of his brand new, stiff cut. I drag him to the other side of the van, away from our incoming buyers. I lean in close to his face and speak with the most intimidating voice I can make, which is usually pretty scary. "This is your first test as a Prospect, don't fuck it up." His brown eyes watch me carefully, like watching a coiled-up snake, waiting for it to dart out and attack. "This is the type of meeting that is only talked about between brothers, no one else. This is the type of shit you don't walk away from if you fuck it up. Got it?"

Lennox rubs his hand over his short, cropped, brown hair, his deep brown eyes darting around the place.

"Shit. Yeah, I got it, Finn."

My eyes run down his body, looking for anything off. "You good?"

His gaze snaps back to me. "Yeah, sorry. I didn't know I would be thrown into shit so quickly, I just wasn't expecting it. I'm good. You don't have to worry about me."

The sound of heavy metal doors opening and slamming shut pulls my attention from Nox and I quickly look behind me. I need to hurry this little chat up. "I'll be watching you." Nox nods his head quickly and I push him back in the direction of the group.

Killian and Conor have stepped out of the fucking beautiful classic green Maserati, a few guys standing around a pickup that's parked behind the little coupe. I've decided now that my next rebuild will be a classic Masi. I ogle the damn thing every time we meet with them, contemplating if the punishment of stealing it would be worth it. Since death would probably be the punishment, I've talked myself out of it—but it is tempting.

Killian hugs Ronan and Ro meets my eyes over Killian's shoulder. I nod so he knows that Nox is taken care of.

"I see you've got a new member." Conor eyes Nox warily from beside Killian. His icy blue eyes look extra menacing when narrowed like that.

"He's good, been vetted by one of ours," Ronan says. Conor nods once, accepting that answer. "Go ahead, Wyatt." Ro motions for Wyatt and Nox to start loading the boxes full of ammo into the back of the pickup, and the O'Connells load the black duffle bags of cash into our van.

"I think this will be our last exchange for a while," Killian finally speaks, looking at Ronan.

"Anything I should know about?" Ronan asks, taking his eyes off of the exchange and facing Killian.

Killian shakes his head. "No, the shit between the Segretos just ended. We were able to come to a mutual understanding, and we don't need as much ammo anymore."

"Alright." Ronan shrugs. "Just call when you need more."

Killian nods. "I will, and I put some others in contact with you, including Sebastian again."

Ro smiles, big and broad. "Oh, he won't be a problem anymore? That must have been quite an understanding to share your ammo connection, are you sure shit won't pop off again?"

"No, I think we're good now," Killian answers.

Conor barks a quick laugh and wipes at the corner of his smirking mouth. "At least with *that* Segreto."

Killian glares at Conor, but Conor only laughs and meets Killian's stare without backing down.

"We good?" Saint asks Wyatt, breaking the stare-off between the Irish cousins.

Wyatt nods, closing the back doors of the van. "That's everything, VP."

"Hey!" One of the O'Connells guys yells from the front of the pickup advancing towards us quickly. "Who the fuck are you?" His thick Irish accent hangs in the air and all of us snap our heads around, following the guy's finger pointing behind us.

I take off immediately, running blind in the direction the Irish were heading. Nox passes me and runs into the trees. "Nox!" I yell. I lose sight of him immediately, but I pick up the pace when I hear grunting and thrashing in front of me.

It's so dark that I almost trip over Nox and a man grappling in the grass, but as soon as I get there, Nox delivers a brutal elbow to the guy's temple and knocks him out.

Nodding in approval, I watch as Nox stands and wipes the blood running from his nose. "Good eye," I say, watching him pull a white bandana from his cut to wipe his face.

We carry the unconscious man back to the group, Cale and the Irish man following behind us. Nox and I drop the guy on the ground and everyone looks at one another, not sure what to do now.

"I'm assuming you have somewhere to take him?" Killian asks, eyeing the guy laying on his back on the ground.

"Yeah." Ronan drags his hand through his thick dark hair.

"We'll follow you there." Conor smiles, a manic sort of glint in his eyes, and it sets even me on edge.

42

FINN

Grunts and the occasional scream are the only sound in the basement of the cabin. Killian, Ro, Saint, Cale, and I stand around by the wall while Conor drags an iron bristle brush over the exposed arms of the man we found in the lumber yard.

"This is starting to feel like deja vu, Ro." I watch Conor dig the brush in deeper and the man whimpers.

"Who do you work for?" Conor hisses, leaning in close to the man's face.

Ronan looks at me. "You think he's a part of The Brother's Coalition?"

I shrug with my hands. "Maybe."

Killian is standing with his shoulders against the wall. "The what?"

Ronan purses his lips before answering. "We had someone spying on us a few months ago, he was a part of an underground intelligence group called The Brother's Coalition. That was all he let slip." The zaps of the cattle prod make us all look over before turning back to the conversation. "One of the club's Old Ladies had a stalker and we're pretty sure he sent the spy, but this is feeling pretty fucking familiar." Screams pierce the air, along with the pungent smell of burning skin.

Killian licks his lips, watching his cousin intently. "Let Conor work, he's never had a man leave unbroken."

We watch for a while longer with Conor yelling questions that continue to go unanswered.

"We gotta take a different approach, this isn't getting us anywhere," Saint whispers so only we can hear him.

Killian's phone starts vibrating in his pocket and he pulls it out to check the screen. Clearing his throat he slides the phone back into his pocket and walks over to the metal table, picking up a hunting knife. Conor senses him and drops the pliers next to the discarded bloody fingernails on the ground. Killian leans down into the man's face and cocks his head, watching him.

"Are you with The Brother's Coalition?" he asks. The man doesn't answer. "So be it. I have somewhere to be, so I'll leave my touch with you." Before I can blink, he's plunged the knife into one of the man's eyes and twists. The man screams and jerks, but Conor stands behind the metal chair holding it tightly. Killian pulls the knife from his skull, his eyeball pierced on the end. The knife makes a loud clang when he drops it on the table and picks up a packet of QuikClot, rips it open, and dumps it over the wounded eye.

The man continues to thrash and wail in pain. Killian walks away, with Conor following. The spy falls over in his chair, landing hard on the concrete floor.

"Let me know what you find out, I'll ask around about The Brother's Coalition," Killian says before he and Conor walk up the stairs and leave the cabin.

Ronan watches the man whimpering on the floor. "Pick him up, turn off the lights, turn on Mickey Mouse Clubhouse as loud as possible, and meet us upstairs." Ronan heads for the stairs followed by Saint, but Cale stays with me, turning on the stereo while I haul our newest captor back onto his chair legs.

Upstairs, Ronan is sitting at the small kitchen table with a beer and Saint is sitting on the counter, tracing something on the top of it with his finger.

"He's not going to break," I say when we walk into the small kitchen. Cale walks over to the fridge and pulls it open, grabbing a beer and leaning against the refrigerator door. I rest my shoulder against the kitchen entrance. Thankfully the basement is fully soundproof so we don't have to listen to the Mickey Mouse Clubhouse theme song on repeat at a deafening level.

"What if we let him go?" Saint stares at the floor.

Ronan's dark brows pull together. "Elaborate, because I know you didn't just say something that out of pocket without a plan."

Saint sighs. "What if we make him believe he's escaped and follow him? Either figure out who he's working for or gather information that will *make* him break. Wife, kids, mom, whatever. Find something to threaten him with."

"It'd have to be believable. If he's trained for this shit, which he obviously is, then he won't fall for some half-assed plan," Cale interjects.

"We keep him here and tied up until after my wedding, then send Leo here in a Prospect cut pretending to be hung over. An arrogant, young kid who's not paying attention and doesn't care."

Ronan nods slowly, his eyes focused on the window next to Saint. "That could work."

Saint looks at me. "I like it."

"Alright. Cut the music and let's get out of here. I'll have one of the kids come check on him in the morning, feed him a little, and then we'll check on him again after the wedding." Ronan stands and walks to me. He smiles and puts his hands on my shoulders. "Now get the fuck out of here, you're getting married tomorrow." My face breaks into a smile and we leave the cabin.

Cale stops by the fusebox to cut electricity in the basement so the stereo turns off. We all head to our bikes and start to get on.

"Tell Huntley I'm sorry for keeping you out so late the night before her big day," Ronan yells over the bike engines.

"I'm staying at Cale's tonight, she didn't want us to see each other before the ceremony," I say, smiling. I can't fucking stop. I'm so excited to marry Huntley tomorrow.

Saint rolls his eyes. "Women and their traditions. Have fun on the couch!" He guns his bike and takes off, kicking up dirt as he goes.

I turn to Cale. "You wouldn't make me sleep on the couch, right, Cale?"

Callum shakes his head laughing. "Never, Finny. You can sleep with me."

Ronan's rough laugh almost echoes, it was so loud. "What about the Princess?"

"Oh fuck. Guess you're in the spare room, Finn," Cale says before we all leave the cabin and take the long road back into Merrill Hill.

43

HUNTLEY

THE HOUSE IS CHAOTIC. RANDY HURRIES BETWEEN THE KITCHEN and the shop making the food for the reception. All of the guys are transforming the shop, moving in tables, chairs, all the flowers, and DJ equipment. The guys were here early this morning moving all of Finn's cars to the body shop. All but one. The Hellcat.

Allie is going back and forth between supervising the guys and talking with Reese, Farryn, and me in the master bedroom. I knew Finn would want Callum as his best man, so I asked Reese to be my maid of honor. Well, that, and I do love her. She's the sweetest little spitfire I've ever met.

"Quit ogling your man and get over here. It's time for hair!" Allie snaps lightly, walking into the room. I drop the curtains and walk over to the barstool that we brought into the room.

Reese and Allie's friend, Sophie, is setting up her hair tools and makeup in front of the large mirror in the bathroom. The giant window that takes up the entire wall behind the bathtub is letting in the best amount of light, so we decided to get ready here.

The bathroom overlooks the backyard and I watch Finn and

the others start to arrange the chairs and toss the ball around for Noctem. Sophie curls my hair and twists and pins it into a large, low bun, leaving curled pieces out in front. Allie is doing Reese's makeup, Farryn is steaming my dress, and when my phone starts vibrating on the bathroom counter, she reaches over and hands it to me. My dad is calling.

"I'm going to step out and take this," I say, looking at my phone. My dad wasn't happy that we were going through with the wedding, but he said he would support me anyways. I thought he would have been here by now—the wedding is in a little over two hours—but I understand if he wanted to be around Finn as little as possible. It hurts, but I understand. I step out of the bathroom, close the door almost all the way, and walk over to the bed. "Hey, daddy! Are you on your way?"

"I'm sorry, Princess," his voice rumbles down the phone.

No, no, no, no, no. Not today. Please, not today. "Sorry for what?" I try to keep my voice enthusiastic, trying not to give in to the dread.

"I can't support this wedding, Huntley. I cannot support you marrying someone you barely know," he says, almost sounding sorry.

"Daddy, please," I whimper. Tears fill my eyes, but I stare at the ceiling so they won't fall.

He sighs. "He's going to hurt you, Princess, and I can't stand around and watch you both agree to spend your life together only for him to leave you for the next piece of ass that walks his way, or for him to wind up in prison!" He starts to raise his voice. "I won't watch you throw your life away for him."

My hand shakes in my lap and my lower lip trembles. How could he do this to me today? How could my dad call me two hours before he's supposed to walk me down the aisle and say he's not coming? I take a deep breath and blow it out. "I'm going to go marry the man that saved my life. I'd love for you to be here, but I won't beg you." I hang up on him, not giving him a chance to say anything. I allow myself two minutes of tears before I have to pull it together. I won't let him ruin today.

The bed dips beside me and I pick my eyes up from the floor, wiping the tears from my cheeks. I hadn't realized that Allie came into the room. "My dad doesn't understand me either, but I've never had the guts to stand up to him like you just did." Allie hands me a tissue and I dab under my eyes.

"Who's supposed to walk me down the aisle now?" I ask, panic laughing.

Allie takes my hand in her small gentle one. Her mint eyes are bright, like a light is lit from behind them. "Let me worry about that while you go get your makeup done." She pulls me up and gently pushes me toward the bathroom.

A little way into my makeup, I hear all of the guys come into the house. Their loud laughs and voices echo through the house as they head to the upstairs bedrooms and bathrooms to get ready.

Allie walks into the bathroom and takes the curling iron from Farryn to finish Reese's hair. "Randy said he would love to walk you, but we need to know if you still want him to walk Noctem or have someone else do it?" Allie watches me in the bathroom mirror.

"I really liked the idea of him walking Noxy down the aisle, but he could walk us both maybe?" I say, thinking out loud.

"Well he wasn't the only one to volunteer, so we have options." Allie hands the curling iron to Reese and pulls her phone from the waistband of her leggings. She taps out a message before sliding it back in and taking the iron back from Reese.

Sophie finishes my makeup, Reese and Allie finish just a few minutes earlier, and Farryn holds my dress for me. A knock on the bedroom door interrupts us, and Sophie goes to check it.

"Huntley, it's for you!" she calls into the bathroom.

I wrap my robe tighter around my body and walk into the bedroom. Ronan is standing just inside the doorway, his hands in his pockets. His black hair is slicked back, and his short beard is trimmed. He's dressed in a crisp white dress shirt with the sleeves rolled up, his cut, black slacks, and shiny dress shoes.

"You make a very beautiful bride, Huntley," he says, smiling shyly.

"Thank you," I say, looking at him expectantly. I have an idea of why he's here.

He clears his throat, looking around at the other girls moving around the room getting their dresses ready and putting on jewelry. "Look, I know I'm not your first choice, but I'd be honored to walk you down the aisle today. Finn is like a little brother to me. I've watched him grow up and become who he is today, and I'd love to be a part of this next journey for both of you. If you'll have me of course."

"It's not bothering you?" I ask.

Ronan shakes his head. "Of course not. I want to make today the best day possible for the both of you, any way that I can."

I purse my lips, moved that he cares this much about today. "I'd really like that, thank you."

Ronan smiles, biting his lip. "Okay, I'll wait for you in the living room. The guys are making their way downstairs and outside. We're ready when you are." With that, he turns and leaves the room, closing the door behind him.

Sophie, Allie, Reese, Farryn, and I put our dresses on. Sophie, Allie, and Farryn leave to find a seat in the backyard for the ceremony. Not that it will be that hard; the only people invited were the club, Farryn, some of my friends from pole, and Finn's dad. Reese is considered a part of the club since she's engaged to Cale, and Allie and Sophie are Reese's friends, and they helped with today, so they were of course invited to stay for the wedding.

Reese is about to open the door to leave when she turns around and grabs my hands in hers. "Before we leave, I just want to say something." I stare at her, urging her to continue. "Thank you. Thank you for teaching me self-defense and giving me a small amount of bravery when it came to Eli. Thank you for not hating me when Finn was shot trying to protect me. Thank you for looking after Cale when we broke up. Thank you for allowing me to be a part of your wedding. Thank you so much for being my friend, Huntley. I'm so glad I met you." Tears well in Reese's eyes and I have to look away.

"Reese, get your ass out of this room before I start crying," I laugh, nudging her towards the door.

"You're right. Okay, let's go get you married." Reese turns the knob and walks down the long hallway into the living area with me following behind her.

Randy, Noctem, Cale, and Ronan are sitting in the living room, talking and laughing at something that someone said. Everyone stops when we enter the room. Randy pushes off from the armchair, walking to me.

He smiles widely and pulls me into a hug. Pulling away and holding onto my elbows, he keeps me close. "I can see why Finn calls you Angel. You look absolutely heavenly today."

I lower my head, smiling. "Thank you."

Randy sighs. "I wish Olivia were here today. She'd be a fucking mess, but she'd be so excited to finally have a daughter. Actually," he clears his throat and reaches into the pocket of his black slacks. Pulling out a small black jewelry box, he opens it and presents it to me. "She would want you to have these. She wore these on our wedding day." Inside is a pair of beautiful teardrop sapphire earrings with a diamond halo.

I take the box from him and stare at the beautiful earrings.

"They're beautiful. My mother left when I was a baby. I don't have anything to remember her by. This means the world to me, truly." I look up at Randy and see a small tear running down his tan face. Goddamnit, we all need to stop crying! I hand him back the box and start to take out the plain diamond studs I had in.

Randy chuckles. "I guess the earrings aren't the only thing you'll be wearing of Olivia's today."

"Excuse me?" I ask with my hands lifted to my ear. I notice him staring at my engagement ring.

He smiles, pointing to my ring. "One of the diamonds on the side of the ruby is from Olivia's engagement ring. Finn asked for it the night he was shot, but when I saw your ring from a distance I only noticed the red stone. I just thought he decided not to use it or you didn't like it."

I drop my hand and stare at my ring, a wave of love washing over me. "He didn't tell me he used her diamond."

Randy shrugs. "I know it had to mean a lot to him."

Nodding silently, I finish removing my studs, replacing them with the beautiful sapphire earrings from Randy. He places the box with my earrings now in it on the kitchen island and bends to pick up Noctem, who was watching us from the couch.

Bending down I place a kiss on her head and hold my arm out for Ronan. I look around and catch Reese huddled under Cale's arm, dabbing at her eyes with a tissue. Shaking my head and laughing, she bursts into laughter too.

"I couldn't help it, that was the sweetest thing I've ever seen!" She laughs more.

Cale leans over and kisses her temple. "Come on, Red. We gotta get our practice in for our wedding." He pulls her towards the sliding back door, leading to the patio and the backyard beyond it.

Randy gives me another hug, squeezing me tightly. "Thank you for loving my boy. I can't wait to have you as my daughter," he says into my hair, then pulls away and walks with Noctem on her leash out of the patio doors.

I watch Randy walk down the stairs, Noctem almost pulling him with her excitement. Cale and Reese wait for him to get to the end of the aisle and sit down in the front row before they descend the stairs arm in arm.

"Ready, sweet girl?" Ronan asks, looking down at me. I nod and we walk to the door, waiting for Cale and Reese to get to the end of the aisle and stand at the altar.

Stepping out onto the patio overlooking everything is surreal; the warm weather that feels like a light blanket laying over your skin, the soft breeze, the golden hour before the sun starts to set. The chairs are lined up and face the altar, decorated with flowers that fall like lines of string lights. Everyone who loves us stands and watches me slowly walk down the wooden stairs of the patio. Finally, my eyes land on Finn, already watching me. He stands at the altar, tall and strong, a dark contrast to the green grass, and the white flowers on the altar. His black hair is slicked back, his black dress shirt tucked into black slacks with black shiny shoes, and his cut. He looks perfect —everything is perfect. I just wish my dad was here.

Ronan lays his hand over my arm that's entangled with his, and squeezes it as we step onto the grass. I wore my white converse for this very reason—I was not about to worry about my heels sinking into the grass. Reese paired a black pair of wedges with her long black dress, which was a smart choice as well.

We're one step into the aisle when my dad shouts from the edge of the house. "Wait!" Ronan and I turn around and watch him run toward us.

I open my mouth, not sure if I want to yell at him or fall into his arms and cry, but he speaks before I can. "I can't let you walk down this aisle without me, Princess."

"But you said—"

"I was wrong," he interrupts me. He brushes the curl of white blonde hair out of my face. "I don't trust him." He takes a long pause and I roll my eyes, tired of him thinking so badly of a man who has only ever been good to me. "But I'm sure he will earn my trust over time. For now, I just want to support you and your happiness." Nodding, I take his hand and pull him into a hug. He squeezes me so tightly I can't breathe. Pulling away he asks, "Can I still give you away?"

"Of course, daddy," I say, smiling.

Now everything is perfect.

Ronan places his hand on my shoulder. "I'm gonna go have a seat." He holds his hand out to my dad to shake. "It's good to see you, Nik." They shake hands, but before Ronan can leave, I reach for his arm.

"Could you walk me as well?" I look back and forth between him and my dad, very aware that the song I was supposed to walk out to has made a loop and is playing for the second time. Ronan opens his mouth, but I speak before he can. "It's important to me that you approve of me and Finn."

Ronan's smile almost splits his face, it's so wide. "I've always approved of you, Huntley. You're the best thing that ever happened to him." He holds out his arm again and I loop one arm through his, my other with dad.

An instrumental version of "Control" by Zoe Wees starts from the beginning and the three of us slowly walk down the aisle. I chose this song because it reminded me of the night that Finn brought me back to life. That night, I never thought that I would be marrying Finn. Staring at his tattooed back while he turned away so I could undress privately, I never thought we would end up here.

I'm so glad we did, though.

44

———

FINN

MY BREATH CATCHES WHEN SHE WALKS OUT OF THE HOUSE—THE house that I unknowingly built for her a few years ago. She looks every bit of the name that I always call her, floating along the patio and down the stairs, her white satin dress falling over her body like water. The slit on the side is so high that I know for certain she isn't wearing any panties. I can't take my eyes off her, scared that if I do, she'll disappear; that this day will all have been a dream; that the last few months with her have been a dream.

A yell breaks the haze I had fallen in. Nik runs to Huntley and Ronan, dressed in his black suit. I guess my call worked.

AN HOUR AGO...

"Hey!" Allie yells, causing all of us to look over at her. My brothers and I are in the backyard arranging the chairs for the ceremony and putting the altar together. "We have a problem," she says slowly when everyone has stopped talking to listen to her.

"No." I stalk toward her. "Not fucking today."

271

She bites the inside of her lip, looking at someone behind me before finally looking into my eyes. "Huntley's dad isn't coming."

Narrowing my eyes at her I ask, "Is he in the hospital or something?" There can't be any other reason he would miss walking his only child down the aisle. Allie shakes her head, her eyes darting behind me again. I catch onto what she's not saying. "He's not coming because of me."

Allie looks at her bare feet in the grass and tucks her blonde hair behind her ear. "I need someone to walk Huntley down the aisle. Randy is walking with Noctem, so I need a second option to present to Huntley," she says to my brothers standing behind me.

I lightly grip Allie's arm, getting her attention. She turns her head to look at me again, but she keeps her chin raised. I like that I don't intimidate her, or at least that she acts like I don't. I respect it. "How is she?" Allie looks back at me and shakes her head. That's all I need to know.

Rage pulses through my body as I walk through the backyard and around the house to the front. I want to go check on Huntley, but I know not seeing each other is important to her. I go back and forth for a while; should I call him, should I not? Fuck it, my anger gets the better of me. Getting my phone from the pocket of my workout shorts, I dial Nik's number.

"Hello?" he answers, probably not expecting me since he never actually gave me his number.

"That's some shit bailing on Huntley today." I stare out at the packed circle driveway, all of my brothers and dad here to help us, to celebrate us.

"I don't trust you, Finn. You're going to hurt her." He spits down the line.

"No, Nik. You're the one hurting her," I growl. "I don't give a fuck if you're her dad, I will not allow people in her life that hurt her. She is about to be my wife, and I will protect her until I die, I don't care who that's against." I take a deep breath to calm myself down. Looking out

at the trees surrounding my property. The clear sky. It's a beautiful day. The perfect day for a wedding. "You can hate me, but I'm not going anywhere. I love Huntley with everything that I am, and I really hope for her sake and the sake of our future family that you can figure out how to accept me and see that all I've ever done is protect and love your daughter." He doesn't say anything, and I don't want to waste any more of my wedding day trying to prove myself when I don't need to. Huntley is the only person I need to prove myself to. "Figure it the fuck out, Nik." I hang up and slip my phone back into my pocket.

Footsteps on the wooden porch capture my attention and I turn toward them. Cale is walking to me, holding two glasses of amber liquid.

Handing one to me he says, "Ro is gonna ask to walk with Huntley." I nod. Leave it to Ronan to step in when everything is falling apart. "Come on, let's go get ready." Sighing, I follow him inside and up the stairs.

Present...

When Nik, Huntley, and Ronan make it to the end of the aisle, Ronan hugs Huntley and takes a seat in the front row next to Saint, leaving Nik and Huntley standing in front of me. He hands me Huntley's hand, but before letting go, he says, "I don't care who your club is, or what you do for them. If you break my daughter's heart, I will hunt you down and show no mercy. I'll bring her back your heart."

"And I'd let you," I answer without hesitation.

After a sigh, he lets go and takes a seat next to my dad. I look at my old man and the empty seat on the other side of him, with a small plaque that reads *"Reserved for the Mother of the Groom."* My heart constricts and I have to look away.

Instead, I hold my bride's hands and look into her beautiful eyes—the first thing about her that ever held me captive. Jack starts the ceremony, reading from a piece of paper tucked inside a small black book. He gets to the vows and gestures to me.

I clear my throat and pull a piece of paper from my back pocket, keeping hold of one of Huntley's hands. "I told you that I was yours on our first date, but to be honest, I've been yours since I saw you at Second. I will be with you until my last breath. I will always protect you, no matter the cost, and I will love you harder than anything you've ever experienced. I am yours to wield as you please. Forever, till the end of time." I stop looking at my note, already knowing everything I want to say is already in my heart. I watch Huntley, the entire world fading away and leaving only the two of us. I'm only speaking to her right now. "Nothing will separate us, not even death. I will continue to wait for you until we find each other again in whatever afterlife we find ourselves in."

"Wow," Huntley breathes. "Finn, you met me when I was a ghost of a person. Walking through life without a purpose. You breathed life into me and gave me something I didn't think I would ever have again: peace of mind. You've changed my life just by loving me, and I can't wait to start the rest of our lives together. I will love you until the end of time, until there is nothing left of you and me, not physically or spiritually. I am your Angel and you are my Devil and this world is ours to rule."

A tear I didn't realize was there falls down my cheek, and Huntley brushes it away with her delicate thumb. Sliding her hand down my cheek and to my chin, she pulls me down to her lips and I gladly kiss her. I love her, so much more than I could ever articulate. More than this world, than my family, than my brothers. She is everything to me and I will prove that to her until I'm taking my last breath.

Jack clears his throat and Huntley pulls away from me laughing. "That was supposed to be after the 'I Do's.'"

"Well get on with it then!" I snap lightly.

"Huntley Alina Novikoff, do you take Finn to be your lawfully wedded husband?" Jack asks flatly.

"I do." Huntley bites her lip to keep from smiling, but she fails, her smile popping wide despite her efforts.

"Finn Michael Evans, do you take Huntley to be your lawfully wedded wife?" Jack continues.

"Abso-fucking-lutely!" I lick my bottom lip, never taking my eyes off of my Angel.

My wife.

Mine.

"Because of a lost bet and some scammy website, I now pronounce you hus—" Jack cuts off when I bury my hand into Huntley's hair and yank her head back, kissing her.

Whoops and whistles ring out through our small crowd and when I reluctantly pull away, everyone is standing and clapping with smiles on their faces. I place one last kiss on Huntley's lips before we walk down the aisle hand in hand, everyone else following us to the shop for dinner and partying.

———

THE DANCE IS FINALLY SETTLING down. People are tired of dancing and most are sitting around and talking, and enjoying the open bar. The parents, some of Huntley's friends, Tobi, Nate, and one of Little Red's friends went home. Leaving my brothers, Little Red, Allie, and Farryn still here.

"We'd better do your wedding present before either of us gets too wasted," Saint says, setting his short tumbler down on the round table.

The shop was completely transformed; it doesn't even look like a shop anymore. A few round tables with white tablecloths and light wooden chairs were brought in, a large area in the middle left open for dancing, and flowers everywhere. Flower arches, flower backdrops, small flower centerpieces, and flower petals everywhere. I keep the shop clean and without the cars in it, it's just a large building with tall ceilings, white walls, and heated tile floors.

"Yeah, I guess so." I push back from the table and stand.

Saint turns and starts for the door. "Come on, you can help me bring everything in," he calls over his shoulder.

After bringing in Saint's travel bed and kit, I'm laying shirtless on my side, with Saint prepping his gun and ink. Huntley sits behind me, watching Saint set everything out and prep my ribs.

The needle pierces my skin and I close my eyes, enjoying getting another tattoo for my girl. My wife. My Old Lady.

"What's the first date?" Huntley asks, leaning over to watch Saint work.

I make sure to keep my breathing even during the short tattoo. "My parent's wedding date. It was my first tattoo. I kept the spot under it open for whenever I met my dream girl and married her."

Huntley leans down and gently kisses my cheek, not disturbing Saint.

"6/11/2022" is inked into my skin in roman numerals, just like the one above it.

"I want one too," Huntley says to Saint as I'm sitting up from the table.

"Alright, where do you want it?" Saint pulls off his gloves and starts to clean up the used materials.

Huntley lays down on the bed, moving her hair off of her neck. "Here." She glides her slim finger along the side of her neck.

Saint gets set up again and I kneel at the head of the bed, grabbing one of Huntley's hands and holding it.

"Okay." Saint leans forward, gloves on and ready to go. "What am I doing?"

Huntley inclines her head to look at me. "'A Devil owns me' in a fine script."

I watch Huntley the entire time, though Saint did have to move her head to face forward for the tattoo, I never take my eyes off of her. Lying there in her wedding dress, getting a tattoo for me.

She's fucking right. I do own her ass.

Then something blue catches my eye. Her sapphire earrings glitter in the Christmas lights that are covering the ceiling.

Huntley closes her eyes and squeezes my hand, taking slow and calm breaths during the tattoo. Saint finishes and cleans it up, placing a protective wrap on it.

I guide Huntley to her feet by her hand and pull her into me with my hands on her waist. Looking into each other's eyes, we stay silent. So much more is said between us when we don't say anything at all.

"Since my shit is out, who wants tattoos to celebrate Finny and Huntley's wedding?" Saint calls to everyone sitting around a table watching us and talking.

Huntley pulls my face closer to hers and whispers into my ear. "I have a wedding gift for you."

"I do too," I whisper back.

She pulls away and wiggles her eyebrows. "What did you get me?" she asks.

I take her hand and pull her toward the large garage door that is opened. "I'll show you. It's in the garage."

"Of course it is," she laughs from behind me.

Looking over my shoulder, I watch her walk behind me, holding my hand. Her hair is still perfectly in place, her white blonde hair framing her beautiful face, her plush lips painted a deep maroon, her lashes long and thick. Her dress is beautiful, with the v-neckline, the thin straps over her shoulders, and the deep cut of the back of the dress that hits just above her ass, leaving her entire back on display.

I fully take in the moment we're in; what we celebrated today.

I'm married.

To the most strong, fearless, and amazing woman that I've ever met. I watched my dad love my mom and me more than anything in the world. I waited my entire life to find the person that I would love that much. She's everything I ever wanted and more. She's perfect for me.

Made for me, but definitely not made in Heaven.

"Do you want me to carry you?" I ask. She's been on her feet all day.

"Sure." She smiles. I bend down with my back to her and she laughs, climbing onto my back and wrapping her arms around my neck. "This is not what I had in mind when you said you would carry me."

"What? Did you expect something more intimate?" I walk us around the front of the house and toward the garage.

"Well we *are* married now," she whispers against my neck, kissing down until she

meets my shoulder and then biting me hard.

I groan at the pain and she immediately kisses the area to soothe it. "We have all night for that, Angel, and I intend for it to take all night."

I hold onto her with one arm wrapped under her leg and type in the code to the garage door. We wait while it slides open and I step inside, setting her down next to her new 2023 Jaguar F-TYPE Coupe, a shiny deep gray with a big red bow sitting on the hood.

She walks around the car, her finger sliding along the body. "Wow," she finally whispers.

"Pretty, huh?" I watch her staring at the car. "Wanna take it for a spin?"

Huntley bites her lower lip, looking at me from the opposite side of the car. "Yes." She nods her head.

I open the driver's side door for Huntley and rest my arms on top of it, waiting for her. When she comes to the door, I take the key fob out of my pocket and hand it to her. She slides into the deep red leather seat and I shut her door, walking to the other side to get in.

"The car isn't your only gift." I press the small button to open the glove compartment and pull out her other gift.

She examines the papers, reading them. "Building permits?"

I try to turn in the seat, but the cabin is a little small, so I turn as much as I can to face her. "I got a permit to build a studio next to Evan's Body Shop. You can use it for whatever you want, but I thought you might like someplace that you can teach your self-defense classes out of, or just blow off some steam on a heavy bag." Her mouth drops open. "Building it at the shop keeps strangers away from the house. You can design it however you want, or not at all. Whatever you want."

She leans over, cutting off my speech with a kiss. "Thank you." She smiles against my lips.

"Let's go, Angel." I kiss her one more time.

"What about our guests?" she asks as she starts the car and it silently starts, not even letting anyone know we're leaving. A cool feature about the Jag.

"Today is about you and me, so why don't we spend the rest of it together? They'll all get the hint when they can't find us."

She nods and turns back to the front, putting the car in reverse and backing out of the garage. I click the door button closed and she slowly drives down the driveway and turns onto the deserted road, pressing her foot into the gas and sending the car shooting forward. She giggles nervously, holding the wheel tightly.

After a few miles of her testing the limits of her new car, she finally slows down and relaxes into the seat, resting her head against the headrest. Her eyes trail up, noticing the panoramic roof. "Wow, the stars are beautiful tonight."

"Not as beautiful as you." I take one of her hands and kiss the back of it. "I love you."

She turns to me, a smile on her face. "I love you too."

I enjoy the ride with her, listening to her plans for her new studio and the new enrichment toy she found for Noctem. I don't even notice we're at the clubhouse until she pulls up and stops at the gate. I side-eye her but give her the gate code regardless. She taps it into the little box, I get the alert to my phone, and I allow us access. She slowly pulls us in and parks near the door.

"What are we doing here?" I ask, shutting the car door and walking around it toward her.

"Being alone." She smirks and steps around me, walking to the clubhouse door.

I follow her through the dark clubhouse, the lights around the bar dimly lighting the large main room. I follow her to the doors of Purgatory. She pushes the doors open and steps into the pitch-black room. She flips the lights on, the red lights illuminate the room, basking all of the black furniture into a deep maroon color.

"Take a seat, husband." Huntley stands in front of the sound system, typing something into her phone.

The speakers hum, indicating that a phone was connected. "What is this?" I ask, walking to one of the chairs that sit in front of the stage and pulling it to the edge.

She walks to the stage. "This is your bachelor party and your wedding present all in one."

Huntley sits on the edge of the stage, scrolling through her phone and pulling off her converse and socks. "Wicked Games" by The Weeknd fills Purgatory, and Huntley steps onto the stage. She slides the thin straps of her dress over her shoulders and lets the dress pool at her feet on the floor, her naked body taking on the deep red glow of the LEDs. She turns around, her back to me, and when the beat drops she falls into the splits, her back still toward me, her hips moving in a wave to the beat. She turns out of the split and moves to her knees, crawling before sliding down onto her stomach and lifting her ass in the air, running her hands up her legs and over her butt. I watch in rapture as she places her hands on the floor and pushes herself up and sits down, spinning to face forward, her legs spread wide for me to see. She leans down and pulls herself forward, her head facing me and legs together behind her. She lifts her ass into the air again, dropping it side to side on the floor. Spinning out of that, and into a sitting position, she moves to the pole and climbs the pole to the top, spinning around it and holding onto it. She comes around and opens her legs, turning herself upside down and straddling the pole. I suck in a quiet breath. I've watched plenty of women do inverted tricks on the pole, but it's different when it's your girl. What if she falls? She lets go and drops her back, her leg going out behind her, before twisting her body around the pole and spinning faster. Slowing herself down she splits her legs again and holds onto one leg with one hand, the other extended down toward the ground and wrapped around the pole. Without thinking, I stand and walk to the stage. She drops the other leg and grabs it, pulling her body into a bow-and-arrow-looking position, with her legs in the splits and both hands each holding onto a leg. Pulling herself into a ball she slowly spins down the pole, she lets go and turns to move, but the sight of my shoes stops her.

Her eyes run up my body, all the way to my eyes, and I have to admit, I love seeing her kneeling before me.

She crawls to me and places her hands on my thighs, staring up at me, like she's asking permission. I shake my head slowly, making a come here motion with my finger. She stands and I quickly pick her up, my hands holding her beneath her thighs. My shoes click on the stairs to the stage but go silent when I make it to the bottom and hit the carpet. I lay Huntley down on the stage and kneel before her. She sucks in a breath at the cold flooring against her bare back.

I push her legs wide and my tongue draws a line from the side of her knee to her thigh, then I bite the sensitive spot on the inside of her thigh. She yelps and grabs me by the hair, pulling me into her pussy.

"Is this where you want me, Angel?" I slowly lick a long line from her opening up to her clit.

"Shut up, Finny," Huntley groans, her fingers tightening in my hair.

My tongue makes slow circles over her clit. I flatten my tongue and apply just a bit of pressure. Huntley's moans spur me on and I pick up my pace, doing faster up-and-down motions. Her moans mimic my pace and they pick up in pitch the faster I go. Stopping just when she's close to cumming, I pull my tongue away and do slow licks, pulling away after each one. She raises her hips, following my face when I pull away again.

"So eager for my tongue, aren't you, Angel?" I chuckle, diving back into her clit and picking up the fast up and down I know she likes. This time, I don't slow down when she's close and instead keep the same measure. She cries out through her orgasm and I gently massage her clit with my tongue, seeing her through the tremors. When she's back to me, I suck her clit into my mouth hard and she half gasps and half moans.

Standing, I pull Huntley to her feet and shove my lips

against hers, forcing my tongue into her mouth and letting her taste herself. She moans against my mouth and I pull away, turning her around and falling into the chair that I pulled up to the stage. I undo my pants and pull them down, letting them rest at my ankles.

I grab Huntley's wrist and pull her towards me, turning her around by her waist and pulling her onto my lap. Then I wrap my arms under her thighs and behind her head and pull them open wide.

"Slide me into you, baby," I demand into her hair.

Her hand wraps around my cock and guides me to her soaking opening. I slowly start to slide inside her, her head resting heavily in my hands. I keep pushing in slowly, her tight pussy gripping me the whole way. When I'm balls deep, I rest my head against the back of the chair, taking a deep breath before I lift my hips, put my feet onto the stage, and start pumping into Huntley's sweet pussy.

"Play with your pussy, Angel," I grunt, my hips bucking into her wildly. I feel her arm squeeze in between my arm and her thigh, on its way to work her clit. "Match my pace." Huntley whimpers as we work her roughly, and a short time later she sucks in a breath and lets out a groan. Liquid rushes over my cock and drips onto my balls, the sloshing noise a clear indicator that she squirted.

Dropping her legs, I grab the front of her throat and guide her to the stage, bending her over it. I move my hand to the back of her throat, pushing her turned face into the stage. I slam back into her, without warning and without a care.

"Yes. More," Huntley moans.

I bend over the top of her, squeezing the back of her neck painfully, and drive my hips into her roughly. Her hips will no doubt have bruises from slamming against the edge of the stage, but neither of us cares right now. Huntley's moans can be heard over the song that's playing through the speakers, and the red lights wash out her pale skin, leaving her skin looking as red as the lights. I pump into her harder. Claiming her.

"I'm gonna fill this sweet pussy so full of my cum, it's going to be dripping out of you for a week," I growl into her ear.

"Oh fuck, Finn," Huntley groans, her eyes closing with the pounding of my hips.

A smile spreads across my face, all teeth. "That's right, Angel. Who's fucking you?"

"My husband!" Huntley screams, her pussy pulsing around my dick, and as much as I want to hold off, I can't. Her orgasm and her calling me her husband send me to my climax. I push into her as deep as I can, and spill all of my hot cum into her tight pussy with a roar.

I pull out of her and fall into the chair behind me, pulling her with me. She lands in my lap limply, and I move her around so I'm cradling her, looking into her eyes.

"You're so fucking perfect," I whisper over her lips, placing a gentle kiss there.

Huntley smiles, her eyes still closed. "I love you," she whispers back.

"I love you too. Forever." I pull away and watch her. Her head lulls a little bit, falling against my shoulder. That's when I notice her earrings again. "Are you wearing my mom's wedding earrings?" I ask, watching the red LEDs glint off of the sapphire teardrops.

Huntley licks her lips before answering. "I am."

My finger slides under the earring, lifting it slightly. "She would have loved you, and she would have loved that you wore these today. Thank you."

Her eyes slightly open and she looks me in the eyes. "Why didn't you tell me that you had my ring made with your mom's diamond?"

I bite the inside of my lip, thinking. "I wanted you to love the ring because you loved it, not because I guilted you into loving it." I want to look away, but I hold her eyes.

She raises her hand to my cheek, holding my face to hers. "I love my ring, and I love it even more now that I know how special it is."

"Good." I bend down to kiss her, running my hand down her thigh and collecting my cum that's leaked out of her pussy. I scoop it up on my fingers and push it back inside her still wet snatch. Huntley pulls away from my lips and moans, her head falling backward. "Wanna go fuck against your new car?" I ask against her neck, biting down hard. She sucks in a breath and then a moan when I run my tongue over the red mark. "I'll take that as a yes." I kick my pants the rest of the way off and stand up with Huntley draped over my arms. Walking us through the clubhouse and outside to her new Jaguar.

45

FINN

IT'S TOO FUCKING EARLY FOR HOW LATE WE STAYED OUT LAST night, but I still pull up to the cabin in my white '66 Shelby GT350. The weather is nice and I haven't taken it out much this year. Maybe Huntley and I will take it on our honeymoon. Leo and Mason pull up in Mason's pickup and park behind me in the dirt circle driveway.

We gather between the vehicles before going inside. "Okay, so I thought Leo and I could go inside and wait for him to escape and then follow him on foot, following the tracker. Mase, you can drive around and pick us up if needed, we're a long way from town, and we'll probably need something along the way."

"Got it," Mason says, turning around and setting his tablet on the hood of his pickup and tapping the screen.

"Who placed the tracker?" I ask. Leo holds a stiff cut in his hand and leans back against Mason's truck. He must have borrowed it from Nox. His dark sunglasses shade his eyes and his dark brown hair is a mess.

He pulls a pill bottle out of the pocket of his gray joggers and pops a couple in his mouth. Aspirin I think. "Saint. He took Allie home last night, so he said he would swing by here after.

Injected him with something and when he passed out, he injected the tracker too."

I nod. That's good. "If anyone was going to do it, it's best that it was Dr. Viotto. Alright. Let's go."

Mason gets into his truck and pulls around my car and out of the driveway, while Leo and I go through the front door of the cabin.

"How do you wanna do this?" Leo pulls his sunglasses off of his face and sets them on the back of the couch, which he leans against. His brown eyes are bloodshot and there are slight purple bags under his eyes. Looks like he won't have to fake being hungover.

"You sure you're up for tracking through the woods?" I watch him. He doesn't seem too bad.

He waves away my question. "This is nothing."

I shrug. He knows how important this is, Leo wouldn't let the club down because he was too busy killing his liver last night. "I brought some breakfast. Take it down to him, make a big show of being hungover, and then I'll call you. Rush out of there and leave him able to escape. I'll wait for you in the garage and once he's made it out we can follow." I offer the white paper bag to Leo.

Leo takes the bag and peeks inside. "Give me a few minutes to eat this and then call." He stands up and walks over to the wall, opening the hidden door and going down into the basement.

When the door is closed, I make my way back outside and pull my car into the garage. We want the spy to think that Leo drove off, so a car in the driveway will have him second-guessing us. I grab a cap and pull it on backwards, then lean against the wall and wait.

I give Leo a few minutes like he asked, and I text him a question mark. He responds with a thumbs up, so I know I can call him. I dial his number and after a few rings he picks up.

"We all good?" I ask.

"Are you serious?" he asks, sounding annoyed. "Fuck! Okay, I'm on my way." He pulls the phone away from his ear and I hear another "fuck" before he hangs up.

Not long after, Leo quietly slips into the garage from the door that leads behind the house. I incline my head as he steps towards me.

"Saint changed his binds last night to rope, so I undid his hands but left his legs tied. When you called, I left some bolt cutters out and slammed the door so hard that it bounced back open," Leo says, smiling. Fucking proud of himself. "I even dropped my breakfast burrito when I ran out of there."

I snort, holding my hand to my mouth. What a fucking idiot. "Why did Saint change his binds?"

Leo shrugs off the Prospect cut and pulls his phone from his pocket and pulls up the map for the tracking device. "So that he could escape easier. He dipped the rope in peppermint oil so that it would sting and cause a rash, so it seemed like more torture."

"I'm impressed." I look over his shoulder at the dot. It stays still for a while, but finally, it starts to move.

When it gets a short distance from the house, Leo and I sneak out of the garage and follow the dot into the woods. I dial Mason and keep him on the line through an earpiece, neither of us saying anything, but we keep the line open in case we need to.

We track him for about five miles. Leo and I slowly follow the moving dot through the thick vegetation and soaring trees.

"He's moving toward the road," Leo whispers to me.

I nod, then speak into my earpiece. "He's heading for the road, Mase. Make sure he doesn't get into a car."

"Got it." Mason clips then goes silent again.

Leo and I keep walking, making sure to stay quiet and watching the tracker.

"I'm gonna pick him up." Mason comes through the phone.

"No!" I snap, picking up my pace.

I hear rustling on Mason's end before he answers. "He's never seen me. I'll offer to drive him somewhere. It'll be faster than trekking through the woods or following a car with a do-gooding citizen."

"Fuck," I sigh. "Fine, but keep the line open," I demand.

"No can do. He'll know. I'll call when I got something." The line goes dead before I can say anything else.

"Goddamnit." I grab Leo's arm to stop him. "Mason's picking him up, let's go back to the cabin and wait for him."

Leo shakes his head, turning around to go back the way we came. "Fucking Mase."

After making it back to the cabin we wait and watch the moving tracker for about half an hour.

"I'm really surprised he never figured out we tagged him," Leo says, laying across the leather couch.

"Me too, guess he wasn't as advanced as we thought. Guess we didn't have to follow him after all." I watch the driveway through the window in the living room, waiting for Mason.

Finally my phone rings. I click on speaker and hold my phone so I can talk into it. Twirling my lighter with the other. "You good?"

"Yeah." Mason's voice floats down the line, and I see Leo's shoulders relax a little after hearing Mase's voice. "I offered to take him to a hospital, but of course he refused. I dropped him off at a house about five minutes ago."

I lean over and pick up Leo's phone, zooming in on the map. "He's in Los Lobos territory." I bite my lip, thinking. "Is that his house?"

"I'm not sure, he didn't say, and I didn't want to press and raise suspicion. I was going to go back to the clubhouse and run the address through the County Assessor's Office and find out what I could about the house," Mase says.

"Okay, I'll drop Leo off. You two fill everyone else in on what happened today. Huntley and I need to get on the road."

"Got it, brother." Mason hangs up.

Leo and I stand and leave the cabin, locking up and heading to my car in the garage.

The spy may live in Los Lobos territory, but it's also possible that he was visiting someone, an underground doctor maybe. We did fuck him up pretty bad. I mean, Killian did take out his fucking eye. The most chilling scenario is that he could be working for a Lobo. They don't have the numbers to go against us though, so it would be a very poor idea for them to try. They could be watching us for harmless reasons, making sure we don't cross their territory, that we're not planning to move in on their operations, shit like that. It could also mean they're planning an attack. This also calls into question who the first spy we found was working for. Was it Eli like we originally suspected, or whoever hired this guy?

I rub my index finger between my eyebrows, my mind working a million miles an hour. It's the perfect time for a little vacation with my wife. Or maybe it's not. I guess we'll find out when we get back in two weeks.

EPILOGUE
HUNTLEY

"Life's A Mess" by Juice WRLD bleeds through the speakers, and the water and trees blur together through the car window. I spread my legs wider, pressing my head into the back of the red leather seats of my Jaguar.

"Damn, you're really making me work for it today, aren't you, Angel?" Finn's fingers pump into me faster, the heel of his palm pressing into my clit in a downward motion.

"I'm about to cum," I groan, and Finn's fingers curl and start to massage the spot inside of me, effectively bringing me to orgasm.

Finn pulls his fingers from me and slips them into his mouth, sucking my cum off.

"That would have been over a long time ago if you had pulled over and fucked me like I asked." I use a wipe to clean myself up and slide my panties and shorts back on.

Finn barks out a laugh, passing about the millionth car since we left Alaska. "Asked? Angel, you begged for my cock." He licks his lips and grins. "We're already late as it is, and if you still want to stop by the house to change and shower then we don't have time to stop." He looks over at me, his deep blue eyes sparkling with dirty promises. "But don't worry, when we get to the party tonight, I'll kick everyone out of Purgatory and you can put on another show for me."

"Fine," I sigh, turning my attention to the window.

I watch as the sea passes us by, remembering our perfect Alaskan honeymoon. We spent our time hiking, lounging in the cabin with Noctem, and taking a boat out and fishing or stand-up paddle boarding. It was relaxing and fun, and nice to spend time with just the three of us. Noctem is exhausted. When we got into the car to come home, she immediately climbed onto Finn's lap and fell asleep. His big hand rests on her little body, reaching up to scratch behind her ears every few minutes. She was so interested in all of the wildlife that trekked through the backyard of the cabin. Turning my head, I lean it against the back of the seat and watch Finn drive. His tattooed hand wrapped around the leather steering wheel, passing yet another car in his haste to get home. I think about the last few months together. Him handling me with such care, but also letting me stand on my own. Never smothering me, trusting me to take care of things on my own, and allowing me to do so. He gave me my peace of mind back, my sanity, and he's made me feel safe since the first night I met him. Now that he's in my life, I can't imagine my life without him. It's a life I wouldn't want to live, I guess. I'm excited for the first time in a long time, having a future to look forward to that doesn't include looking over my shoulder every time I step foot out of my apartment.

Speaking of my apartment, we need to move my things out. My lease ends this month, but it's been paid for anyway by my very generous anonymous donor.

An hour later, we pull into the driveway and I hurry inside while Finn takes Noctem to the grass. I unlock the door and swing it open, flipping on the light as I step inside. The bright overhead light illuminates the living room and kitchen and I stop in my tracks when I see the new art hanging on the walls. Two giant black, white, and gray murals of a woman's body hang on the walls. Different poses, both covering the private bits, but it's clear that it's a naked woman's body. The murals are only from neck to thigh, with no face, but as I make my way into our bedroom, two more murals hang over the bed. This one is clear who the woman in the mural is. Me. My Medusa tattoo is included in this mural, and in this one I'm not covering anything. I stand and stare at it. It looks good. I look good.

The taps of Noctem's nails enter from the hallway and I hear Finn's heavy footsteps following.

"What do you think?" he asks, stepping up behind me and wrapping his arms around my stomach.

"Are these all of me?" I ask, still staring at the mural.

"Of course," he scoffs. "These are the pictures I took of you that night, I sent them to a very talented painter and she painted you." He kisses my temple and continues. "I told you that you were a work of art and you deserved to be worshiped. I hoped that this would help with your body image. To see your body as a part of something else."

I lean back into Finn. "They're beautiful, thank you."

"You're beautiful. Now come on. Saint has already texted me asking where we are and dads on his way to get Noctem." He bites my shoulder and then pushes me forward, smacking my ass.

I reach back and grab his hand, pulling him with me into the bathroom. I turn on the water and we undress each other, getting into the steamy shower. Finn washes my back, and I return the favor, then make him bend down so I can massage the shampoo into his hair. He rinses it out and turns back around, facing me. His blue eyes sparkle in the dim light of the bathroom, water dripping off of his thick eyelashes. Finn's eyes are as blue as the ocean and just as deep. I could get lost in them, and I guess I did.

Saint

I LOOK around at all of my friends.

My family.

They're happy. I'm happy.

We overcame some crazy shit this year, and still have a lot to figure out, but right now is our time to enjoy our brotherhood. Only one man is missing, but I know he'll be here soon. My phone vibrates in my pocket and I pull it out to see Robinson's name. I answer the call and put the phone to my ear, watching two of my brothers toss their shirts aside and step into the ring, big grins on all of our faces. Before I can even say a greeting, the club pocket cop is saying one of the only things that could ever truly rip my heart out of my goddamn chest. I hang up, ending the phone call without even saying a fucking word, and gently place the phone on the table in front of me; my eyes staying trained on nothing.

"Hey you okay, man?" someone says next to me as they gently push my shoulder, but I'm too zoned out to know who it is.

"Saint," the voice says again, more stern this time.

I'm faintly aware of people starting to pay attention to me, but fuck them, this can't be happening right now. I quickly stand up, my chair toppling over in my rush. I search the crowd for him, praying this was a mistake. I can't see him.

He's not here.

I jump on top of the table to get a better look, beer bottles fall over and smash on the concrete.

"What the fuck are you doing, jackass?" someone snaps, but I ignore them, my head snapping around to look, and me turning in a complete circle.

Searching.

Please.

Strong hands pull me off of the table and turn me around to face them. Blue eyes, concerned blue eyes that force me to accept this is real. "Saint what—"

"He's dead."

To be continued...

ACKNOWLEDGMENTS

I'm so excited to be writing another one of these, but with a second book came more doubts than with the first. I hope I was able to live up to any expectations that Only The Strong left with you. I hope I was able to tell another story that you loved and that captured your attention until the very end.

Finn and Huntley flowed out of me like water. It was the fastest I've ever written. These characters spoke to me better than anyone has so far, and I felt them come alive inside of me. I hope that translates to the page. I hope you love them as much as I do. I've started the next book, and it's hard. I'm going into uncharted territory for me, and these characters are stubborn, not only with themselves but also with talking to me. I'm going to have to pull this story out of them, but I think it's going to be a good one. I hope it will be a good one.

I have so many people to thank. So many people who hyped me up and made me want to keep writing. I told myself that the Outlaws were going to be written even if no one ever read it, and they will be, they've been in my head for too long and I need to put them to paper. But with all of the support I've received, I've found something that I love, a community that I love.

So I would like to thank anyone who beta or ARC reads for me. Your input and reviews are so invaluable. The first time I heard someone mention my book in a TikTok, I about died. I squealed like a child and cried. You have made me the happiest I've been in a long time. This last year was rough, I unexpectedly lost my mom, and then seven months later we lost our youngest dog, a dog who was my son. But you gave something to me that I will always hold dear. It was you all and being able to stick my head in my writing that has pulled me through. Thank you so fucking much if you've ever supported me in any way. I seriously can't put into words how much it has meant to me.

I want to personally thank Emi for being so kind to me and offering to edit this book. You were only supposed to ARC read OTS, but you came back with edits that I missed. I'm so glad my leftover mistakes lead me to you and where we are today. Your eagle eye is what will make you an amazing editor. I can't wait to grow with you and see where you take your business. I wish you an absurd amount of success! If you ever need anything, all you have to do is ask. I adore you.

I would also like to thank Shay for all of the TikToks you made for OTS and for always commenting and liking my videos. I love listening to your recs and watching the creative videos you make. I also really love your profile picture and I was serious about you cover modeling. You're gorgeous, you should do it!

Kortnee. If I wrote books like I wrote to you, the Devil's Outlaws would be completed lol. I know sometimes it takes me a few days to reply. I get caught up in life and writing, and I forget. But I love that no matter how long has passed between messages, we always pick up right where we left off. You have become a true friend to me and I am so grateful to you! If you ever come down for a game, we have to meet up!

Alyssa, your voice soothes me and I love watching your TikToks. You are such a sweet soul. Thank you for continuing to rock with me and my over the top bikers.

If I missed anyone, I greatly apologize. I have met so many kick ass people through publishing.

To all of my readers:

Thank you so much for your love and support. Thank you for encouraging me to continue doing what I love. I appreciate you all so much.

Bethany

FOR EXTRA CONTENT

To discuss spoilers, theories, cliffhanger rants, and read deleted scenes for Will Survive, join our Facebook group, The DO Chapel.

You can also follow me on TikTok @queenb17, Instagram @bethanydawnauthor, and my Facebook page @BethanyDawnAuthor

ALSO BY BETHANY DAWN

The Devil's Outlaws:

Only The Strong (book 1)

Will Survive

This Mess (May 2023)

Of Bikes and Men (September 2023)

Outlaws Never Die (January 2024)

The Devil Always Wins (May 2024)

The Devil Didn't Want Me (September 2024)

A Devil's Forever (December 2024)